Odds & Ends
Luck of the Draw

Blake Alb
Lieh Pena

World Castle Publishing, LLC
Pensacola, Florida
Copyright © 2024 Blake Alb
Hardcover ISBN: 9798325442445
Paperback ISBN: 9798891262126
eBook ISBN: 9798891262133
First Edition World Castle Publishing, LLC, May 27, 2024
http://www.worldcastlepublishing.com

Cover & Illustrator: Lieh Pena
Editor: Karen Fuller

ACKNOWLEDGEMENTS

Blake Alb: I would like to thank LIeh Pena for his excellent illustrations, Denise and Darrell for their many hours proof-reading and test-reading, Karen Fuller for her hard work editing, Hermione Lee for her encouragement and faith in me as a writer, family, friends, those that are no longer with us, and others I failed to mention.

Lieh Pena: It is always an exciting experience to work on illustrations for a new book. For this I would really like to first thank Blake Alb, since without his text, that would not be possible. And to my wife, Raila Pena, I am not really sure if "THANK YOU" would be enough to express my gratitude for all the support she has given me during all these years illustrating. I would also like to thank Darrel for trying to keep us motivated with his words, and Denise for the corrections to my texts.

It's the year 3154. Many, if not most, have heard of Euclid and Autumn Hux and their supposed grand adventures. Many of these tales include legends, songs, and folk tales told in passing, whispered under candlelight, or sung in earnest by bards, poets, and storytellers (using the 26 letters of the alphabet). One cannot say the Hux heroes went unsung. But to what extent does the veracity of these lofty tales hold true? By and by, some academics have gone so far as to assert that their legends of wanderlust are so much larger than life that it remains doubtful that the events existed at all.

But not all is for naught. A treasure trove of correspondence was just recently discovered in a dusty attic in the far reaches of cyberspace, giving credence to the myths and legends regarding the existence of these illustrious heroes. Using the "correspondence method" of storytelling, the communiques between Autumn and Euclid are currently being compiled and organized by cyberspace historians.

But that is just on the outside. What about the inner workings of the illustrious Euclid and Autumn Hux? What makes them tick on a cellular level? Thanks to "impression decoding," the noisy hormonal, electrical, genetic, and neurotransmitter communications between key neurons, sperm cells, egg cells, and nanobots inside Euclid's and Autumn's bodies have also been decoded. In fact, it could be said that the adventures of one certain alliance of sperm are equally as fascinating as the adventures of Euclid and Autumn Hux themselves. So, let's join these five sperm in their quest as they chronicle their journey to reach the egg.

The curators of this treasure trove of communiques will allow the correspondence to speak for itself and weave a tale without the bardsman's superfluous hyperbole or poet's penchant for embellishment. What you see below are the actual communiques as they were originally sent, received, and decoded. Enjoy!

CHAPTER 1

The A Letters
Subject: Humble beginnings
Date: 02/02/2182 (Saturday)
Location: Country of Repro
Sender: Random sperm cell
Recipient: Prime Minister of the Country of Neuron

To the Prime Minister of the country of Neuron in the brain region,

I am a random sperm cell, gamete, or haploid from the reproductive system and country of Repro (way down in Euclid's reproductive system). I have always admired your country from afar, as I am fascinated by how memories, emotions, and learning are made manifest by the prefrontal cortex, amygdala, hypocampus, limbic system, and temporal lobes. I don't mean to sound cavalier, but I request your audience on a most serious matter of significant scientific importance (not to mention the opportunity of a lifetime). I am but a three-day-old gamete, haploid, and sperm cell (the longest a sperm cell can live at most is around seventy-five days). You can consider this to be a May Day, distress call, or S.O.S. for reasons that will soon become apparent. But rest easy, for time is not of the essence (yet). So, for the interim, you can consider this to be an orange alert.

Please do not think of me as one of those certain ilk who reaches out only when necessity requires a monetary safety net, lump sum, or bailout. There are far too many such solicitors and philanthropists on their knees begging for financial compensation for this, that, and the other thing, replete with their corresponding tragic tales of woe. Either such tragedies are conjured out of imagination and the appeals of emotion, or they are a dime a dozen, revealing once and for all that the world really is a cesspool of despicableness and heartbreak. And the charlatans who make up such tales of melancholy only diminish the veracity of those with the humility and honor to tell the truth (invariably leading to a sort of "Boy that Cried Wolf" situation). But to claim that the sky is not falling when it is would be every bit as egregious.

I am an inquisitive sort by nature, a connoisseur of organic and non-organic technology (whether skin, muscle, bone, or the stuff of smoke, steam, and metal). For many tech-savants, old technology goes unappreciated as it is discarded into obsolescence and left to atrophy in the annals of time. But for technology buffs with a proclivity for history, there is more nuance than that. Like a Tempranillo wine, these relics demand much more appreciation and approbation.

As you know, we get most of our culture, knowledge, and media information from the mind of our twenty-seven-year-old human host, Euclid Hux. But it's also no secret that Euclid Hux is also a decorated reproductive scientist, and very few are privy to his innermost knowledge and secrets. But the fact that Euclid has this knowledge places an auspicious opportunity right on our doorstep. After all, as a brain cell, you are privy to the academic knowledge and memories tucked away in the sealed vaults of Euclid's brain and memory banks. We are also privy to the hundreds if not thousands of nanobots scattered throughout Euclid's body for the purposes of his cellular muscular regeneration. These conditions conjure a milieu that is rife for scientific inquiry. With your access to Euclid's knowledge, coupled with the nanobots, we can chronicle the new frontier as we embark on a pilgrimage from the testes to the urethra. No haploid has ever reported what kind of world exists beyond the rim of the urethra. And if we do not embark on this mission, it's doubtful anyone ever will.

These nanobots can transfer DNA, hormones, drugs, stem cells, and electrical neural impulses between cellular and genetic systems. This is nothing novel for 2182. More impressive is the recent operating LAN that allows each and every nanobot in this body to pass data and information between one another (allowing cell-folk in all 11 countries to send and receive electronic mail back and forth between cells in all organ systems).

To say that I have not spent many an hour pacing to and fro in the confines of my modest house, contemplating whether or not I should reach out to you, would be a bald-faced lie. And while part of this hesitation was due to procrastination, social awkwardness, or being too lazy to labor myself, the fact remains that these sentiments were tenuous excuses. And this is not to mention that prior to the establishment of the nanobot LAN, sending and receiving communiques was an arduous and time-consuming affair, lending itself to the further justification of my complacency. Like the old man who walked to school uphill both ways, I was resigned to relying on electrical, chemical, and hormonal messages being passed from nanobot to nanobot like buckets of water in an old-fashioned fire brigade.

But times have changed since our new LAN network was up and running a mere month ago. We can now fling messages back and forth with ease, burning fewer calories than dipping a pen in an inkwell. With this newfound LAN, I ran out of excuses to rationalize my avoidance. But today is different. I am choosing you as my first recipient of electronic mail. Not only will I get this letter off to the races, but it's a perfect opportunity to practice my hand at this new Goliath and titan of technology. Consider this email to be my way of killing two birds with one stone (without taking aim at messenger pigeons). Allow me grace as I navigate the nether regions of cyberspace. I have so much to learn from the cell folks in the 11 countries on planet Euclid: Music, Endo, Repro, Uri, Cardio, Skel, Lymph, Integ, Digi, Neuron, and Resp.

And today is just the beginning.

Who begins a distress call with small talk and pleasantries? We both know that this is nary the standard decorum of your run of the mill Mayday or distress call, not even one of "modest importance." There's always an ask. And you have no reason to believe that I am not among the charlatans I mentioned. I am in the same position as they to appeal to your gut feelings and empathetic sensibilities in the matter. All I ask is that you refrain from uprooting a cruciform flower from the soil, only to yank off each of the four petals one by one, proclaiming "I trust him" and "I trust him not" in rapid succession.

It is not fame or fortune that I seek! That is what I am not doing. So, what is it that I am seeking? I am not seeking but rather beseeching that you do not squander the post you hold. We have within our grasp the memory stores of Euclid's hippocampus, neocortex, and amygdala.

There is a school of thought that we are all driven by our own selfish desires. My motivation is the same as any other scientist. I suppose it all comes down to wanderlust and sheer curiosity. I yearn to examine and chronicle the experiential knowledge gleaned as I travel from testes to urethra. But I won't stop there. I will chronicle what exists outside the rim of the urethra. Even you must have cast a wistful gaze at the memory vaults, yearning for access to the existential knowledge that only Euclid Hux holds. What we have here are the answers to the questions of the very universe. How could we not be elevated to titans, veritable gods among mortals?

We are not limited to the textbook knowledge from Euclid Hux's memory stores, short-term memory, and long-term memory. My journey will also chronicle my first-hand experience and experiential knowledge as I pound the pavement at the school of hard knocks. We have all heard the rumors that only one sperm out of millions makes it to the end alive. And there are tales of a wonderful prize, a pot of gold at the vestiges of the rainbow, in the form of a magical egg in the innermost sanctum of an alien host. But even modest legends are indeterminate. nd with access to new territories beyond our meager confines, we can separate fact from fiction. But the journey will require resources. And only you possess the secret knowledge that is essential not only for the interests of science or the greater good but for my very survival.

You would be a fool to not have some skepticism. "Why must we acquiesce to such a requisition from a random sperm cell in the small country of Repro?"

We are just like you, confined to the jail cells of our cellular bodies as if being relegated to cages that keep us from taking flight. I am a rare haploid, emboldened to learn the what, how, wherefore, and why (and risk my very life in the process). Curiosity and bravery must not be confused.

If you are still reading this, I have accomplished more than I expected. And I am appreciative that you seized the time to read until the bittersweet end. If you should humor me with a reply, all the better, and I should be ever more grateful to be at your behest.

Most sincerely,

Just a random sperm cell

P.S. In the spirit of full disclosure, I have a history of feeling jealous of neurons, with their beautiful axons, dendrites, synapses, and beautiful language systems that rely on electrical impulses and neurotransmitters.

The A Letters
Subject: Re: Humble beginnings
Date: 2/4/2182 (Monday)
Location: Country of Neuron
Sender: Ron Une (mail and email screener for Office of the Prime Minister of Neuron)
Recipient: Just a random sperm cell

Dear random sperm cell, I work for the Office of the Prime

Minister in the country of Neuron! I am not the Prime Minister, but I am the chap who screens mail for any threats or security risks that might come his way. I am still getting acclimated to the LAN, as evidenced by the fact that the original letter I wrote you an hour ago is now deleted and sent to the cyber dead letter office! If this letter seems a bit short, it's only because I didn't want to write all of that tripe all over again. Maybe I will opt for the good old days of paper transcripts of the information shared by hormones, neural impulses, chemical transfers, or other rudimentary but familiar methods!

I find it odd, in a good way, that you would write a letter of such significance straight to the Office of the Prime Minister! What in the hell were you thinking? What you are asking for is tantamount to treason! The MacGuffin you are requesting is the "key to the castle," the top-tier knowledge that is not available to any other cell in the body (including myself). You may take me for some regal sort, working alongside the Prime Minister and all, but make no mistake. I only play the butler to his Batman. My "career" feels more like the stuff of a layman's factory job. Do you know what I do all day? I red-flag letters, much like the one you wrote, as potential security risks. Last week, I sifted through a few thousand of them (most of them still paper), and there were just five of them worthy of a red flag. Boring employments leaves one to reach for reassurances if only to preserve one's own sanity. "At least it's a job" has been my go-to catchphrase for the last few months, although I am not sure how much I really believe it!

Your letter may just be an orange alert to you. But in my world, it's worthy of a red flag. But to save you from any legal hullabaloo, I will not forward this letter to the Prime Minister. Lucky for you, I believe your intentions hold merit and are laudable and well-intentioned, even if you laid them down a bit thick. Do not mistake this as a boilerplate and disingenuous rejection letter. You know the type, the old "best of luck in your future pursuits" kind of tripe. Talk about wasting words on a whole lot of nothing.

But as you said, there is always an ask. And you are not alone in your zest and zeal for adventure. My only ask is that you count me in! But why risk my own neck, hide, and career to humor you in a game of cops and robbers? Make no mistake. I am no glutton for punishment. There are times when the "bravest" among us have something left to hide but nothing left to lose. And some of the most nefarious arch nemeses come from within ourselves. Still, I suppose I am stricken with the very same wanderlust you describe. And you are more right than wrong that I have been tempted to open the Pandora's Box of Euclid's mind since day one. Who doesn't like secrets? It's keeping them that's the tricky part! I suppose we should consider ourselves lucky. Without the nanobots, we wouldn't have access to Euclid's mind and hence access to all manner of human popular culture, from music, movies, to books.

Make no mistake. I will need to probe very deep into the dark recesses of Euclid's brain for what you inquire and desire. And there may be mental blocks on private thoughts or memories, and it's not a simple task to surpass these locks (many of which are self-imposed by Euclid himself). Do not forget that I am risking my hide, hair, and neck by even writing you about this tripe. You and I must both keep mum about any hint of this. Our lives depend on it.

Do not kid yourself. You are naive to think that you and you alone are alone in this boyhood yearning for adventure. And you are not the only one who understands the opportunities that Euclid Hux's mind can grant us. In fact, you are not even the first to send such a requisition to this office (but you will be the last). You are the fifth and final adventurer, and from henceforth, you will be named as "Adventurer 5."

There are four others who have reached out to me for such secrets. After all, it's common knowledge that Euclid is a reproduction scientist. You will receive ample opportunity to meet and greet them. In the beginning, I was going to solicit others to see who would be willing to take on this mission. Not only was there a dearth of interest, but it just wasn't worth the risk of being discovered for breaching security at the Office of the Prime Minister. So, instead of bringing Mohamed to the mountain, I waited for the mountains to come to Mohamed. And after securing four good men, I still needed a leader. There were a couple of applicants that didn't make the cut for one reason or another. But when I perused your letter, I sensed a kindred spirit. Your eagerness for adventure was seeping out of your pores like milk through a colander. As such, I would be honored to appoint you the leader of our rowdy rabble. I can't control how the five of you will mingle and get along, but I trust in your abilities to bolster teamwork regardless of any disparity in personality. Do not make friends with your battalion. Speak with conviction, charisma, and assertiveness. And carry a big stick if you must.

Being up here in Neuron and with you five being down there in Repro, I won't be able to join you in physical form. But I can communicate with you through the nanobot LAN and give guidance based on the knowledge I extract from Euclid's brain. Think of me as a sort of Control or Master Splinter (a promotion from playing Robin to the Prime Minster's Batman).

I will alert the others that with you on board we now have our Captain's catch. With the benefits of my intel, the five of you will garner an advantage in the adventures ahead. But do not resort to hubris! Your advantages can only carry you so far. Use my information with caution, and do not relay it to anyone outside our group of freedom fighters. Even when you discuss matters amongst yourselves, make sure nobody else is in earshot or spitting distance. Loyalty and trust are crucial. As such, we can write individual communiques to each other or to the group. You can also forward messages as you see fit. But in the spirit of transparency, if you must refer to someone else in our battalion, be respectful and write the letter "as if" the haploid you are talking about is right there with you. Gossip and back-stabbing will only destroy our group from within. Divide and Conquer is the oldest trick in the book. Over and out.

P.S. You are on fire! Now stop, drop, and rock and roll!

CHAPTER 2

The B Letters
Subject: The Great Wait
Sender: Adventurer 5 (formerly known as a random sperm cell)
Date: 02/08/2182 (Friday)
Location: Crystal Gate (Repro)
Recipient: Ron Une

Hello Ron, I must say that it's a great pleasure to receive any bit of your correspondence. I suppose, in hindsight, my requisition was maudlin and dramatic, if not rife with desperation. My only defense is that I was overcome with passion as if a drunken and smitten hopeless romantic texting a long-lost paramour. At the very least, I sensed a kindred spirit.

I am not an assertive sort by nature, but I will play the part of an austere ship captain until my forthright words and stoic demeanor shall become entrenched in the fabric of my muscle memory and fibers of my being. I will go now and write my fellow comrades a communique.

Flattered and honored, in that order,
Adventurer 5

P.S. I will keep mum about any and all manner of this top-secret matter. Consider it a gag order (not to be confused with a doctor's orders to induce vomiting).

The B Letters

Subject: Re: The Great Wait
Sender: Adventurer 5 (formerly a random sperm cell)
Date: 02/08/2182 (Friday)
Location: Crystal Gate (Repro)
Recipient: Adventurers 1-4
CC: Ron Une

Greetings, fellow gametes (Adventurers 1-4). I trust that all of you have been informed under the tutelage of Ron Une that each of us has been gifted with the opportunity to be ushered in as one of the king's men. This is a powerful post. And with power comes responsibility. And just like that rush of emotion that comes with being ingratiated into the arms of an elite university, we can allow ourselves a moment to feel that conglomeration of emotion that comes with "making the cut" and being ushered into this once in a lifetime opportunity. If you feel some anxiety, don't fret. This comes from the apprehension of not knowing what lies ahead and beyond the rim.

Whether from intuition or intoxication, Ron Une saw something in me and delegated me as our leader. Rest un-assured, any leadership ability I have acquired is either embedded in my DNA or due to my time spent at the school of hard knocks. But I do know that a solid leader aims for the "sweet spot" between bossy asperity on one end of the continuum and being a passive pushover on the other. My first "command," as it were, is to myself. I will not envy my assigned post. I will feel no preponderance of superiority in the manner in which I perceive and conduct myself in the presence of the lot of you. It is not a role I would choose. And my ask is that you, too, refrain from any and all manner of envy towards such a so-called regal post. The last thing we need is a "too many cooks in the kitchen" kind of rivalry that lends itself to team implosion. I will aim to be tough but fair, as a leader ought to be.

I also know that camaraderie is germane to any successful band of allies. So, let us get to know our quirks, personalities, strengths, and weaknesses. I suppose one could call it an icebreaker exercise. As leader, I will take the icy plunge first.

Adventurer 5:
Age (haploid years): 35
Favorite outfit: Suit and tie
Strength: Curiosity-driven philosopher, ability to find the sweet spot between extremes for max efficiency, devout follower of Murphy's Law
Example of strength: Bought two smoke alarms in case one crapped out, the house would have burned down if the second smoke detector didn't "smell the smoke"
Weakness: Penchant for cynicism, more questions than answers, dysthymia
Example of weakness: Made a friend cry on his birthday for reminding him that he's one step closer to the grave
Most embarrassing moment: The first time I saw a nanobot, I thought it was an alien trying to kill me
Favorite classic movie (before 2030): Everything, Everywhere, All at Once
Favorite expression: "If it can go wrong, it will go wrong." Many think this is pessimistic, but I find it proactive and even soothing.

The B Letters
Subject: Re: The Great Wait
Sender: Adventurer 3
Date: 02/09/2182 (Saturday)
Location: Repro
Recipient: Adventurers 1, 2, 4, and 5
CC: Ron Une

Hi, partners in crime! This is Adventurer 3. I can't believe we are doing this! As soon as I caught wind that Euclid Hux was a reproductive scientist some years ago, I put on my sneakers, put the rubber on the road, and hit the ground running. I joined

"Champ Camp," which is more taxing than boot camp (as it's designed for Olympian swimmers). I have been dying for this moment since high school. I have never lost a race or a fight, and I have twenty-three gold medals to prove it. I hope that I can use these abilities for our mission! Let's hit 'em where it hurts!

Name: Adventurer 3
Age (haploid years): 23
Favorite outfit: Track suit, tennis shoes
Strength: Physical fitness, adrenaline junkie
Example of strength: First place in too many competitions to count
Weakness (according to some): Overconfidence, poor risk analyses, poor loser, poor winner
Example of weakness: During my time in "Champ Camp," I challenged three sperm to a fight (and I went KO during the very first round)
Most embarrassing moment: In middle school, I told the entire school that I would ride a nanobot through the urinary tract (and smelled like piss for a haploid week)
Favorite classic old movie (before 2030): The Karate Kid
Favorite expression: "No pain, no gain."

The B Letters
Subject: Re: The Great Wait
Sender: Adventurer 1
Date: 02/10/2182 (Sunday)
Location: Repro
Recipient: Adventurers 2-5
CC: Ron Une

Greetings, newfound friends. I will alert you now that I am the slowest lion in the pack. I also have meager amounts of fortitude, and I am surprised I made the cut. My one and only risk in my pathetic life was taking part in the Eric Hux World Math

Championship (and I had to twist each arm with the other to do it). Despite my hesitation, I was overcome with euphoria when I took home first prize. I abstained from even going to university (although I learned all I could about math and mechanics on my own accord). I am obstinate and rigid when it comes to managing my impression and "public self." I know full well how "first impressions are lasting impressions" (Primacy Effect). And I also know that "last impressions are lasting impressions" (Recency Effect).

Consider this adventure to be my second wind. I am at the point where the low notes of my regrets are outnumbering my one and only high note. How many high notes can one have? More than one would make my life. Just don't enable me to slow you down. I may not be as intrepid as the rest of you lot. But if it comes down to a battle of wits, I can be a veritable titan. And that's a statement of fact, not an attempt at showing off. That is not the hill I wish to die on.

Name: Adventurer 1
Age (in haploid years): 40
Favorite outfit: Lab coat
Strength: Mathematical ability, mechanically inclined
Example of strength: Memorized pi to 300 decimal places, took apart a nanobot piece by piece, and put it together again
Weakness: Afraid of small spaces, fear of failure, tendency to self-handicap and end on a high note
Example of weakness: After taking home the prize in the Eric Hux World Math Championship, I had a peculiar need to "protect" this memory. The math championship was my "high note" in life I chose to end on. I rested on my laurels ever since. And that was ten years ago (haploid time).
Most embarrassing moment: One day in elementary school, the nurse came and gave inoculations to curtail STDs. I hid in the closet the entire time. My cover was blown when the nurse opened up the closet to get a box of Bandaids.

Favorite classic old movie (before 2030): A Beautiful Mind
Favorite expression: Do the Math

The B Letters
Subject: Re: The Great Wait
Sender: Adventurer 4
Date: 02/11/2182 (Monday)
Location: Repro
Recipient: Adventurers 1, 2, 3, 5
CC: Ron Une

Hey, fellow gamete game-mates!! I am writing this during a sort of manic high, so I may regret reading this later. The truth is, I don't know what Ron Une sees in me. I just had a whim one day to write him. And he wrote back. And here I am! Time will tell if it was a moment of impulsive weakness or a moment of healthy spontaneity! It's possible this manic high will diminish, and I will soon realize what I signed up for. But right now, I am over the moon! Yee-haw!

Name: Adventurer 4
Age (in haploid years): 29
Favorite outfit: Oversized sweater
Strength: Can see humor in any situation, love making metaphors
Example of strength: I was bullied in school, and I would cope with it by watching and writing improv comedy
Weakness: Over-using humor to avoid feeling
Example of weakness: Telling dark jokes at a funeral to (try) and lighten the mood
Most embarrassing moment: Having a laugh-attack during a moment of silence
Favorite classic old movie (before 2030): The Jerk
Favorite expression: Happiness is the best revenge. If you don't laugh, you cry

The B Letters
Subject: Re: The Great Wait
Sender: Ron Une
Date: 02/11/2182 (Monday)
Location: Neuron
Recipient: All adventurers

Many thanks to you all for partaking in our "lame" icebreaker! Many cell-folks are far too coy, too trendy, or lack the self-awareness to engage with a proper icebreaker. I appreciate the specificity and level of detail. We have yet to hear from Adventurer 2, and I do pray that he does not have "cold tail" about this whole thing (I mean, this mission does meet the criteria for insanity). And thank you all for CC'ing me on these self-descriptions. Still, please do not feel the need to CC me on each and every bit of correspondence. It would crush me to be one of those pesky micromanagers who are deprived of any trust in their fellow team members. We want to cultivate a milieu of trust and loyalty. With that said, please respect this level of fast and loose flexibility. Gossip and backstabbing are not nutrients that grow and foster trust and camaraderie. Morale is contagious, and when members don't feel "in it to win it," the entire team will suffer.

Now listen up, gentlemen. It's time for brass tacks. I need all of you to congregate at the campsite not far from the Crystal Gate in the testes. You know the one, the massive arched door that leads to the ducts, tunnels, and catacombs that wind their way to the urethra. Be there at 8:00am, sharp as Cheddar, February 14 (human time). From what I have been able to gather from Euclid's brain, that is the "day of love" in human culture, called "Valentine's Day." As such, there is a very good chance Euclid and Autumn will get together, and the doors of the Crystal Gate will open sometime on that day. Valentine's Day is not well known in Repro, especially given that any and all knowledge of the day is banned by the Prime Minister. So keep this intel on the hush-hush.

Sperm are a homogeneous bunch, so you will require an inconspicuous means of identification. I suggest something noticeable, but still doesn't draw too much attention. Perhaps something to the tune of holding a can of soda in each hand or wearing a cap tilted to one particular side. Eccentric but not weird!

In the interim, until February 14, I will break as many more locks as I can, being as covert and discreet as possible. It will help to do this while Euclid is inebriated, and most of his brain cells are under the influence. I will print as much as I can to allow me to pore over the materials in the safety of my private quarters without the ever-present watchful gaze of the powers that be.

In anticipation of your arrival at the campsite, I will use the LAN and delegate five nanobots from the muscular system in the country of Musc to saunter your way with haste (these nanobots will be energetic and excited to see you as this variety shares the personality traits of Shetland sheepdogs). These are the same nanobots that Euclid uses for his genetic muscle enhancements for the purposes of keeping up his strength under the duress of his Korsakoff Syndrome. That man drinks too much.

The nanobots will grant you three assets.

GPS Trackers: The specialized nanobots will outfit each of you with a GPS tracker on your left ear (it will not be placed deep inside, as the trackers are also equipped to monitor proximate sensory activity from the environment). These will allow me to track your whereabouts (not as a micromanager, but like a scientist studying the migration habits of geese). What's good for the goose is good for the gander, eh? Between the intel from Euclid's brain (including anatomical maps of the human body) coupled with the GPS trackers, I can relay intel on how best to navigate the murky depths, mazes, and corridors of the reproductive system. The trackers also have audio, in case I need to tell you something urgent. Still, it will behoove us to stick to email when possible (there are always eavesdroppers afoot chomping at the bit to hear anything from gossip to life-saving advice). For the purposes of science, these cute little trackers will record every second of your journey. Collecting data from all five senses, they will catch every sight, sound, tactile information, gustatory readings, and olfactory information. Keep in mind that all nanobots also record everything around them, and this data can be accessed via the LAN as well.

Body enhancement: The nanobots will inject genetic material in your bodies that will enhance your physical attributes (strength, speed, physique, stamina, etc.). All five of you will become super soldiers (Adventurer 3 will be even more super than he already is). Just don't let this get to his head.

Organ detection: As you may or may not know, all nanobots in this body are equipped with organ detection software. The tech is based on X-ray technology and sound waves, among other things I don't understand. They can identify and locate organs by their cellular and molecular composition (like the old-fashioned facial recognition technology from years ago).

All this will grant you an advantage over the millions of sperm that will be your adversaries. They would, if given any opportunity, kill you for them. All gloves are off when survival is at stake (all except brass knuckles, of course). Be on the lookout for these five peppy nanobots at the campsite at the Crystal Gate, as they will be sent to that very location when our day of truth comes (the nanobots will have shining red eyes, unlike the usual yellow). But again, they will also be expecting you as well. When you meet these adorable puppy-dogs, they will demand a password. It is "peptide." They will then place the GPS trackers inside your left ear. At that time, they will also implant the genetic material into your bodies to enhance your physical abilities. These procedures will be painful, but it's imperative that you do not attract attention with your grunts, groans, and/or moans. When you have all the payload procured, keep the five nanobots with you at the Crystal Gate. They must go through the barrier with you (as we do not know how many nanobots will be present at your place of destination). Some nanobots always pass through the urethra with the sperm, but we lose touch with them when they go beyond the geofence. But since the nanobots are now part of a LAN network, it should be possible to establish a link between the male LAN and whatever LAN that may exist in the expansiveness of the new frontier (as long as someone knows how to interface the two networks). The five nanobots can be "loosely" programmed to head towards the egress of the urethra. Even still, you must be vigilant to protect them at all costs and guide them a bit should they stray or veer too far off course!

Advantages aside, you will have to deal with the other sperms' varying swimming and fighting abilities. You will have an edge, but the quest will be far from easy. Statistics alone predict your demise. Rely on the support of your platoon and maintain ample amounts of morale and loyalty. Your first mission will be to barge through the Crystal Gate like a battering ram. You will have to maintain this momentum and inertia as if a steam train or bowling ball. It will not be a cakewalk as you snake your way through the winding tunnels and ducts. With luck and skill, you will locate the egress of the urethra and burst into the brave new world! If it's true that you will be in the belly of an alien being, let's hope and pray that this alien is a benevolent one!

Just making it this far will be a monumental triumph, as no haploid who has exited the urethra has ever returned to talk about it. It is not a far journey, but a crucial one. And the trackers should record every bit of it. As with any stage of your adventure, use everything you can muster: knowledge, serendipity, creativity, luck, strength, speed, perseverance, providence, and resourcefulness (just to name a few).

Recording devices can't capture everything. I ask Adventurer 5 to proffer frequent status reports to keep me abreast of where things are at in the mission (only use the audio if an emergency). I expect Adventurer 5 and I will correspond with each other the most, for obvious reasons, but CC or write anyone as you see fit. Just be mindful of not allowing any inter-member criticisms to slip (as such a thing could be a detriment to team morale). If gossiping becomes a problem, I will have to rethink our free-writing privileges. In the interests of science, give me the important facts (the nanobots will be collecting data as well, so you don't have to do all the work). Embellish as you wish, as I do like a good war story. Include a brief summary of any important conversations that take place within your platoon. And if you must be a harbinger of bad tidings, save any bad news for the bitter end, if possible. Being stricken with grief may preclude me from bothering to finish the message in its entirety.

I will act as a guide and helper when I can. I apologize, but I cannot do more from my "Ivory Tower." But do not be deceived by appearances, as I am in much more danger than you may realize. And when this is all said and done, I will have done more than enough to justify not only termination from work but termination from life itself!

I will end with this. Remember that a "Fool's Hope" is better than no hope at all. You can do this. You must bolster morale in your mates (feign confidence if you must). Go through the motions. I, too, will do my part to bolster this morale. My faith in you is genuine and unwavering!

Sincerely,

Ron Une

Office of Prime Minister: Security Screener of Mail

Country: Neuron

The B Letters

Subject: Re: The Great Wait

Sender: Ron Une

Date: 2/11/2182 (Monday)

Location: Neuron

Recipients: All Adventurers

Greetings Adventurers,

By now, I trust that the details surrounding February 14 are etched into your brain like a wood carving and burned into your muscle memory like a brand from a branding iron! Just don't spill any beans that are not worth spilling. Do not divulge the "low-down" on what we are up to.

While you are an alliance, a veritable "brothers in arms," there will come a time when you must compete with each other. But I would be remiss if I did not dissuade each of you from any gregarious fraternizing. Alliances are a wonderful thing, but they serve a strategic purpose! And by design, they benefit a group for only a short while. Congenial bonds will undermine the mission when push comes to shove, and stab comes to kill. Keep things professional, if only for your own sakes. Abstain from using your real names. Refer to yourselves as Adventurer 1, 2, 3, 4, and 5. I get that being named a number is not very personal. But it's a far cry better than being called "a random sperm cell." Do what's best for the mission. Please do not take this for nagging, insulting your intelligence, or stating the obvious.

I discovered some useful intel, but it wasn't from Euclid's memory or knowledge stores. I was able to retrieve a menagerie of brief, rudimentary, and fragmented Wi-Fi signals from the nanobots that passed Euclid's urethra during his last bout of sexual intercourse. As the nanobots left the urethra, they were able to maintain the Wi-Fi signal for only a brief moment. On their own, it was just static or white noise. But when I spliced the signals together like puzzle pieces, I gleaned a consistent flow of information, and a clearer picture began to emerge!

It appears that only 2 million sperm out of 50 million or so make it to the next milestone or goal post beyond the urethra. From statistics alone, this translates into a scant 1/25 chance of survival for each of you. But your advantages will improve these odds by a lofty margin. Leave no stone unturned, make no assumptions, and consider nothing as inconsequential! The planning stage is the easy part. Figurines and toy tanks on a battle map look cool but trust me, they do not shoot back!

Seize the five nanobots and take them with you as you leave the urethra (they will do their best to follow as well). This may put you at a temporary disadvantage because their weight may slow you down. I suggest you each tether yourselves to one of them and help guide it to the extraction point. Don't listen to that saying, "work smarter, not harder!" Work smarter AND harder! They are not mutually exclusive! You will need both to get to the end. Reach out to me if you need anything. Otherwise, just meet the nanos at the campsite and follow the previous instructions to the letter. I have faith in you! And I trust that such sentiment is mutual! Let's stop, drop, and rock & roll!
Sincerely,
Ron Une

P.S. My main goal will be to break Euclid's memory lock and gain access to top-tier information. His Korsakoff Syndrome has left many of my fellow cells in a state of atrophy. As a result, some of his memories are hazy and spotty. Between Euclid's knowledge and the data from your nanobots, I can extract geographical information on where you are headed and how best to get there.

The B Letters
Subject: Re: The Great Wait
Sender: Adventurer 5
Date: 02/12/2182 (Tuesday)
Location: Repro
Recipients: Ron Une

Hello Ron Une,

Your brass tacks are most welcome (and much more welcome than ass-tacks on a chair). You leave no stone unturned. And I will offer my reassurances that we will keep mum and "keep the low-down on the down-low." There are traitors amok, and even alliances are not immune from someone turning coat.

This is a dead horse worth beating, and you do not belabor the issue by mentioning it on an intermittent basis. There is no need to heap additional trouble on our already troublesome affair. Even the most cynical among us are not gluttons for punishment, and we hope to find the calm in the eye of the hurricane even during times we feel resigned to rain on the parade with a deluge of acidic rain. And last but not least, I will also be intentional to avoid any "bad news" until the end. I can only imagine how difficult it must be to read a letter where the very next sentence might be the one that describes one of our deaths. Talk about a death sentence!

The training wheels are off. The safety net has been rolled up and cast aside. But we still lack an ironclad plan. Adventurer 2 has not yet joined us. The rest of us have been scrunched together in my tiny home since this morning, brainstorming ideas on how to ensure the five nanobots make it across the threshold. Adventurers 3 and 4 did not waste a microsecond to claim my leather sofa as if it was a life raft on a sinking shop or unclaimed territory in a land rush. Adventurer 1 settled for my favorite bar stool (as he fidgeted with his fidget spinner). As for me, I didn't hunker down. I suppose it made it easier for me to give standing orders. Even with this level of body distribution, we were still elbow to elbow. I can't say I am well-versed on how neurons live in your country, but tiny houses are the norm for us haploids here in Repro (at least for nocturnal rest, as most gametes spend most of their time outside).

Even thought we were indoors, we took care that our secrets were conveyed only through the medium of whispers, body language, and the written word. As far as I was concerned, even grapevines could be tapped. I can assure you (Ron) that maintaining a whisper during an argument is no small feat. This is especially true when the volume of flying spittle exceeds the volume of the spoken words.

I stood at my wall whiteboard, clutching a dry-erase marker as if poised for battle. I had your last letter printed and tucked in my shirt pocket. I read it aloud, word by word. Hearing words once makes an impression. And hearing them again solidifies that impression.

"Any questions?" I asked. They murmured "no" and shook their heads from side to side. I placed the document in my paper shredder near the main door leading outside.

I coughed into my hand. "Okay, the first thing we need to do is come up with a means of identifying each other at the campsite. Ideas?"

Adventurer 4 raised his hand and was called on. "Why can't we keep it simple and just look for the picnic table with a potted cactus at each of the four corners? I say we bring treats as well. I will bring homemade fortune cookies with my favorite bits of wisdom, some cooked up by me!"

"Not sure if horticulture makes us appear as a force to be reckoned with, but it will do," said Adventurer 3. "Chalk it up to a form of hustling and poker faces. As for me, I will complement Adventurer 4's fortune cookies with protein bars."

"What about Adventurer 1," said Adventurer 3. "Is he trying to get out of bringing food?"

I looked at Adventurer 1. "What about it? Care to bring anything to the table? I will bring the cacti and macaroni salad. Not that we really need the cacti, given our food plans."

"Sorry for not jumping in," said Adventurer 1. "Don't worry, I'm not trying to get out of anything. I will bring the bratwursts and buns."

"Should be fun," said Adventurer 4, smiling and clapping his hands together.

"Okay, next order of business," I replied. "We need to deliver the five nanobots across the threshold. What can we do to ensure their safe delivery?"

Adventurer 3 raised his hand but did not wait to be called on. "I say we leave them behind. Didn't Ron say some nanobots always manage to cross the barrier on their own accord anyway? He made it sound like they are akin to guard dogs. We may have trouble losing them if anything."

"Yeah, we don't need them if there are nanobots in the new frontier," whispered Adventurer 4. "They will only slow us down."

I drew a crude map of our surroundings and pointed at the various milestones. "Ron said we maintained internet contact for a brief moment. We do not know if those nanobots made it to the new frontier in the uncharted territories. The signal was lost just moments after they crossed the urethra."

Adventurer 3 huffed. "Those things will just drag us to our doom, no matter how many gold medals I have for strength and speed."

Adventurer 4 smirked. "How does Adventurer 3 manage to find an opportunity to brag in every conversation?"

"What's that supposed to mean?" asked Adventurer 3. "I think this Adventurer 4 guy is all hat and no cattle."

I put up my palm to reassure. "Calm those nerves, gentlemen. We are not 'fixin' to die.' Ron himself suggested we each commandeer a nanobot and tether ourselves to it. Maybe we can ride it like a nautical vessel."

Adventurer 3 shook his head. "That sounds about as easy as riding a bull in a rodeo. What good are the nanobots if we can't even make it out alive? I think we should just chance it and hope for the best."

I looked at Adventurer 1. "You have been rather discreet, Adventurer 1. Do you care to proffer an educated opinion on the matter?"

"You sure?" whispered Adventurer 1.

Adventurer 3 groaned and shook his head. "Man, what a beta-softie."

"Go on," I said towards Adventurer 1. "You have the floor."

Adventurer 1 cleared his throat. "Well, since you asked. There is one way to circumvent our little bottleneck. As you know, I never went to university. But I am an autodidactic learner. I studied nanobot technology inside and out at my own leisure. I know how to program them to follow our GPS trackers. Tethering ourselves to the bots is not even necessary."

Adventurer 3 sighed. "And to think we were heading to our deaths because Adventurer 1 was too shy to interject his opinion. Being shy is one thing. Allowing others to march to their doom is another."

"It's okay," said Adventurer 4. "Better late than never is what I like to say."

The excitement in our group was palpable. I can't thank you enough for humoring our unsatiated thirst for adventure (and yours as well). The nanobot payload is most welcome (GPS coordinates, genetic material, tracker, stem cells, etc.). We are poised and ready to ready our poise.

P.S. After the squad took their egress to their own devices in their own tiny houses, I sprawled myself out on the sofa as I allowed myself a loud groan. My thoughts began in a worldly fashion, kind of like when you are staring out a first story window and can spot the makes and models of the nanobots and describe them with fine and copious detail. But my thoughts became more existential and big-picture, like when you ascend to the tenth floor and can count the vehicles and identify their colors but can no longer discern the makes and models. But in order to mitigate this loss in detail, you now have a clearer view of the very heavens and the beyond. But as I got more sleepy, my thoughts melded into each other. The last thing I remember before falling asleep was the word "wanderlust." I didn't think of it at the time, but now I just realized that the words "wonder" and "wander" are more similar than different. I understand that "wanderlust" is a noun and "wonder" is a verb. Even still, they both conjure images of curiosity, the impetus to adventure. The lot of us are no doubt "wondering wanderers."

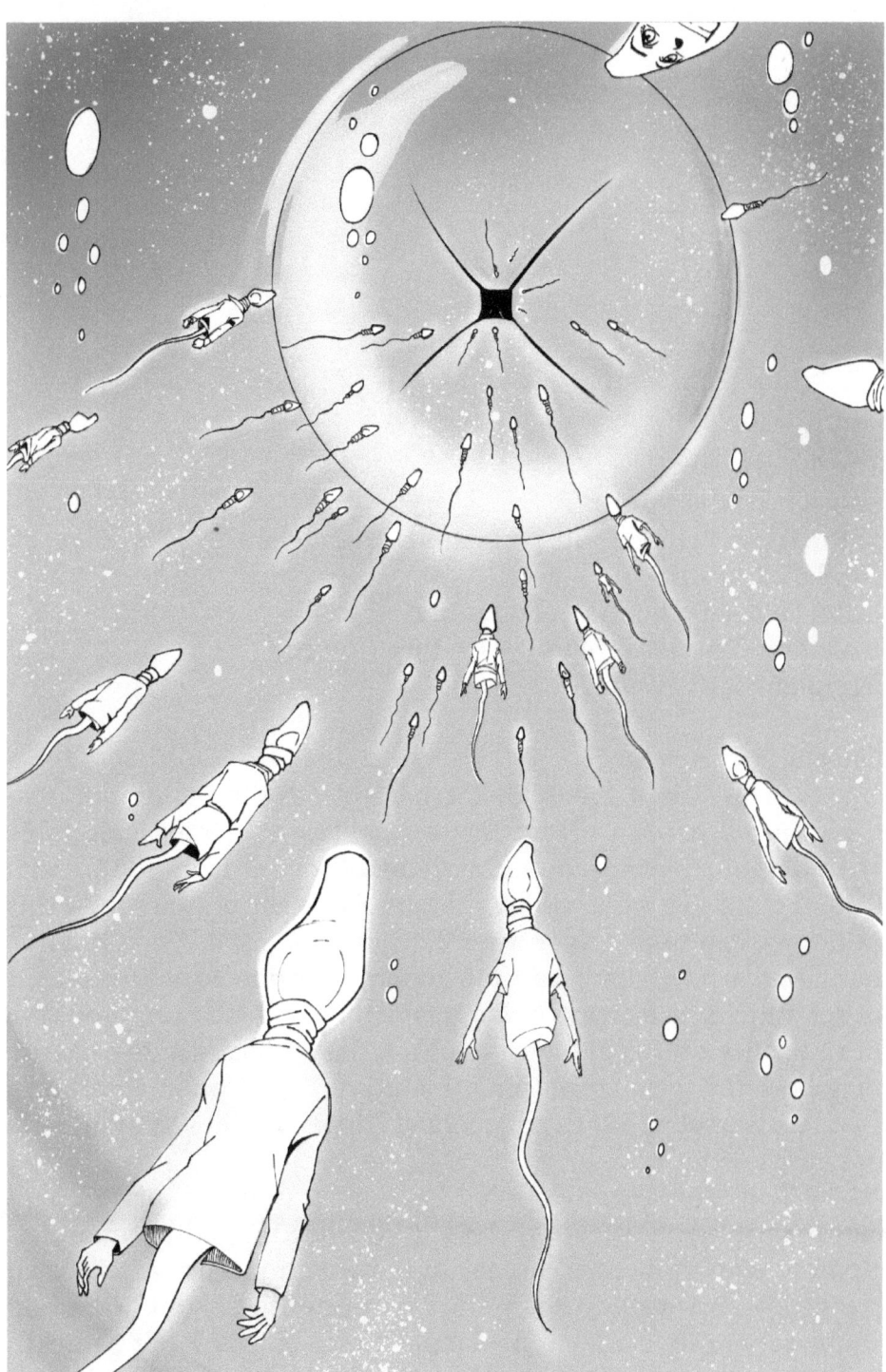

CHAPTER 3

The C Letters
Subject: To the Cervix
Battle type: Cellular survival games, flight class *
Sender: Ron Une
Date: February 14, 2182 (Thursday)
Location: Crystal Gate to the urethra (Repro)
Recipient: Adventurer 5

Cheers, Adventurer 5!

Please read the relevant parts of this missive aloud to the group when all of you have assembled at the picnic table with the four plants. The location is not too far from the Crystal Gate. I trust that you will be there early to get prepared. At this point, we can take Adventurer 2 off our CC lists. When the five nanobots arrive, don't call too much attention to yourselves. I don't anticipate anyone being suspicious and hassling you. It's not uncommon for gametes to check the web or use the nearby nanobots for various reasons, including medication injections. Just be discreet about the injections! Especially those of you who are needle-shy!

I won't regurgitate what I expounded on January 12. You can read it again for yourselves if you need a gentle reminder. By now, we know and can assume this is not a tip-toe through the tulips or a walk in the park. Not even the Boston Marathon can compare to the level of danger here. This is a life or death competition. Just making it through the Crystal Gate will be a daunting task, as there are going to be over 50 million gametes in waiting. And every one of them is motivated by their fear of death, just like us. Is there a stronger motivator? Not even money wields that kind of power! I do not say this to strike fear into your hearts. But I must relay the gravity of the situation. It is foolhardy to march through a blizzard without a winter survival kit. I say all this because I believe in you. If I lacked this faith in you, I would order you to pack it in and traverse home again while you still can. That's what Adventurer 2 did. And I'm not sure any of us can blame him!

I cracked a few blocks in Euclid Hux's memory stores and obtained some vital intel. Euclid Hux is a "male host," and the country of "Repro" consists of "male reproductive organs." And lest Euclid's Korsakoff has rendered him delusional, the new frontier should involve a similar "female host" with similar organ systems. This means we are headed for a brave new planet with its own set of continents and countries. It appears that most of the countries and organ placements are almost identical, save for the very disparate reproductive systems. Like our Euclid Hux, our twenty-eight-year-old female host and partner to Euclid (whose full name will be Autumn Hux on January 17 when they become married).

Breaching the Crystal Gate will be the most challenging aspect of this sub-quest due to the excessive numbers of sperm trying to break through the small gate. When you breach the gate, you will find yourselves navigating through a series of winding corridors that lurch their way towards the urethra like vines. With equal helpings of luck and skill, you will happen upon the cervix region of the female reproductive system. Here, you can find a moment of reprieve from the big race. Extract all wisdom you can from this sub-quest, as it appears the next phase of this quest will involve another gate as well. But we won't stress about that now. We will cross that rickety rope bridge when we get there!

I surmise that if you are fortunate enough to make it

through the Crystal Gate, you will find yourselves in a swimming race, so prepare your swimming and racing abilities in advance. Allow Adventurer 1 ample time to sync the five nanobots with the GPS trackers. Swim as fast as you can, and they will follow you like ducklings to their mother. You will find the nanobots to be a sprightly bunch.

Your bodies will soon feel the effects of the enhanced abilities given by the nanobots. Trust that the muscle enhancements are doing something, even if you don't feel any different. The genetic material will buff your speed, stamina, endurance, power, and strength. There is always good news, and the Crystal Gate leading to the cervix has been opening less often these days. As such, the number of gametes at the gate is more sparse than usual. And the ones that are there have become more complacent and unprepared.

Humans have an expression: "luck of the draw." This will be our metaphor for what we are stacked up against. Like a duel between cowboys, every phase of this quest will require both luck and skill. The "luck side" can include circumstantial variables such as the tightness of the holster, accuracy of the pistol, or even the length of their finger nails as they reach for their side arm. The skill variables can include things like reaction time, aiming ability, and hand/eye coordination. Do not let the low odds of success paint a bleak picture. At first I was considering withholding the odds of success to you, but further thought on the matter convinced me that without some element of fear, you may not be as vigilant. And we don't want our platoon to be rife with complacency and atrophy like some of the folks near the Crystal Gate!

P.S. You may be wondering why I began the letter with "Cheers" instead of placing it at the end. Let's just suffice to say I drink my nightcaps in the morning (no thanks to Euclid Hux).

The C Letters

Subject: Re: To the Cervix
Survival Type: Cellular competition (flight class)
Author: Adventurer 3 (AKA "Brawn")
Date: February 14, 2182 (Thursday)
Location: Crystal Gate (Repro)
Recipient: Ron Une
CC: All adventurers

Hiya my man Ron Uno,

We are stoked for adventure (at least I am). And while each of our motivations may differ, we share a common destiny. It's hard to believe that we will be the very first to give a proper report from beyond the urethra (other than the brief amount of static you were able to retrieve). This is cray-cray!

Sure, we have patches of textbook knowledge that you have extracted from the knowledge and memory stores of Euclid's mind. But who cares! We will be the ones in the trenches, not the cozy confines of the ivory tower! As far as we are concerned, the Crystal Gate leads to the great unknown, and I reckon we may never see our humble country of Repro again. What really lies beyond our human host, Euclid Hux? It's hard to say! But we are at the cusp of something great (and I look forward to reaping the fanfare and financial rewards that are sure to follow).

When I arrived at the camp, I spotted Adventurer 5 waving at me from the picnic table (along with the awkward stares of other bystanders trying to see who that crazy guy was waving at). I sauntered over and spotted the four potted plants positioned with perfect symmetry (not that they were necessary, given the waving flag and abundance of pasta salad on the table). I set down my granola bars next to the several cases of pale ale (which must have come from the new thirty-something guy at the table, given the three empty bottles next to him). The little but evolving shindig was nice and helped dissolve any low spirits brought on by the cloudy and drizzly weather.

Adventurer 5 stood up. "Let me introduce you to

Adventurer 2."

The new dude clasped my hand in the tightest hand-shake I had ever felt. So how about that Ron Une? Adventurer 2 made it after all! Talk about a pleasant surprise. It wasn't long until the others arrived as well, with their foodstuffs in tow. Adventurer 5 allowed us ample time to sit down and meet, greet, and eat to allow us to get a "feel" for our physical presence and personas. We also used this time to make sure Adventurer 2 was caught up to speed on everything that has transpired so far (although it turns out he did read all the CC'd correspondence, he just didn't bother to reply in kind).

The new guy stood up as if making a toast at a wedding (with glazed eyes and a small stagger to his swagger). "I must apologize for my tardiness and lack of reply. I had to take a series of stress management classes after I was caught smashing the nanobot mail courier. And I just got done working and paying for the damages. I like to think I learned my lesson. But I must level with you. Crimes of passion are the most difficult to deter."

"Why the chip on your shoulder, if you don't mind my asking," said Adventurer 5.

Adventurer 2 hesitated and scratched his shoulder. "Well, I was expecting my monthly military pay. When it didn't arrive on time, I did what I was supposed to and told myself, 'It's better late than never.'. I took it in stride and waited until the next day. The next day, it didn't arrive either. And while I did swear at the poor nanobot, I was happy I didn't take a swing at the poor fellow. Well, when it didn't arrive on the third day, I guess you could say I 'advocated for myself.'"

"Is that therapist-speak for knocking sense into their heads?" asked Adventurer 4. "Did you at least get the money?"

"The very next day," Adventurer 2 mumbled. "But not really, as I had to spend it all to replace the nanobot postman."

Everyone laughed, except for Adventurer 2 (at least at first). And then his boisterous guffaws became the loudest of the pack. You should have been there, Ron. The vibe was raucous and raw.

I can't say that the five nanobots were as punctual as the rest of the gang. It took another haploid hour for them to arrive (which wasn't the end of the world, as we just spent the time relaxing and listening to Adventurer 2's war stories). We didn't even need the nanobots' red eyes as a cue.

"Look out!" shouted Adventurer 1 as a pack of five nanobots with red eyes came at us. "We are under siege!"

Adventurer 1 curled up in fetal position. One of the nanobots nuzzled against Adventurer 4 and pushed him out of fetal position. All five of them were jumping and engaging in zoomies.

"If I'm not mistaken, I would say they are happy to have found us," I said.

"Fetal position, Adventurer 1?" asked Adventurer 3. "Was that necessary?"

I laughed. "Hold the phone, Adventurer 3. Remember that fetal position is better than fatal position."

After the nanobots settled down, I volunteered to receive the nanobot injection and GPS tracker first (I used to be a fitness instructor, after all). I felt awkward seeing nosy bystanders peer at us as if we were prepping to rob a bank. Adventurer 2 went next. And then Adventurers 4 and 5 took their turn.

A rando approached us. "Whatcha guys doin'?"

"None of your business!" said Adventurer 2.

Adventurer 5 held up his palm. "At ease, gents."

"I have never seen anyone get inoculations way out here before," said the rando. "I never thought of this place as a field hospital. I'm just curious, as it's kinda weird."

Adventurer 5 spoke with such conviction I almost believed him myself. "We are receiving our Germ-Sperm inoculations. Now, move along. Nothing to see, taste, touch, smell, or hear here."

The stranger must have been a glutton for punishment. "I have never heard of Germ-Sperm. Is it contagious?"

"I'm afraid so," said Adventurer 5. "In fact, you may have gotten too close already. You may want to slide back a few paces."

"No worries," said the rando as he slid backwards while facing us and holding up his palms. "Sorry for intruding. I hope you all feel better soon."

I tell you, Ron, it's one thing to wield a believable excuse. It's quite another to give the opposing party a reason to stop hassling you! And this time, it worked on both counts!

"So what about you, Adventurer 1?" asked Adventurer 5.

Adventurer 1 stuttered and stumbled over his words. "Um, I think I might be allergic to these inoculations. I better opt out."

"No chance," said Adventurer 5. "Ron Une said it is almost impossible for a muscle-enhanced sperm cell to trigger an antigen immune response."

"I think what we got here is a needle-shy coward," said Adventurer 2.

"None of that, Adventurer 2," said Adventurer 5. "If anything, denying muscle enhancements could be construed as an act of bravery, after a fashion."

Adventurer 2 put up his palms. "Have it your way. It's not worth the trouble. Sounds like another opportunity to practice my anger management skills."

"Owowow" shouted Adventurer 1 as he took the brunt of the needle injection. Several bystanders gazed at us as if we were naked in the streets. They must have felt second-hand embarrassment as they went on their merry (awkward) way. While we don't see or feel any physical advantages as of yet, at least our bodies are tolerating the implants (so far). And with my stamina, the implants are a bonus, but nothing I really needed. If personality has a genetic component, it's a shame we couldn't use genetic modification procedures to augment our personality traits or even gain new ones.

I don't know how many additional hours we spent at the campsite (pivoting between peals of laughter, heartbreak, and fisticuffs). At least it gave Adventurer 2 some time to sober up. Adventurer 1 used the entire time rigging the nanobots to follow our GPS trackers. Was he the strong and silent type? Well, so far, he proved the latter "silent" part. But his needle phobia sure made me question the former part.

"Done," said Adventurer 1, slamming the wrench down like a shot glass downed in one gulp to the tune of hoots, hollers, and applause from the group.

"Splendid," said Adventurer 5. "Now, let's get to the gate. We shouldn't be too complacent. That door could open at any time."

"Let's each read a fortune first," said Adventurer 3, handing each of us a home-made fortune cookie. "I wrote the fortunes myself."

Adventurer 4 revealed the paper as he chomped on the fortune cookie. "We will be victorious."

Adventurer 2 mumbled into my ear. "Good advice, but hardly clever."

Adventurer 5 unraveled his and likewise popped the cookie into his mouth. "Life is like a bag of fortune cookies. You never know what unexpected advice you are going to get."

"Sage advice, but hardly original," whispered Adventurer 2.

I opened mine next. "Keep your friends closer and enemies closest."

"Getting better," I whispered back to Adventurer 2.

Adventurer 1 tossed his cookie to the ground.

"Tossing your cookies?" asked Adventurer 5. "You feeling alright?"

"Sorry," said Adventurer 1. "I appreciate the thought. But I think fortune cookies are bad luck."

"Ugh," said Adventurer 2. "Here we go. Time to practice more anger management, I see."

"And you?" asked Adventurer 5, looking at me.

"Time is like perfume, it is of the essence."

"Nice," said Adventurer 5. "A perfect segue to make ourselves to the gate."

We have all spent leisure time at this Crystal Gate many times before. After all, it's a popular jam for gametes to have parties. But today was different, even despite our little party. And while the crowd may have been fewer and farther between than usual, there were still millions of sperm in waiting (many of them rowdy as they whipped their tails and arms around their immediate vicinity to create space). Sperm were packed around the door like sardines (not to mention that sperm resemble fish as well). At least there was no indication of pushing (yet). Since the door has not been opening much these days, many of the gametes have no doubt become complacent. But Adventurer 5 had us maintain our vigilance regardless, knowing that the door could open at any moment. We all understood the importance of reaction time in a situation like this (and we remained hopeful that the physical enhancements would give us more of that, too). Not that I needed any, mind!

"Today, the Crystal Gate is not just a tourist trap," said Adventurer 5. "It's a trap in more ways than one." Likewise, the Crystal Gate itself seemed somehow taller than before, as if some holy shrine. It occurred to me that the gate was both an entrance to strange new worlds and an exit away from home. There was a glimmering green emerald at the very top, like a crown on a king. An ominous question mark adorned the left door, and an exclamation point on the right. There have been many legends and fables about what these symbols meant, and I remember having great fun during school days sharing with others on what they could mean. But today, it wasn't just subject matter for chit-chat and chin-wags. If anything, knowing what it all meant could really help us in our journey.

But it wasn't just pasta salad and cacti that Adventurer 5 brought. He also lugged a large spool of very thin wire with him. (Could these items be any more random?) And Adventurer 2 didn't just bring the ale. He also brought some military tear gas canisters. I never even thought to bring anything non-food related. After all, I have heard the expression "Never bring a knife to a gunfight," but "Never bring a spool of wire to a rat race" was new to me! We didn't expend much time and energy on battering down the door (it was so tight I wondered if there was some sort of spiritual seal). Besides, if I couldn't budge it, nobody could!

To your relief and ours, there were a handful of nanobots in the group, waiting to be ushered into the tunnel like a small mass of groupies of an obscure rock outfit. But for your peace of mind (as well as our own), we brought our five to the gate.

Adventurer 4 walked in front of Adventurer 5 as the latter began laying the trip wire across the front of the Crystal Gate. I smiled when I heard their contrived conversation about sports and weather (the last thing either of them cared about). When they returned, Adventurer 2 handed us each a teargas canister and a Swiss Army Knife. But today, the weather wasn't just a topic of small talk. Storm clouds gathered, and the weather soon became inclement. A deluge of rain beat into the mob. Sure, it made things harder for the five of us, but at least it made it harder for everyone else, too. Talk about grading on a curve.

After the brief storm, the gate was still closed. And then boredom became our worst enemy. We made the best of it and spent time reviewing each other's strengths and weaknesses from our ice-breaker before. It felt like we were "different but equal" RPG characters with varying attributes in range, distance, stamina, strength, intellect, or speed (although I had several of these advantages).

After a time, the lot of us just stood in line, not saying a word, with glazed-over eyes.

Adventurer 4 snapped his fingers. "Hey, we should have nicknames. You know, to shake things up and make it more fun."

"I don't know," I returned. "Ron made it clear that we shouldn't humanize each other too much. We may be an alliance for now, but we are still enemies."

"Adventurer 4 is right," said Adventurer 5. "I mean no disrespect, but the Pygmalion Effect does have survival value."

"Pygmalion effect?" asked Adventurer 2. "What are you going on about? The Three Little Pigs?"

I rolled my eyes. "Only you can wear ignorance as if a badge of honor."

"You wanna say that to my face?" asked Adventurer 2.

"Stop it, gents," said Adventurer 5. "The Pygmalion Effect refers to self-fulfilling prophecy. The way we view and see ourselves and others can have an effect on drawing out those very same traits, even unconsciously. In other words, if we all start calling Adventurer 2 'Unhinged,' he might adopt and exaggerate his pissy posturings all the more."

"Hey, I resent that," said Adventurer 2.

"See?" returned Adventurer 5. "It's working already. But let's focus on our strengths. What should we call Adventurer 1?"

Adventurer 4 chimed in. "Since he is mathematical, I think we should call him Brain."

"But that doesn't acknowledge his knowledge in mechanics," I said. "How about Abacus, as it is a mechanical device that also does math?"

"How does that sound?" asked Adventurer 5, looking at Adventurer 1.

"That suits me just fine," said Adventurer 1 (Abacus) as he spun his fidget spinner with a hastier velocity. It made me wonder if he really was fine or just being a pathetic sycophant. But I agreed Abacus had a nice ring to it.

Adventurer 5 looked at Adventurer 2. "Come to think of it, you never did do our little ice-breaker. Could you explain your greatest strength and greatest shortcoming?"

Adventurer 2 stared at the ground and kicked a pebble around. "Well, okay. My situation is difficult, see, because my strength and weakness are the same."

"Ah, how does that work?" I asked. "That doesn't make sense."

Adventurer 5 held up his palm towards me. "It's okay, let him speak."

Adventurer 2 continued. "Rage is my gift and my curse. When channeled and focused, it can be a force to be reckoned with. It's a natural motivator, and I can feel the power coercing through my veins. But when you know what buttons to push, my anger can be directed and wasted on the wrong target."

"That makes sense," said Adventurer 5. "And it can lead to unintentional impertinence or belligerence. Like a chameleon, you are an irascible sort and very sensitive to environmental stimuli. As if a chameleon turning green with envy on a lily pad or hot-red on a red wagon. We just have to know what buttons NOT to push."

Adventurer 3 looked at everyone. "How about Bellicose for a nickname? It has a military ring to it."

"A bit too pejorative, I think," said Adventurer 5.

"Animus," I suggested. "That has a similar meaning, but sounds more like a super hero."

"Let's let you four put it to a vote," said Adventurer 2.

It was three to one in favor of Animus, so Animus it was!

"Adventurer 3?" asked Adventurer 5, looking around. "Any druthers?"

Adventurer 5 paused. "It's highly irregular to give yourself a nickname."

"And arrogant," said Animus. "It's like knighting yourself! I say we call him Butterfingers. He's always dropping stuff."

I couldn't control myself. "I would rather be Butterfingers than Butterface, which is the name for this clown."

Adventurer 5's voice thundered. "All right, gentlemen, that's enough. This is a trivial thing to get worked up about. Our patience will only be tested much more than this in the days ahead. I think 'Brawn' rather suits him. He can match Adventurer 1's brain with brawn."

"Then it's settled," I said.

"I guess I'm next," said Adventurer 4. "I'm not sure my

strengths will be all that beneficial."

"Nonsense," said Animus. "He's a funny guy. He can be our comic relief character."

"I see the connection," said Adventurer 5. "But I don't want to minimize his importance to the mission. We need a word that also emphasizes his ability to maintain a sense of humor in the darkest of times and the most tumultuous of situations."

"I want to hear what Abacus thinks," said Animus. "He nary said a word this whole time."

Adventurer 5 looked at Abacus. "Well, what do you think, Abacus?"

Abacus stared at the ground. "Levity."

"I like it," said Adventurer 4. "Works for me."

"Then Levity it is," said Adventurer 5. "I guess I'm last but not least."

Levity spoke. "Adventurer 5 may not always see the glass half full, but he always gives nuggets of wisdom."

Animus scrunched up his mouth into a stink face. "You want to call him Nugget? Like a puppy?"

Levity glared at Animus. "No, I was thinking something more like Guru!"

"Too self-important," said Adventurer 5. "I would fancy something a bit more modest."

Levity was bound and determined to find a suitable epithet. "How about Sage? It can be a noun or a verb."

"I would be honored and flattered," said Adventurer 5 (Sage). "In that order. We now each have a coat of arms to be proud of. Every time we say it, we will reinforce the respective images of power in our brains and muscle memories."

"What about Ron Une?" asked Levity.

"Yes, what about him?" I asked. "We wouldn't even be here if it weren't for him."

"Unlike Sage here, I think he's a glass half full kinda guy," said Animus. "No offense to Sage."

"None taken," Sage said. "I think."

Abacus raised his hand.

"Just spit it out, Abacus," shouted Animus. "No need to pussyfoot around like a meek and timid kitten."

Abacus cleared his throat. "How about Morale? Ron Une has a certain proclivity for raising morale."

"I like it," said Sage. "Now let us live up to our epithets as if they were ideals to strive for and titles to be earned!"

As our intoxications began to taper down, our conversation turned to the "Nanobot Fury" demolition derby competitions held in the endocrine system in the country of Endo. The event was televised here in Repro (as contestants build their own nanobots from spare parts and race or fight them with each other). And just as I was sharing about a local championship race here in Repro a few haploid years ago, the gates flew open like the gate at a rodeo. But unlike a rodeo, this felt more like the "running of the bulls" with all the mayhem and bedlam that ensued! Haploids were punching, tail-whipping, trampling, shoulder checking, head-butting, slapping, and any other "contact sport" they could conjure. I was able to sneak a peek through a tiny crevice of swaying bodies, and I could see a gargantuan cavern housing a small lake. There was a soft orange flickering glow inside, indicating there were lit torches adorning the walls. And just to think that all this time, I thought "go jump in a lake" was piss-poor advice.

The gate became clogged like a broken cork lodged in a bottleneck, and nobody could press through it. Some of us were lucky to have enough belly space to breathe. Many haploids were crushed to unconsciousness or death while still standing and being pressed forward. Others fell to the ground and were trampled upon like ironic "welcome mats." Others retreated and escaped back to the park near Crystal Gate with a sudden change of plans and change of heart. Some wielded weapons such as brass knuckles, tools, rods, scissors, sticks, stones, and everything in between.

I made eye contact with Levity just a meter or two away.

"It's standing room only, Levity! Hold your ground! As for me, I'm gonna try to use my dodging and running skills. A good offense is a good defense."

"Running skills?" shouted Animus. "Sounds like something track-star cowards say."

I huffed. "You got better ideas, Animus?"

"I'm gonna put the fight back in fight vs flight," returned Animus. "I'm gonna start by breaking their arms. And then their legs. And finally, their head! By the time I'm done with them, they will be in a full body cast."

"I guess Animus has a different take on the idea of a caste system," said Sage. "I shudder at how he celebrates Boxing Day. But I'm getting the impression that you two are more concerned about competing with each other than our antagonists. I want you two to bury the hatchet with each other and focus on burying the hatchet into the bodies of the enemy."

Animus grunted. "I think that can be arranged."

"Let's use teamwork," added Sage. "Link your fingers like a fence, but don't get too close to the trip wire. And let's swing our linked arms forward as if a header on a farm implement to suck the sperms inside."

Levity smiled as we knocked over sperms like bowling pins. "Keep your friends closer and your enemies closest, eh gentlemen?"

"I should have never accepted and opened that damn fortune cookie," I returned. "Who knew that the advice would turn out to be so literal."

"What are friends for," said Levity.

"Who needs friends when you got enemies," said Abacus in a quiet voice.

"Given the fact we are holding hands like Christmas carolers, we must be mortal enemies," added Animus.

"It's martial law with martial arts," Sage shouted as we found ourselves in the middle of the fray.

We had to break our "combine header" technique as our

defenses were breached. But we still had the trip wire, which proved somewhat practical, as many of the competitors made the mistake of holding their gaze at the horizon once they got past our windmill. The downside was that this just made the opening at the gate all the more clogged as the sperms that tripped were trampled into oblivion.

Good things don't last forever (that should have been one of Levity's fortune cookies). Once word got out that there was a trip wire, it was only a matter of time for some of the haploids to remove the trip wire. Not to brag (well, maybe a little), my height, strength, long arms, and stamina were assets as I clotheslined my tree-branch arms and swiped multiple haploids with one fell swoop like a crazy lumberjack (okay, maybe it took a couple of swoops). The rest of our platoon waved Swiss army knives around, slashing any arm or body that was in spitting distance. Many say "right out of the gate" as if you just hit the ground running. This gate was not that kind of gate! Hitting the ground running was a goal in and of itself! Millions of sperm were now clogging up the entry space like gunk in a drain. I stood tall and steadfast at the gate, trying my best to outstretch my arms to push others away to clear space so that my mates could go under my arms and get inside. The five nanobots were sticking to us like children to their mother's apron (and we were sticking to them with a similar vigor).

"Quick, toss your tear gas canisters and get inside," I shouted.

"But you will be hit with the tear gas," Sage shouted.

"In Champ Camp, I won a gold medal for holding my breath the longest," I said.

"Bragging during an all-out brawl?" returned Animus. "Your narcissism knows no bounds!"

A thought went through my head. "Sorry for trying to save your life, Animus!"

Levity, Animus, and Abacus tossed their tear-gas canisters just before they ducked under my arms to hobble their way inside the cavern (I held my breath). Sage was playing hero to a fault due to his laudable (and obstinate) fixation of "Leave no man behind."

"Don't be a hero," I shouted.

When Sage realized that I had to waste breath just saying those four words, he ducked under my arm as he sneezed and teared up on his way inside. I could hear his coughs die down as he joined the three others inside the cavern.

I shouted to the mob. "If you have anything to cry about, now is the time!"

My breath was spent after my flippant remark, and it wasn't long before I realized that the sarcasm wasn't worth it. The tear gas was intense, and my vision became foggy, as if I had cataracts. This was further compounded by the tear gas in the cavern that Sage must have tossed before diving into the abyss. I had no choice but to feel my way towards the lake. Feeling the water against my eyes was a sight for sore eyes!

It may have felt nice, but the water was so dark and murky I couldn't see much better than before.

I felt a hand on my shoulder. "Hey Brawn, Sage here. Let's find the others."

How about that? Sage waited for me! And between our GPS trackers and my speed/strength, we were able to locate our platoon in no time. When we coalesced together, Sage commanded us to use a similar "wing formation" like we did before when we linked hands. I took the middle (for obvious reasons), and I knitted my fingers to Abacus's hand on my left and Sage's hand on my right. Abacus also held on to Levity, and Sage held on to Animus.

This was a moment of truth for me. It would have been easy to let go and fly solo (after all, the others just slowed me down). After all, I spent most of my life competing with others and feeling no mercy leaving them in the dust. But this was starting to feel different. I suppose maybe I'm bragging to you by saying this, but I am proud to say that the thought of absconding didn't even trespass into my mind. By now, loyalty was part of my muscle memory, and I proved it not only to myself but to the others as well. My resolve remains unwavering!

Our arms were now bonded together like a wire fence as before, but this time, the plan had more to do with maintaining stamina for swimming (so we wouldn't have to fight the current). I guess it was the same logic as a tandem bicycle. This sounded good on paper, but it was all less reassuring to notice other haploids blow past us as if we were still anchored and docked at the marina!

To this sight, Animus took umbrage. "Come now, Sage, this is no time to hold hands like frolicking apple pie boys! Look at everyone shooting past us!"

"It sounds like we went from wassailing to a pie-eating contest," shouted Levity. "I think we are moving up in life."

"Consider it a lateral move," grumbled Animus.

Sage shouted to Animus. "Speaking of apple pie, there is a sweet spot between speed and stamina. Our strategy will pay off when those in front become too tired to press on. We may not tear through the finish line like sprinters, but we will hobble through it first. They are playing checkers, and we are playing chess. "

"Will it be more useful than my up and coming three-in-one shampoo, shampoo, conditioner, and toothpaste?"

"Don't quit your day job," said Animus. "But it might be a step up from your fortune cookie company."

Animus wasn't the only one who harbored some doubts with Sage's plan. I just had enough impulse control to not voice it! Sage's was a risky strategy, and it relied on assuming our opponents would become winded. The silver lining was that not only did I have the genetic predisposition for swimming and the training for swimming, but I also had the bonus of physical enhancements (which in a normal race would get me disqualified faster than a weightlifter taking steroids).

"See, Animus?" said Sage as we began to notice the same

sperm that shot past us near the start of the race. "That's what victory tastes like when you take the time to cleanse the palate first."

Animus grumbled. "No need for gloating."

"You almost sound let down," returned Sage. "One might think you would prefer to be dead and right than wrong and alive."

As I am composing this letter at this very moment, Sage just motioned for me to wrap it up.

"Let Morale know more about the punchline and less about the clothesline," Sage whispered as if you could hear him as if I was talking to you on the phone.

All right, so in the end, all five of us made it to the cervix with the rest of the two million "lucky ones" (only two of the five nanobots made the journey intact as some sperm caught up with them and pulled them down into the mob to be destroyed). I saw nanobots at the cervix, giving me the hunch that Autumn did indeed have nanobot implants of her own, just like Euclid. When/if we can get the male and female LANs connected, we can see just how vast this new network is!

When I set my tail on dry land, it felt like I found the gold at the end of the rainbow. But I reminded myself that it was too early to take a victory lap. After all, we still have to hit the home run! The cervix was comprised of a spacious organic room, large enough for two million gametes. It was decorated (if not intentionally) with red carmine pulsating walls that sounded like a slow heart rate. The ground was squishy. I noticed that my tail would sink an entire inch as I snaked ahead. The five of us hunkered down near a pulsating wall, away from the others. It made the sound of a heartbeat with each and every "pulse."

The Cervical Gate further down stole some of my excitement. There's just something ominous about something that is mysterious. After all, none of us really knew what was beyond that door.

Levity must have spotted the apprehension written on my

wrinkled face.

"I feel you, Brawn," said Levity. "The gates around here don't seem to lead to pretentious gated communities with founts and white picket fences."

Sage nodded. "That gate right there is more of a 'bacon in the pan' than a 'beacon in the night.' Make no mistake. Out of the frying pan and into the fire. Expect no air conditioner or hair conditioner there."

The door was more disheveled than the Crystal Gate from before. It was more akin to a doorway into a haunted house or dungeon. It appeared to be made from fossil, and you could see fossilized snail shells and various sea life embedded in the hard rock. There was an antique brass lion door knocker, but the ring part was missing (so knocking on the door the formal way was out of the question). Although lions were often lauded for being kings of the jungle, this one had a conniving and mischievous smirk, as evidenced by its pursed lips and squinted eyes. It reminded me of a gargoyle, beckoning us to enter as if to say, "If you dare." The blood stains and spider webs did precious little to dispel the ominous haunted house motif. Regardless of what insufferable madness lay waiting beyond that gate, at that moment, getting this far was cause for celebration. Well, at least in theory and on paper.

Sage cleared his throat. "Enjoy the victory and the ardor that goes with it. But we also have no time to waste. Abacus, can you combine the nanobot LAN from the male host with the nanobot LAN in this female host?"

"I was just thinking the same thing," said Abacus as he pushed one of the two retained "Euclid" nanobots towards one of the "Autumn" nanobots near the Cervical Gate. The rest of us stood there slack-jawed, entranced by Abacus's ability to combine the two LANS so that every nanobot in both bodies were synced. At least he had something to fiddle with other than that damn fidget spinner.

"Abacus is a shy sort," said Sage. "His work is impressive,

but we should let him work in peace."

"It's okay," said Abacus. "I'm almost done. It's just a matter of pairing the LANS together. Morale will soon witness the burgeoning of a brave new world and all its forms of flora, fauna, and organic and mechanized entities. For now, we can call it Planet Autumn."

"Wow," said Levity. "I can only imagine we are the talk of the town in Repro on Planet Euclid. It's easy to forget that when we are isolated here in Planet Autumn."

Sage grinned. "And let's not forget these new nanobots can convey information from all five senses through the LANS. They have the capacity to transfer digital versions of taste, smell, touch, sound, and sight. For Ron, it will be just as if he was here with us, a very virtual reality."

"Monumental stuff," I stated. "I can already see the financial opportunities lurking on the horizon."

Animus sneered. "If you joined this suicide mission to make money, you made a big mistake."

I shot back. "I guess your intentions appear to be much more noble than mine. We should petition your Sainthood."

"Hold it, gentlemen," said Sage, holding out his hands, palms vertical. "That's not the sort of camaraderie Ron Une is counting on us for. Now shake hands."

"Are you serious?" asked Animus. "What are we, third graders?"

Sage raised his voice. "You are lucky it's just a hand shake. Next time, I will ask for a hug."

Animus grumbled as he snatched my hand and gave me the softest hand shake I have ever received.

"That's about a tenth as firm as the one he gave me at the campsite," I added.

"A handshake is a shake of the hand," said Sage. "Now, let's move on."

I changed the subject. "But Sage, I don't feel any different in terms of physical prowess."

"Me neither," blurted Levity, looking at himself flex his muscles.

Animus said, "Yeah, what gives?"

Abacus chimed in. "I guess in the end, we survived, so maybe the concoction did something."

Sage rubbed his triceps and biceps. "I have to say, I don't feel any different either. But I would like to think they did something. Maybe Morale can tell us more."

P.S. Hey Morale, you may want to put a cap on the nightcaps, as too many can brutalize brain cells. Of course, you can't do much about it since Euclid is the one that tips the bottle.

CHAPTER 4

The D Letters
Subject: To the Uterus
Survival Type: Cellular competition (flight class)
Author: Morale
Date: February 14, 2182 (Thursday)
Location: Neuron
Recipient: Adventurer 3 (Brawn)

Dear Adventurer 3 (Brawn),

This is no mere superficial salutation! All five of you are dear to me (in the most professional sense of the word)! What a pleasant message I received on this diminutive nearby nanobot that you are all alive and well (well, alive anyway). I even took the time to pet the nanobot like a puppy (although it purred like a cat).

I must have presented like a blushing newlywed to the pedestrian-pedestrians buzzing around me when Planet Autumn appeared on my radar as if a new planet being born from the big bang. But how amazing it is when bliss can trump and over-ride social awkwardness! You have made Planet Autumn a reality (a real reality for you and a virtual reality for me). I have already partaken in soaking up data from all five senses from the nanobots at your current location.

I am grateful you saved any bad news for the bitter end! Spoilers in fiction are one thing, but in non-fiction, it's quite another! Your safety is of paramount significance and importance to me! This is why you mustn't get too comfortable despite the increased odds of succeeding in our next phase. But like some of my academic peers say, take statistics with a grain of salt (or at least a low-sodium diet).

I do feel the need to apologize, but only a little (a half-apology, if you will). I felt it was in your best interests if I risked a "white lie." But the fact I am telling you the truth now means something. In the end, I know you can handle the truth, if not right away.

Let's just say that I was fully aware that your genetic enhancements would have no effect (yet). Consider it a harmless experiment on the Placebo Effect. I aimed to prove to you just how powerful confidence, morale, and drive can be. I snagged the idea when probing Euclid's memory stores and retrieved knowledge about studies on self-fulfilling prophecy. My hope was that your belief in your superhuman abilities would help turn the tide! I'm over the moon that it worked (and you should be as well)! I must admit that I held some concern that Adventurer 3 might veer off into a state of hubris, but all is well that ends well, eh? Just don't throw stones at me just yet. Consider it a lesson in tough love.

The moral of the story is that part of your success will be mind over matter (I would know, being up here in Neuron). Don't forget that the most efficacious physical abilities mean nothing unless they are augmented with copious amounts of fortitude, drive, and determination! Think of me as the maestro to your orchestra, where each of you plays a different but valuable role, from tympani to trombone! After all, it is all of you who gifted me the lovely epithet of "Morale!"

Without further white lies, the (actual) effects of the body enhancements should take place soon (around the time you reach the female reproductive organ called the uterus). Of course, since I lied once, you may be hesitant to believe further comment from this particular "boy that cried wolf."

Brass tacks. One million of the two million sperm in the safety of the cervix right now will make it through the Cervical

Gate and land safe and sound in the warm embrace of the uterus (a 50% chance based on stats alone). Despite the enhanced odds, treat this journey with the same amount of delicate TLC as before. Sage himself would remind you that a fifty-fifty chance of survival is also a fifty-fifty chance of death! I would suggest adopting Euclid's hero Stanislavski's "Magic If" and acting "as if" your chances of survival were less than 25%. Own the belief! Fear can be pragmatic, but too much fear can make you trip and fall down (like the tropes in horror movies). Tap into those strengths of yours from back when we did our icebreakers. Think of yourselves as super-heroes if you must. After all, that is how I view you!

And while my white lie about the performance enhancements was intentional, I underestimated how much of a "battle element" there was in your previous race to get to the cervix. My supposition was an oversight, and I must thank you, Animus and Sage, for bringing the wire, tear gas, and Swiss army knives to the frenzy. Fight vs. flight is one thing. Fight AND flight is quite another!

I am well aware of the debate that exists between the optimists vs. pessimists regarding Murphy's Law and how the latter find utility in "assuming the worst" or how it's "better to be safe than sorry" even at the expense of wasted time or energy. As a glass-half-full sort of sort, Sage must realize that there is merit in having some semblance of faith that things will work out! Can't live under a rock all your life, eh? Well, unless you are some sort of turtle or crab, I suppose. But before Sage puts his big ugly finger under my nose to say, "I told you so," you have my permission to tell him that while his decision to bring contingency supplies, resources, and weapons to the fight may have paid off, this time, there will be just as many occasions where all that work and time could have been better spent on other pursuits. Why build a bomb shelter when there is no threat of war?

I am flattered by the title you have given me, to be sure, but forgive me if I must refrain from indulging too much in such sensibilities. I feel I must carry an air of neutrality, even if it makes me seem uncaring and aloof. By rights, I shouldn't allow you all to even use them with each other. I can't stress enough, do not become too close! It's for your own good! There could be a time when you have to turn on your mates for the sake of your own survival. There are better things in life to "take a stab at" than right in your friend's back (I might suggest curling or scrap booking). Color me a weak softie, but I will humor your use of nicknames only insofar that I include them in parenthesis after your more formal names of Adventurer 1, Adventurer 2, Adventurer 3, Adventurer 4, and Adventurer 5. We will see whose system grows on each other the fastest.

P.S. Tell Adventurer 2 (Animus) to harness the power of his anger as if it were a super power, but to remember that with power comes much responsibility! His power is like an archetypal MacGuffin! Ensure he does not waste his energy on quibbles, squabbles, and trifles! He only gets one hill to die on, so don't waste it fighting with Jack and Jill! Appearances might suggest that I am at a comfortable distance from the crazy that you find yourselves in. I can assure you that while I have an abode, it is not a humble one. And complacent, I am not. Every time I take a deep-dive in Euclid's head, I risk being fired and killed (in that order, of course).

The D Letters
Subject: Re: To the Uterus
Survival Type: Cellular competition (flight class)
Author: Animus
Date: February 14, 2182 (Thursday)
Location: Cervical gate (Repro 2: Autumn's body)
Recipient: Morale

Dear Morale,
        I seized the liberty to treat you on a first name basis (since

you rejected your deserving title of "Morale." You can refer to me however you like (most go with "hot head" or "jerk"). You mentioned a "fight" phase near the end of your letter, and just as my appetite for battle was salivating, you cut the conversation! What gives? It's like telling half a joke and not revealing the punchline! I have half a mind to give you my own version of a punchline. And this would be for the best, as I seized your letter from Levity's weak little baby hands, and it was not very flattering towards me, let me tell you!

You were a clever one to tell us the concoction of physical enhancements was working when it really wasn't (but still a confidence trickster). If you keep up this penchant for fibbing, we may have a "boy that cried wolf" situation on our hands (you being the boy, of course). At least we won, Placebo Effect or otherwise. It appears our natural abilities were enough. If that was your goal, well done (which might seem like a compliment, but it's no way to eat a steak).

I will provide the status report as to what happened during our leisurely jaunt to the uterus. And just like me, competitors were raucous, rowdy, and dead-set on living (and not just out of the gate, but AT the gate). Everyone knew what to expect by now and were fixin' to barge the door down if the situation demanded it. They might as well have given the mob hay-forks and torches. I can't say I blame them, as I, too, pounded, bashed, smacked, whacked, and tail-whipped at the door to no avail (although it was therapeutic for my anger management).

It only took a few scant hours (haploid time) before the door started to open (but unlike before, it was creeping upwards with the insidious nature of the minute hand on a grandfather clock). And as bad luck would have it, it was at that moment of all times that we could sense our performance enhancements kicking in! This put us at a disadvantage, if anything, as it allowed the smaller gametes to go through the door before we could! Could our confounded luck be any worse? We were now at less than 50/50 odds of survival! Talk about lies, damn lies, and statistics!

But this time, we were ready for equal helpings of flight and fight. I made sure of it!

"Elbow Fence," shouted Sage as the gate began creeping upwards. "Lock elbows and place your hands on your hips. Hold that position for dear life."

The five of us linked elbows and placed our hands on our hips, a variation of the "finger-linked combine header" strat from earlier.

"What are we, some sort of dance troop or cheerleading squad?" I asked.

"I think you found your calling," Brawn retorted.

"Enough, said Sage. "Save it for the locker room."

But in all seriousness, Sage's plan wasn't cutting the mustard. Other gametes were just slipping around us or playing red rover by slamming their fists down against our linked arms, which was very painful (for us and them). Even Sage was sweating, and it wasn't from too much exercise.

"If we keep this up, we may literally go down swinging," I said. "It's not a cowardly way to go, but you got any other cards in that deck of cards of yours?"

"Something better than an old maid would be nice," said Levity.

"Go fish, Levity," chimed Sage. "I got something better. Neck Wreck!"

"Now we're talking!" I said. "Now that's my kind of "wild card."

If the clever name didn't do it enough justice, this meant that we were to bring our linked arms up and clock the enemies in the jaw. But our arm strength was waning, even Brawn's. But we did clock at least ten haploids to the point of KO (every little bit helps). Ten for the price of one? I will take it. As long as we could put some of them out of commission before getting through the gate, all the better.

As soon as the crack under the gate became a sliver, the smaller and medium-sized sperm were being ushered in, sneaking under and around our chain-linked arms and sliding under the narrow opening at the bottom of the door. So even "Neck Wreck" was showing its age. We disbanded our linked fence. Brawn went to the rising wall and gave it a good heave-ho to try and expedite its speed, but to no avail.

I slapped Brawn's shoulder. "I suppose you regret all that weight lifting right about now. Not only are you unable to open that gate, but now all that bulk is just a disadvantage as all the scrawnies slide under that gate."

Brawn grumbled. "If you keep it up, you might be the one to regret how much weight lifting I have done."

I couldn't help but notice the rising amount of dead bodies around. They still had wide-eyed expressions of fear etched on their faces as if their final expression of cowardice was etched in the stones of perpetuity. At least their actions died with courage (even if their faces didn't show it).

"Better them than me," I mumbled. "Sucks to be them."

"Show some respect for the dead," Sage asserted. "It's just the way the ball bounces, or the 'wrecking ball smashes,' as it were. The only difference between winners and losers is the luck of the draw."

"What's that supposed to mean?" I asked.

"Figure it out," returned Sage.

I saw Abacus nod in agreement to Sage's comment. Was he taking Sage's side? Or was he displaying some sort of disdain towards me? Either way, he pissed me off. How dare he!

By now, most of the gametes had already gone through the opening! It was like watching flour fall through a sieve. And we were like the big chunks too fat and ugly to pass through.

"Damn these confounded ripped bods and six packs," shouted Brawn.

I grunted. "We are almost dead last."

"Did you just say 'dead?'" asked Levity.

"We gotta do something," said Brawn as he tried yet again to lift the gate to coerce it to open faster, as if he was hoping for one of those adrenaline surges you supposedly get when you need to lift something heavy off someone you care about.

"Fall back," said Sage. "That door is not going to open any faster. No sense in wasting our energy on it."

We didn't have a choice but to wait.

"I say we go under as soon as we can fit," I said. "Abacus and Levity are the smallest. They should go first."

"Belay that order," said Sage. "We don't go under until all five of us can at once. We are only as fast as our slowest man."

"No man left behind," I muttered. "I'm starting to think that's a rally cry of the weak, helpless, and stupid."

Sage shot his laser eyes at me. "Wanna say that when the rest of us leave you behind? Didn't think so."

I grumbled a bit. But I think I can speak for everyone in saying that it was painful watching everyone shoot ahead of us as if our tails were lame and broken! I would have ripped out every one of our physical strength enhancements if it could have gotten us under that door faster. Talk about buyer's remorse!

After what felt like an eternity of five minutes, the five of us went under at the same time. I looked behind, and sure enough, we were at the back of the pack. Well, in the land of the living, at least.

After shimmying through the crevice, we found ourselves in yet another cavern.

"Another cavern?" I complained.

"Expecting a tavern?" asked Sage. "I share your dissatisfaction."

"At least we found some common ground," I returned.

"Be it hallowed ground, unhallowed ground, or otherwise," Sage chimed.

This enclosure was much more narrow than the last (after all, there were far fewer haploids this time around). But instead of a lake, there was a massive river cutting through the cave with no end in sight (I took a mental note of how a rock can stop a river, but only up to a point until erosion places the river as the winner of the battle of the elements). The tunnel was well-lit, with torches lining both sides of the cave as far as I could see. So, at least we had the option of swimming "human style" with head above water.

Levity did his best cannonball, splashing water all over us. "Jump in, gents, the water's perfect!"

Brawn, Sage, and myself took the plunge next. Last (and least) was Abacus.

"Well folks, I got good news and bad news," said Sage.

"Oh great," I mumbled. "My favorite opener to a really bad day."

"The good news is that we don't have to worry about grappling with the mob just to get into the river. As you can see, the lake is ours for as long as we want it."

"And the bad news?" asked Abacus with a soft and wavering voice.

Sage paused. "We are shuffled in the back end of the deck. And as nice as this cozy lake is, we cannot stay here long."

I didn't know what to say, so I just let my moans and groans convey whatever thoughts were wrestling for dominance in my mind.

"You know what Morale would say in this situation," said Sage.

"Please elucidate us with his wisdom," I quipped. "From the comforts of his ivory tower."

"Better late than never," replied Sage.

"That's it?" I said. "That one isn't even worth one of Levity's cheap fortune cookies."

With Sage taking the lead, we swam with the vigor of Olympians, doing 360 rotations with our arms like windmills. It was nice not having to fight a current like before.

"At least there's no current this time," I said.

Abacus opened his big little mouth. "Not to be pedantic, but others have this same advantage, so it doesn't really help us in any way. We are just being graded on a curve."

"Not to be pedantic?" I asked. "Then why be pedantic?"

Sage laughed. "I see that Animus's rolling eyes made some waves above and below the water. Now, let's put our performance enhancements to the test. Let's forego the wing formation and fly solo. But let's stay together. And if one of us should get lost in the shuffle, rely on your GPS trackers to find the group."

"So much for 'no man left behind,'" I mumbled.

Sage heard me. "What was that, Animus? We are not leaving anyone behind. But it's your responsibility to keep up the best you can until there is no other way. Our bigger problem is catching up with the enemy. And if we are lucky enough to catch up, we will be greeted with another mob of gametes clogging the river as if wrestling to get a life raft on the Titanic."

"At least we don't have to worry about women and children first," I shouted with a guffaw.

Sage interrupted. "Save your energy, gentlemen."

"Me, gentle?" I returned. "I feel insulted."

We swam along in unison like a flock of geese. It took an entire haploid hour before we could even see the throngs of adversaries ahead.

"We are gaining on them," said Sage. "Clogs ahead, and not the good kind."

"Good kind?" asked Brawn.

"Clog dancing with wooden shoes, of course," said Sage.

I grunted. "Of course? I can't say I'm a fan of either kind of clogging."

Sage continued. "Prepare to get through another bottleneck. Underwater fighting isn't as easy as it looks."

My punches were only effective against the gametes that swam with their heads above water. Well, all except the ones that dared cross Brawn, anyway. He could knock someone out with an underwater punch with the best of them (and he was the best, as much as I am loath to admit).

We pressed on. But for every two steps, we made another one back. It wasn't long until we found ourselves in shallow waters. The water was now up to our waistlines. But there was another clogged drain!

"Now's the chance to get a move on," Sage shouted. "Strike that perfect sweet spot of fight vs. flight to maximize efficiency. We have to put more emphasis on flight."

Sage was right. We were spending more time at the pit stop than the race itself. What good are new tires and fuel when you don't put the rubber on the road or pound the pavement?

"Has anyone ever been to a mosh pit?" asked Levity as we approached.

"Sounds like a deep hole filled with strained peas," I said.

Levity continued. "If you can't beat 'em or join 'em, there is only one thing left to do."

"And what is that pray tell?" Brawn asked.

Levity proceeded to climb atop the clump of haploids.

"Body surfing," said Brawn. "But of course!"

I slapped my palm against my head. "Why didn't I think of that?"

"Your sarcasm is duly noted," said Sage. "You all heard the man. Climb aboard! Just make sure we all join hands so we can pull each other along."

"More hand-holding?" I said. "I don't know how much more of this I can take."

I spotted other gametes trying to do the same, but they were pulled down by the others and prevented from getting to the top. Levity's body enhancements allowed him to scurry up the mass of haploids like a spider over a rope ladder. The rest of us followed Levity's lead and made it to the top with little hassle, save for the occasional sucker punch to the face or abdomen (being accosted by the mob was no match for our buffs and upgrades). The clog in the river was quite dense, with very little opportunity to fall back into the river (although this also meant that you would be trampled as soon as you splashed back into the shallow river, only to drown anyway).

I saw that Levity was not the first to think of this plan.

There were a few dozen "body surfers" floating ahead of us. We did what Sage commanded and joined hands as if we were engaged in a group prayer.

"The mob is trying to yank me down!" shouted Abacus.

Abacus wasn't overreacting as I first thought. There appeared to be a concerted effort by some of the haploids to create a large gap to pull body surfers down into.

"I heard of stomping grounds, but this is ridiculous," said Sage.

"Hold on tight," said Brawn as he hoisted Abacus's half-submerged body back atop the crowd.

We inched ahead while maintaining our tight grip on each other's hands. By now, the cell density was so thick there was nary a chance of falling down (a good thing, I think).

I felt haploids punching me in the back, but they felt like fist bumps against my skin. Nothing my own brand of fist-bumps couldn't fix.

Sage took off his belt and whipped the hands of haploids that tried to pull him down. "Hitting below the belt may be morally questionable. But nobody ever said anything about hitting with a belt."

"Keep rolling like a chicken on a rotisserie," added Brawn. "That way, the punches will be distributed over a wider area."

"Evenly baked," I returned. "Just like Levity's brain."

"We will need to take turns to make sure we maintain our formation," said Abacus. "This has to be done hand over hand."

Sage continued. "Let's go in order of our numbers, Adventurer 1 through 5."

"I have an idea for another fortune cookie," said Levity. "If you can't beat 'em, let 'em beat you."

"Don't quit your day job," I mocked.

When Sage said "rotisserie chicken," he wasn't kidding. By the time we "surfed" our way to the front, I felt fully cooked, if not extra crispy. I could tell the uterus was just ahead. There was a hazy light at the end of the tunnel, flickering as if a strobe light, perhaps due to dancing of a watery surface. It was bigger, badder, and brighter than the meager light being given off by the torches on the walls of the rocky tunnel. If this "light at the end of the tunnel" was a good light or a bad light, it remained to be seen. And just to make our lives more miserable, the stone gate to the uterus was closing from the bottom up. Was there really almost a million sperm that got through already? Were we really this behind?

I was so pissed beads of sweat dropped from my brow. Sage's "leave no man behind" nonsense is gonna get us all killed.

"Just get to the end!" shouted Sage.

"Talk about sage advice," I said. "Maybe Levity can make a fortune cookie out of that one as well."

"I have a better expression," shouted Brawn. "Land ho!"

"Half-right," said Sage. "That is our destination. But don't expect any dry eyes in the house. The uterus appears to be a water-filled safe haven."

I stole a glance behind me and witnessed dozens of haploids getting crushed by the closing gate behind us. I wondered what that would feel like but turned my mind to more pleasant matters. Like that little convenient factoid that we made it out alive.

Some grudges stick like fly paper, and they are not always directed at old rivals. A group of combatants continued their fisticuffs and bar-brawl even in the "safety" of the uterus. As fun as it would have been to join in, I used the opportunity to make a count of survivors. From my rudimentary estimations, I could verify that a million made it out of the original two million (as expected). It's a sperm eat sperm world out there (and not just for the cannibals among us).

The uterus was a sight to behold (and not in a good way). The liquid appeared carbonated, as there were a plethora of air bubbles everywhere (which I could tell gave my movements an airy float to them). There were no pulsating walls this time around, and the floor felt more like concrete than a wet shag carpet. The walls appeared (and felt) like tree bark (but did not smell as such). And before you ask, I didn't opt to do a taste test!

The room revealed no visible gate or door like before (the only means of escape seemed to have closed behind us). We were in the dark on both counts, as it was very dim in the room and there was no exit in sight. Abacus was akin to a blind man as he floundered around, feeling the walls as if hoping his shaky hands would stumble upon a secret lever that would flip a section of the wall around like an old-time Scooby Doo cartoon. And before you ask, my reference to a shag carpet earlier did indeed plant Scooby Doo in my head!

It was bright enough in the enclosure that I could perceive how it formed a sort of bark-lined funnel with slanted and steep walls on all sides. If there was any "silver lining" to this bark-lined chamber, at least the hullabaloo of scouring the room for an exit did give us ample time to get used to our new bodies as we stumbled and ambled around like toddlers learning how to walk.

"You guys are spoiled," said Brawn. "I had to work to get my physique. It's painful seeing all of you get spoon-fed all that muscle with no work at all."

"Want to come here and say that to my pretty face?" returned Brawn. "The enhancements just augment my Hercules body. I am still the strongest in our team."

"Wanna prove it?" I asked.

Brawn and I squared up.

Sage separated us like a recess monitor. "Put an argyle sock in it, you two," said Sage. "Only a foolish soldier wastes energy investing in intentional friendly fire."

Brawn and I walked backwards from each other, still making eye contact.

"We good?" asked Sage. "If not, 'git good' like the video gamers say. That's an order."

"Git good?" asked Levity. "Hey, that would be a good fortune cookie. I should write that down."

All five of us are alive, but I wouldn't go so far as to say "safe and sound." Is this the graveyard where sperm go to die?

The assortment of dead bodies might support that theory. The nanobots in this body have yet to verify that this magical egg even exists. This may be the end of the line.

I am writing this letter in desperation, as it appears we are all in the same boat (although Sage said the boat was more like a submarine). Abacus is at the moment screwing around with a nanobot. I don't know if he has a cunning plan or just found the most expensive fidget in history. I hope you see this email soon at your earliest convenience, or we will end up dead. And you don't want that blood on your hands, do you? So treat this as an S.O.S., code red, May Day, or other popular distress call.

PS. Don't think I didn't notice how you referred to me as that Adventurer 2 (I took the liberty to read your message over Sage's shoulder). You keep tossing darts at me like that, I might consider taking up soldering instead of soldiering.

CHAPTER 5

The E Letters
Subject: To the top
Survival Type: Cellular competition (flight class)
Author: Ron Une
Date: February 14, 2182 (Thursday)
Location: Neuron
Recipient: Adventurer 2 (Animus)

Hello Adventurer 2 (Animus)! I just read your message less than ten haploid minutes ago. I just had to wait a moment for the security guard to make his rounds. You mustn't blow a gasket for every minor trifle. I only say this due to my concern about your health and mental well-being. Besides, such caprice and labile temperament are unbecoming for a soldier! Remember your decorum, man!

I can almost hear you in your mind telling me to "get on with it" (or mumbling it with actual words). I was able to scour Euclid's mind while also sifting through sensory data taken from the nanobots in your general area. I believe I have the intel you seek on how to find the egress that leads out of the uterus.

Some like to say: watch where you are going. Others say: keep your eyes on the horizon. Others will advise: don't look down. What do I say? "Do look up!" The darkness is dense where you are, and the tunnel going upwards is pitch black. It is doubtful very many of the other haploids will dare venture upwards out of the uterus due to the lack of visibility (and lack of GPS trackers). Take advantage of this inclement weather! Sync your trackers together and take the upward plunge. The effervescence of the carbonated liquid should help carry you as well. When you get to the top of the uterus, you can find reprieve on dry land.

Only 10,000 of the million haploids now in that cone-shaped uterus will make it to the summit. Adventurer 1 (Abacus) doesn't have to "do the math" to know that these odds are less than stellar. Take full advantage of your super-soldier abilities of speed, stamina, cunning, and strength. And be positive, Adventurer 2 (Animus)! You could be burning alive right now or drawn and quartered! Be grateful for how much worse things could be!

Go now! Spread the message to your mates! And read the Post Script of this letter later at a place and time that is more convenient and opportune. Keep on the "up and up" gents!
Sincerely,
Morale

P.S. If you are reading this, you better be at a safe haven. Stop picking on your mates! Not all battles are worth fighting! We are playing Chess, not Checkers. The group must not be divided and destroy itself from within! "Divide and conquer" is one of the oldest tricks in the book. This game is just as much about defense as it is about offense. Each of you must be able to detect when a platoon starts to destroy itself from within over time in an insidious war of attrition. And more often than not this disease is planted by the enemy. I want to emphasize the importance of perspective. There are times when we think we are cowards, running away from something foreboding. But what if we are not running away but rather running towards something far greater for the greater good? Did you ever consider that while Adventurer 1 (Abacus) may be afraid of the dentist, he may also be "not afraid" of enduring the torture of cavity pain as he avoids treatment? And what if those "courageous sorts" who are "not afraid" of the dentist are very much afraid of enduring tooth pain? Both sides are fearless and cowardly in their own way. Perspective, my dear boys, perspective! Without morale, we have already lost. I hope you learned something. It's not every day you get a PostScript that's longer than the actual letter.

The E Letters
Subject: Re: To the top
Survival Type: Cellular competition (flight class)
Author: Animus
Date: February 14, 2182 (Thursday)
Recipient: Morale
CC: Adventurers 1, 3-5

Hey Ron, you sure took your sweet time getting back to us. Did you have to print the SOS first and make a cup of weak coffee? Put some lavender on it to make it seem less emergent? I was getting mighty worried my plea was headed to the dead letter office (along with the rest of us). But lo and behold, just when I started cussin' and carryin' on there it came, like a virtual dog through a virtual doggy door. I suppose I should be grateful that you plucked our S.O.S. just in the nick. And worry not, I just read your postscript from your coveted response as we are now enjoying temporary peace of mind at our new safe haven.

Between the time when I sent off the SOS and the receipt of your reply (fifteen haploid minutes), there were at least a thousand gametes venturing upwards like kamikaze pilots or adrenaline junkies through the big black of space with nary an idea of where they were headed. And more than once, an underwater brawl broke out, haploids flying this way and that like bowling pins in the carbonated fluid.

As soon as the nanobot indicated that "you have mail," I motioned everyone to rush over to me to avoid my pain of having to read it aloud again and again. My voice was hoarse enough the way it was. Abacus either didn't hear, was playing hard to get, or giving me the old silent treatment as he was fiddlin' around with another nanobot. I guess that fool had better things to do.

"Hey, you deaf?" I shouted. "I'm not gonna read this more than once."

Abacus just kept right on fiddlin'! What nerve. I shook my head, cleared my throat, and read aloud right up to the PostScript as you indicated.

"We can't waste a second," said Sage. "Go for speed, not grace. It's rather difficult to keep one's gravitas when fighting gravity. Alas, what comes down must go up! Swim to the rim."

"Done," mumbled Abacus.

"Speak up!" I returned. "Why are you interrupting Sage's command to swim to the rim?"

Abacus stood up. "The nanobot is ready to take us up. It's programmed to avoid impending obstacles. So unless you prefer the scenic route, I suggest you hold on tight."

Sage smiled. "It appears Abacus has our back. And front. And sides."

"What are we waiting for?" I shouted (which drew some attention from nearby haploids).

I don't know how Abacus did it, but the nanobot was now able to carry all five of us at the same time! The only downside was that all five of us weighed the nanobot down, causing it to move at a lesser pace than the five nanobots that followed us into the Crystal Gate at the start of our quest. And our genetic upgrades didn't make things easier. And after my comments to Abacus, I would be the first to be thrown overboard to lighten the load. But the fact remains, Morale. If you ever need to hotwire a nanobot, Abacus is your man with the plan.

When others caught wind of our strategy, they wanted a piece of the pie. And while most of them didn't know how to jury rig a bot to carry five haploids, they opted to fight over the sparse individual nanobots and fly solo. As we ascended, I caught a glimpse of the solo flyers below and the adrenaline junkies above. And here we were, right in the middle, like the creme in an Oreo.

But we were not cream puffs (most of us, anyway).

"Hey, Abacus," said Brawn. "I'm glad that the nanobot knows where it's going, but these standard lights are not very bright. We can only see a few haploid meters ahead of us. We might get sucker-punched off this thing. Not that I'm complaining."

"Oops," said Abacus. "I almost forgot."

With the flick of a switch, HID light jettisoned from the makeshift headlamp! Now, we could see ahead a haploid mile. It appeared that Abacus had more than a few tricks up his sleeve and rabbits in his hat (although his Achilles heel was remembering what tricks he had in the first place).

"Sorry I couldn't make it brighter," said Abacus.

I huffed. "You're not very bright! Having any light at all might just save our lives. Enough with all the apologizing already!"

"I'm sorry," said Abacus.

"Good grief," I mumbled to myself.

Brawn grinned. "Did Animus just give Abacus a half-compliment?"

"Perish the thought," Levity returned.

The light was welcome, but as usual, throngs of sperms below us (and above) took advantage of our illuminated path skywards. Once again, our advantage also became their advantage.

"Get your own!" I shouted.

"Again, we are being graded on a curve," said Abacus. "It's not altogether giving us any home-field advantage."

"Listen up," said Sage. "The light is wonderful but delusive. Those above and below are scurrying like moths to use our newfound North Star. We need to turn it off after we tap into our iconic memory."

"What's that?" asked Levity.

"It's the temporary imprint of your surroundings that remains in memory when the lights go out. It's when you flick off your light for the night and can still manage to locate your bed by having some idea of where the furniture is at."

Brawn spoke. "So you want us to memorize what's above us for the next entire haploid mile?"

"That's the nuts and bolts of it," said Sage. "Everyone look skywards and imprint what you see into your muscle memory!"

I grunted. "Oh great, iconic memory and muscle memory. I hope I know the difference!"

Every one of us stared at what was being illuminated by the light beam, the texture of the walls, the general location, speed, and anticipated movements of our fellow combatants. About a quarter mile ahead, the sperm density was the highest at a few hundred haploids. Some of the nanobot riders were so far ahead I couldn't even see them. I wasn't too concerned about the few independent stragglers ahead of the mob. But that was just a hunch (and a hefty dose of wishful thinking).

"Everyone got a glimpse of what's ahead?" asked Sage. "Print it like a printer."

"I think so," said Brawn.

"I hope so," returned Levity.

Sage began counting. "Okay, Abacus, turn off the light on the count of three. One, two, and three!"

I felt more naked without the light than I thought I would. It was as if my eyes were gouged out. Retaining the haploid and nanobot locations in my brain was like holding my breath (their detail and accuracy faded with time). The furniture in my mind Sage mentioned was falling out of the picture fast.

"Use your tails to give us more speed," said Sage.

"So now what do we do, clobber the goons with our one free hand?" I asked.

Sage paused. "I need Levity, Abacus, and Animus to hide behind this nanobot.

"I'm not about to hide like a frightened child!" I said.

Sage raised his voice. "You can and you will. Haven't you played hide and seek before? Hiding is a very refined skill that requires talent and stealth. Besides, we need your tails to maintain our upwards momentum."

"Brawn and I will maintain a double-fisted grip on the exposed sides while we use our tails as whips," said Sage.

"We are gonna go straight through the mobs?" asked Brawn.

"We have no choice," said Sage. "After this, it will be smooth sailing."

I huffed. "This doesn't sound like very sage advice."

"Hang on!" shouted Sage as we smashed right in the middle of the first conglomeration of gametes.

"I didn't have any plans not to," said Levity.

The jolt was so sharp one of my hands lost its grip. At least all of us were still attached, if not as tight as wood ticks on a deer.

"I think Abacus forgot to add airbags," shouted Levity.

My peripheral vision caught Abacus smile in reply, something I had only seen him do a few times. Was he proud of his handiwork? I can't say I wasn't (as much as I wanted to).

It was like a riot as underwater fights were breaking out in an unorganized frenzy as gametes hit, tail-whipped, scratched, pushed, and pulled at each other just to get the tiniest bit of upwards momentum. There was also the challenge to circumvent the downward pull of gravity as if the latter was a troll or ogre trying to pull you down and asunder. A sly smile went across my space as I spotted a former large alliance kill each other from within. Cool! Less work for us! Still, I couldn't help but wonder if that would ever happen to us. Not cool! I suppose loyalty really is a risk based on little else but the ability to read poker faces. And not only that, but how can any of us know that we can really trust ourselves from ever turning coat? They say everyone has a price.

Sage and Brawn kept the haploids near us at bay with their tails. Sage preferred slapping them, while Brawn opted to grab them and cast them asunder.

"Hey Abacus," said Sage. "Is this one of those two-tailed tests in statistics you are always talking about?"

Abacus smiled without saying a word. He and I tried to focus on using our tails to maintain speed and momentum skywards. And this worked for all of five seconds. It wasn't long until a cluster of five gametes with harpoons came out of the watery woodwork. Their harpoons appeared rudimentary as if cut and pasted from nanobot scrap like some post-apocalypse film.

"Look out, scrap-scrappers ahead!" shouted Sage. "And somehow, I doubt their harpoons are the amorous love-struck arrows from Cupid."

"Scrap scrappers?" said the head archer. "More like meet the Harpoon Platoon."

All five of them surrounded our sputtering nanobot. With the reflexes of a cat, the head archer shot his harpoon without even aiming, as if a cowboy shooting from the hip.

"Levity, watch out!" I cried.

And whether it was my warning or Levity's reaction that was too late, the harpoon struck him, leaving both an entry and exit wound right through his shoulder. He went unconscious faster than my fading iconic memory did when we turned off our spotlight. I'm not sure if it was a good thing or bad thing, but the arrow went straight through his body (so at least we didn't have to put him through the agony of pushing the arrow back out).

"Levity, no!" shouted Brawn as he seized him with his tail before he could fall off our paddy wagon. "I got you, buddy!"

The rest of the Harpoon Platoon seized this chaotic moment and approached port, starboard, bow, and stern.

"You did it now, Archie the Archer," I said, aiming my fist at their leader.

"At ease, gents," said Brawn, revealing a coin from his trousers. "Even the Super Bowl begins with a coin toss. Now, do you want heads or tails?"

"We will take neither," said Archie the Archer. "Keep your coins. Render unto Caesar the things that are Caesar's."

Brawn pocketed his coin and nodded towards Sage. Sage

head-butted the main loudmouth as Brawn tail-whipped two of his cronies.

"Well, okay, then," said Brawn. "Head-butts and tail-whips it is."

That took care of three of them, at least for now. There were still two of the Harpoon Platoon left, and they surrounded Abacus as if detecting his beta-male pheromones.

"I think I'm gonna need some help, Animus," said Abacus.

"Two-tailed test?" I asked.

Abacus nodded. "Two-tailed test."

I snagged one rowdy by wrapping my tail around his while Abacus did the same. Our nanobot rocked and creaked as we slammed the two remaining members of the Harpoon Platoon into each other. It took three smashes before they were both knocked out. We released them like walleye in a catch and release program.

"Nice work, Abacus," I said.

Abacus took some deep breaths. "I prefer a battle of wits. But I will do what needs to be done for the sake of our survival. This is war, after all."

But our victory was short-lived. Blood was spilling out of Levity's puncture wound and mingling with the water to creating a burnt sienna cloud.

Sage shouted. "We will get a nanobot to start Levity's cellular repairs as soon as we get a chance. Brawn, keep your grip on him. I will help hold on to him also."

Our navigation system was not so lucky, and it clapped out after bashing through the mob of adrenaline junkies ahead.

Sage shouted. "The navi is out. Hold on tight with both hands and your tail!"

The nanobot was like a top that lost its balance. It jettisoned upwards at an angle, bouncing around the walls of the uterus like a bottle rocket in a closet or a balloon losing its air and whizzing around a room. And while the air bubbles increased our upward velocity, they also caused our craft to sway and spin.

The mob and crowd dispersed to the sides as our nanobot was bouncing around in a random and unpredictable fashion. We were fortunate that the nanobot took out a few stragglers while it bounced through the tunnel like a pinball. While the nanobot lost its poise and grace, this was mitigated by the fact that it was going upwards at an even faster rate than before.

"Abacus, put the headlight back on," said Sage.

"I can't. It's smashed to bits!" shouted Abacus.

I sighed. "Oh great, how are we gonna see the nano-riders ahead of us?"

"Is that a rhetorical question?" asked Sage. "Brace yourself. Expect the worst and hope for the best! And one more thing, don't look down!"

"More sage advice for Levity's fortune cookie company, I see," I said. And what did I do? I did what anyone does when someone says to not look down. He would have been better off telling me not to look up. But when I looked down, all I saw was pitch black, so it wasn't too big an issue.

Sometimes, one's enemies will fall into your hands. The nano-riders above must have heard us crashing against the walls and making a commotion as they were parked against the walls as if flies on a cupboard. I guess they didn't want to get whacked any more than we did. We bounced our way around towards the top, two steps ahead, one step back. The other gametes got out of our way for their own safety (if only it was a sign of respect). Either way, we were now at the top of the food chain! It's good to be king!

At any rate, when we reached the top of the "well" and climbed over the wall onto dry land, we were greeted by the warm luminescence emanating from the wall torches. It was a more diminutive enclosure, with a max 10,000 sperm capacity.

Priorities being what they were, Sage and Brawn seized the liberty to carry Levity to the nearest nanobot to repair his cellular body back to health (Sage took his arms, Brawn his legs). Abacus commandeered the nanobot and proceeded to flip, switch, and hit virtual buttons until he was able to do the necessary cellular repairs (and set up the IV drip).

"Let's set up camp here," said Sage. "Our supportive vibes can tickle Levity back to health. He needs us right now."

"Where am I?" groaned Levity as he realigned with reality.

"He's alive!" said Sage.

The rest of us hollered and clapped our hands.

"Applause?" asked Levity. "Did I just perform a Broadway musical?"

"We almost lost you, Levity," said Brawn.

"You know what they say, grandmas are better than grand mal seizures," said Sage.

"Who says that?" I asked.

"Ah, well, nobody, actually," returned Sage.

"Hey, can I use that for a fortune cookie!?" shouted Levity. "It's so true!"

I slammed his palm against his forehead. "Good grief."

Everyone broke out in peals of laughter. Levity looked around at all of us staring at him.

"What did I miss?" Levity asked.

I guffawed. "You really missed out. We got to bash some heads."

"Got to or had to?" asked Brawn. "I have different ideas on how to spend my vacation."

Abacus interjected. "Levity will be on the mend for several hours. We have no choice but to count on the next door to not open during his much needed period of convalescence."

Other than Levity's wounds, we made it to the top of Mount Everest. But what does Sage do? He rains on the parade even more.

"Like any mountain, getting to the top is only half the battle," Sage said (I gotcha Sage, maybe you should write these down for Levity's fortune cookies. Give him a taste of your brand of cynical optimism).

As throngs of haploids were setting up camps of their own,

roasting marshmallows, playing board games, or just shouting and jumping up and down in a drunken frenzy, I took a gander around our surroundings. Not all "finish lines" are what they seem. Some involve bursting through a banner at a marathon. Others are bait, a veritable "chalk line" ruse drawn in the sand. Was I the only one who spotted the fact that there was more than one path leading out of this hell hole? There was a fork in the road, a gargoyle poised on each side as if each was beckoning you to take their path. And while both paths were shut tight by a round stone, when would they open? Would Levity be okay by then? These thoughts did not bode well for me (let's face it, gargoyles are not famous for their bedside manner). Was this going to be another 50/50 chance situation, like when we went from the cervix to the uterus? I kept mum about my "reservations," as it was not the time to rain on everyone's parade more than Sage already had. Even if it was partly due to upholding my own sanity.

We set up camp, made a campfire, and shared a group story about how we thought our adventure would end up by the end. We took turns offering a section of story, which changed in tone depending on the storyteller. Brawn told tales of grand adventure, and he embellished the details as if we were great heroes of mythology wreaking havoc on our competition.

Brawn cleared his throat. "What is victory, but the mass of muscle weighed against the mass of blood, sweat, and tears of the enemy? The ratio of heroism compared to cowardice? The ratio of the living and the dead?"

As Abacus shared his portion of the narrative, there were fewer themes about brawn and more about brain.

"Why is the pen mightier than the sword?" asked Abacus. "Because the brain is mightier than the bicep or tricep. A peace treaty can prevent a war and save more lives than the sharpest of blades."

"Wanna test that theory?" asked Brawn as he stood up, Abacus backing away. "You taking psychological jabs at me?

How about putting your money where your mouth is?"

"At ease," said Sage. "Please share your story, Abacus, without any political implications, no matter how subtle or intended. Brawn's skills are just as valuable as yours and anyone else's."

Abacus's story had just as happy an ending as Brawn's (but with fewer bumps and bruises). He went on and on about some dystopian future conspiracy where nanobots took over the world. They would accomplish this by using genetic editing, modification, and eugenics to create titan-sized cells in all eleven countries. He claimed he didn't believe it, but his passion and level of knowledge said otherwise.

Everyone was staring at me, and I didn't even notice until the mounting silence compelled me to meet everyone's gaze. I guess that was my cue to share my part of the story! That ominous fork in the road must have put me in a nasty mood, as without constraint, the following words jettisoned out of my mouth like lava from a volcano: "So who among us is going to survive and who will die?"

By now, I could see everyone squirming, fidgeting, and making less eye contact with each other than before. Abacus even pulled out his fidget spinner! Yup, the parade was officially rained upon once again, and I was the storm cloud. Maybe I should stick to giving political speeches.

Levity, naive as he is, turned the conversation. "I think we will find a way where we can all survive. I just know it. Morale will make it happen. I can feel it. There will be action, adventure, pivoting, strategizing, and stories to tell. There is a light at the end of the tunnel. And not a bad light like an explosion or burning building. But a good light. You know, like the light that allows a dentist to spot your cavities."

I huffed. "I think Levity must have also hit his head."

"I heard the wise words of a beautiful fortune cookie," said Sage. "Light in the night and spark in the dark and all that."

Part of me felt like telling Levity that what he said was a

pipe dream and not how the world works. When push comes to shove, even your best friends will stab you in the back when survival is at stake. And haploids, like humans, have varying levels of ability, as each is as unique as a snowflake (and some happen to be snowflakes, like Abacus). Some sperm are bigger, stronger, and faster. It's just the reality of the quagmire we live in. Sorry, Levity. But I was not about to get into a raging political debate and crush the spirits of someone whose bed we still didn't know was a healing bed or deathbed.

Brawn must have detected my umbrage with Levity's comments as he moved the spotlight onto Sage. "What about you, Sage? Want to add to our narrative?"

Sage fiddled with a tree branch and moved it around in the fire as if roasting a marshmallow. "I don't think it's wise to put the cart before the horse. And it's just as unwise to put a feral horse before the cart. If we assume the best, we may be left down. If we assume the worst, it will lead to consternation, and our confidence will suffer. Our confidence must match our competence. I try hard to walk this fine line, but Morale will say I err on the side of caution to a superfluous degree. We need to stay in the present and treat each battle as if it were a war. If we have heroic tales to tell, they will come in due time. No sense in writing a story that hasn't happened yet. We must not put the fan-fare before the gun-fire."

At the moment we are waiting for Levity's treatment to be finished. Abacus estimated it would require an hour total. I don't know what we will do if that gate should open before he is back to his old annoying self again. Levity seems to be in decent spirits. But knowing him, he is putting on a front to seem healthier than he really was. And while that stance is laudable from a position of strength, such dishonesty would piss me off.

P.S. I don't have a P.S. Oops, too late!

CHAPTER 6

The F Letters
Subject: To the uterotubal junction
Survival Type: Cellular competition (flight class)
Author: Morale
Date: February 14, 2182 (Thursday)
Location: Neuron
Recipient: Adventurer 2 (Animus)

Thank you, Adventurer 2 (Animus), for the lovely details surrounding our quest (and for putting the more pleasant content first and foremost). I don't mind spoiler alerts in fiction, but in non-fiction, a tragic event too early in the narrative runs the risk of precluding me from finishing the rest of the letter. Truth be told, when I reached the bit about Levity, it was a slow burn getting to the end of the message. Words cannot express the consternation I felt, wondering if the next thing I would read would be his last! But when I got to the bitter-sweet end, the fact he was alive was solidified. Please disperse the crucial information from this memo to the rest of the platoon. Spare poor Levity the details of your skeptical thoughts regarding the happy ending to his campfire fairy tale.

I know some of you harbor a modicum of resentment for the apparent "safety" of my perch up here in Neuron (not to mention the longer life span of neurons vs. sperm cells). Just remember that the grass only seems greater on the other side of the fence. And for all we know, that grass could be astroturf or the barb-wire fence that surrounds a jail! You know what happens when you keep feeding ducks bird seed? They start to expect it and keep coming back for more! Receiving this intel is a privilege, not a right (and could get me killed). Don't be those entitled ducks! And speaking of ducks, don't forget that famous poster of the duck that looks calm on the surface of the lake but is paddling his poor feet for dear life! So, while I may appear safe and sound in this "humble abode," fret not, for I feel like that poor misunderstood duck!

Enough complaining. I conducted additional research on my end, using the spy-class nanobots to glean more information from the neurons in the tucked-away memory regions of Euclid's brain. With Euclid's LAN connected to Autumn's LAN, every nanobot now has access to the location and cellular structures of every organ in the female reproductive system. Repro is one of the only countries with such disparity in organ structure and placement. The other ten organ countries and organ systems in the human female appear to be almost identical. Your GPS trackers are also synced with the female LAN, so navigation through the corridors of the female reproductive system should not only be feasible but reliable. The organ detection software in the trackers will further enhance the GPS navigation abilities of your trackers. Don't forget that the trackers have manual and autopilot settings. But know this. Unlike Planet Euclid, we do not yet have access to the top-tier knowledge banks of Autumn's brain. There is no brain cell in Neuron 2 willing to risk their hide, neck, and hair like yours truly. So think of that, Animus, the next time you feel like accusing me of "slacking off!"

As advanced as the nanobots and trackers may be, they are not sensitive enough to detect the existence, let alone the location, of the magical egg. We all know the rumors, and for centuries, billions of sperm have been seeking this coveted prize. And this, my boy, is no mere sci-fi MacGuffin! It's the very crux of our adventure, the ambrosia we are seeking, the veritable Fountain of Youth, the gold at the vestige of the rainbow! But what does it do? What is it for? I have yet to find a way to circumvent a series of memory blocks in Euclid's mind to gain access to this vital information (it's almost as if he is too embarrassed to think about it). For whatever reason, sexuality is very taboo with humans, and they tend to freeze up or feel embarrassed when the topic should come up. There is also the fact that the nanobots cannot get close enough to the egg to bear witness to its existence. It's like spotting Sasquatch without a camera.

Five thousand of the remaining ten thousand haploids will choose the correct path (about the same odds as getting to the uterus from the cervix or catching a politician in a lie). To the best of my knowledge, this is another chance mission. Choose the correct path, and you survive, choose the wrong path, and you don't. Simple as that.

So far, you have experienced lakes, rivers, water-filled carbonated caverns, and dry land. This mission will shake things up even more as the tunnel is a low-gravity chamber with a gravity level of 1.50 meters per second squared (just a bit less than the Earth's moon). Once acclimated to the sensation of being weightless, you can make yourselves ambulatory by sort of gliding or swimming through the air after hopping off of solid objects.

All of you may want to sit down for this next bit. I ask that you split up at the fork in the road. I want three of you to take one path and the other two to take the other. I understand that this strategy guarantees that half of our platoon will be eviscerated. But we just can't afford to lose all five of you in one fell swoop. We all knew going into this that, at best, only one of you would make it to the egg, and even expecting that much is beyond the pale miracle. This is why I discouraged all of you from becoming too close to each other in the first place. It came from a place of good intentions, and I wasn't fixin' to be an odious fellow. In fact, I maintain that this is a positive position and will only maximize our mental health in the end.

Brass tacks. As with the egg, our GPS systems are not

sensitive enough to guide us to the correct path at the fork in the road. It will only guide us in the general direction towards the egg chamber. And the information I received from the nanobots was of little help, as the two tunnels looked identical (trust me, I even used a magnifying glass). And if that weren't bad enough, the physical enhancements will not work to your advantage. This challenge is 100% luck like Bingo (where any skill involved translates to serendipity or Divine Providence being on your side). Remain patient. Your body enhancements will show their prowess when the "fight" phase begins.

P.S. Tell Levity to get well soon. That's not a well-wish. It's an order! Respectfully tell him that if he doesn't follow that order, I will toss him down the wishing well myself.

The F Letters
Subject: Re: To the uterotubal junction
Survival Type: Cellular competition (flight class)
Author: Morale (live audio message)
Date: February 14, 2182 (Thursday)
Location: Neuron
Recipients: All adventurers

Attention Adventurers! Do not be alarmed that you are hearing me through your GPS trackers. The burliest messenger pigeon would be ill-equipped to deliver this information to you soon enough.

It has been fifteen minutes (haploid time) since I instructed you to send half the squad down each path to guarantee at least some survivors (a low-risk strategy to break even). This decision was made in error, and my hope is that this error will not turn to negligence. The fork in the road does not boil down to a 50/50 guess, as I thought. But there is an opportunity for recourse, if not ample. But the silver lining is that there is a chance I can save all of you.

From my research into Euclid's memory stores, it appears that the egg's supposed "location" switches from one ovary to the next each month (human time). One to the other, like AM to PM and PM to AM. Last month, the egg's supposed location was in the left path. So that means this month the egg location should be on the right! How about that? As much as I would like to pat myself on the back, this is more than mitigated by my previous egregious error and assumption.

Enough on that. Brass tacks. All of you in the left tunnel must hurry back to the fork in the road. Immediately. If we were fortunate enough to delegate Abacus to the left path, we could have him hot-wire a nanobot for each of you. Without assistance from nanobots, I fear those in the left tunnel will be left behind. All five of you must get to the right utero-tubal junction to be one of the lucky 5,000 of the original 10,000 that makes it out alive. Due to this, it may be possible that taking the right path will guarantee victory, regardless of the haste of our ambulation. But this is not certain. It will behoove us to treat this as any other race. It's difficult to discern how many others took the left vs. right tunnels. And there could be a closing gate.

Go now, put your focus back on the mission at hand. Write me ASAP when you get to the next safe haven! That's an order, soldier, and not the kind you make at a fast foot joint.

The F Letters
Subject: Re: To the uterotubal junction
Survival type: Cellular competition (flight class)
Author: Abacus
Date: February 14, 2182 (Thursday)
Location: Pitch-fork in the road (top of the urethra, the Gargoyle Gates)
Recipient: Morale

Sending us a live audio message via the trackers was an astute idea, given that we would not have received the memo otherwise. Sage commanded us to "hunker down" (as best we could in our low gravity conditions) so we could focus on savoring your each and every word as if it was "mince pie" (his words). I wouldn't berate myself too much if I were you in regards to "guessing wrong." How can you guess wrong about anything? It's illogical. An "educated guess" is a different story.

When you do the math, anyone would assume that it boils down to a 50/50 coin toss. And it's not as if either of the gargoyles put up a solid argument to take one path over the other. Despite guaranteed casualties, I applaud your low-risk strategy of "it's better to lose some than lose them all." If I was calling the shots I would have taken a similar low-risk strategy. Take comfort in the fact that you corrected yourself (and us) before it was too late. I would say you saved lives in the end (although Animus is still trying to grumble about it despite having a hoarse voice from so much carrying on).

This mission was doomed from the start, even at the campsite before the "Gargoyle Gates" opened at the fork in the road. Levity's nanobot exploded halfway through his treatment; sparks, smoke, the lot. Only a fraction of the strength and immune system enhancements made it into his body.

Everyone gathered around Levity, trembling and sweating.

"Is he okay?" asked Brawn.

Levity smiled. "You guys look as if you are about to read me your last rites. It's okay. I don't feel 100%, but a good hale and hearty 75% is not to be taken lightly."

Abacus looked over Levity as if he were a test subject. "Well, that's still a "C" in many math classes. And that's hardly a clean bill of health."

"He swears up and down he is okay," said Animus. "Leave the poor guy alone."

"Easy, Animus," said Sage. "Sounds like you are about to swear up and down yourself. How do you really feel, Levity?"

Levity paused. "My speed will not be affected. My stamina is a different story. But I will do my very best to not slow you all down. I think the mark on my face left from this explosion is the most serious injury."

"Ah yes, the first battle scar," proclaimed Animus. "I remember that day well. Maybe there's a silver lining to that nano blowing up after all."

"Only Animus would consider a battle scar to be a silver lining," said Brawn.

It wasn't long after that nanobot went kaput that the eyes on both gargoyles turned blood red.

"Is that light coming from the gargoyles' eyes?" asked Brawn.

Sage sighed. "I'm afraid so. And the gates are opening! Quick, to the gates!

All five of us sprinted together, leaving the warm glow of the campsite behind. Sage grasped Levity's hand and galloped alongside him. The gargoyles' glowing eyes stared at the fork in the road, shining a spotlight on the fork itself as if calling attention to the impending choice before us. As soon as we made it to the fork, gametes were spilling into both doors in almost equal numbers, giving the message that everybody was guessing and there wasn't even so much as a rumor as to which door was the correct one.

"All right, let's split up and get going," said Animus. "Who is gonna go left, and who is gonna go right?

"Hold on," said Sage, raising his hand. "How many of you want to follow Morale's suggestion and split up between paths?"

"Do we have a choice?" asked Levity. "I don't mean to seem insubordinate, but I would rather go one, go all, if I had the decision. But again, this is the will of Morale."

Animus huffed. "Cowards, the lot of you."

Sage looked at Levity, Brawn, and myself. "Well, thanks to Animus's heart on his sleeve, we know how he feels. And we know how Morale feels. How about you three? How many wish to go one go all?"

Brawn, Levity, and I raised our hands and nodded in

agreement.

Brawn glared at Animus. "You may have no reservations about tossing us to the wolves, but we are not inclined to cast you aside without mercy."

"Hold up, gents," said Sage. "Morale is the best advisor a captain could ask for. His counsel is without fail and without equal. The heads tells me that we should split up. My heart tells me that we should stick together. Nine times out of ten, I will go with the brain. One time out of ten, I will go with the heart. But what about the gut? There is something in my gut, something I cannot put my finger on, that is telling me that it is not wise to split up. I don't know why or how. It's just a superstitious feeling I can't explain but also can't ignore. I understand Morale's logic that "a bird in the hand is worth two in the bush." But I also understand that beating around a burning bush does nobody any good."

"But what about Morale?" I asked.

Sage nodded. "I understand. And I can already hear him Ron-splaining us to abstain from clinging to the inevitable, that most, if not all, of us will die. And that is sage advice. Our memoir is not a fairy tale. There will be no happy ending. There will be more obituaries than photo shoots of heroic poses. It would be tragic enough if only one of us "would" survive. It's all the more calamitous to know that only one of us "could" survive. The two words are only one letter different. But their disparity in meaning is astronomical. And yet, one's emotions have a funny way of pivoting a person's motivation in unexpected and irrational ways. My gut is trying to tell me something, as if in a foreign language. And while I can't make out what it's saying, I can tell by its body language that its message cannot be ignored."

"Let's go!" shouted Brawn. "No haploid second to spare!"

We swam like gold medalists, without nary a clue that we were wasting time and energy going in the wrong direction! Once again, our talents, skills, and physical enhancements only slowed us down! We were thirty minutes into the left tunnel by the time we received your communique! From my estimation, it appeared that just over half of the haploids took the right path.

"Well, now we are all dead," said Animus. "Not only that, but we also went against Morale's orders and will let him down as well. You snooze, you lose, I guess."

"A shame we can't die in our sleep," said Brawn.

"It's not over yet," said Sage. "And if we must die, at least we will do it together."

"Hardly reassuring," said Animus. "But point taken."

Sage paused and turned around a full 360 degrees to gauge his surroundings. "At least there are five of us here to help Abacus outfit some nanobots."

"And I am grateful for the help," I said, seizing the closest nanobot, trying to pry open the toolbox. "You guys ever wonder what's in these locked cubbies on every nanobot?"

"I never cared enough to find out," responded Animus. "I just figured it would be a good liquor cabinet. After all, nanobots can tell when you are above the legal limit."

Brawn peered at the lid. "Well, unless any of you have a key....."

Brawn placed his fingers under the lid and tore it off like a scab on a wound.

"All nanobots come equipped with a basic tool set," I said. "Only certified repairmen have keys for them. Unless you are as ripped as Brawn, of course."

"But I need eight more nanobots," I stated. "Five host machines to get parts from and five receivers to fit them on."

"Ten in total?" asked Animus.

"I can see you did the math," I said.

Animus huffed. "What's that supposed to mean?"

"No offense intended," I said as I meandered my way to a second nanobot I could collect for my repairs.

Animus huffed. "These are the only two nanos I can see in this blasted place!"

"We will have to scout for others and fetch them," said

Sage. "Abacus will start working on the two he has. Levity and Brawn will scout north, and Animus and I will scout south. I trust we are used to the weightlessness by now. When you each find one, sync it with Abacus's tracker, and it will go to him. We each need to find two. Go now."

I proceeded to tear apart one of the nanobots as if disassembling a jigsaw puzzle. I didn't mind the plethora of haploids racing past. After all, they were going in the wrong direction! And this was like a pit stop.

"Sucks to be you," one haploid shouted towards me as he jettisoned past like an asteroid. I just smiled and kept on working. "Sucks to be him!" I muttered to myself.

It took thirty haploid minutes until all ten machines were docked in our little makeshift bay (it looked like a little hobby cattle farm). By the time the tenth one arrived, I had all five hosts disassembled and two of the receivers outfitted with the additional parts.

"Hand me that socket wrench," I instructed Levity.

Levity handed me an Allen wrench.

"Sorry for not speaking louder or clearer," I said. "Please hand me the socket wrench."

And what does Levity do? He hands me a combination wrench!

Animus guffawed. "He heard you the first time, Abacus. He's just a moron. At this rate, this is gonna take all day!"

"Enough, Animus. Go and make yourself useful," said Sage. "Since you are so much more competent at it, you can play Igor to Abacus's Frankenstein and hand him the tools. Levity can take a break. He needs to keep his strength up anyway."

"Maybe Levity is a tool," grumbled Animus.

"I heard that," said Sage.

Levity slapped the Allen wrench in Animus's hand. "See what happens when you are good at something? You get stuck with it! There's a reason they call me Levity instead of Brevity."

It took another fifteen minutes to outfit the fifth and final receiver nanobot to get it modded and fit for travel.

"Claim one nanobot each," I said. "Pair it with your trackers. They will move with twice the magnetic velocity and horsepower of a standard nano. And more durable too with the additional shell-casings I added from the hosts."

Brawn smiled. "In other words, they are souped-up."

"Even that won't save us," said Animus. "It took forty-five minutes putting these damn machines together, not to mention the wasted hour getting this far and having to go back again."

"What if we linked the five nanobots together?" asked Sage. "Like Voltron? Euclid Hux is a big fan."

"Bah," said Animus. Five nanobots, each carrying one of us, is no different than a group of five nanobots carrying all five of us."

"Uno momento," I said. "Sage is on to something. Nanobots move by magnetic propulsion. And while objects have no weight in space, magnets still work. What if I jury-rigged the five together to create an electromagnet!? It will pull all of five of us as if it was only pulling one of us."

"Not to mention it will allow us to tank our way through the crowd like a battering ram," added Brawn.

"You and your battering rams," said Levity.

Brawn blushed. "Well, I am the brawns of the operation."

It took less than ten minutes to make it back to the fork in the road (despite crashing through many haploids head-on as if they were birds on a windshield). Some of the gametes that we whizzed by gave us a double-take as if we didn't know what direction we were headed. Others turned around and followed us, assuming we must have had secret intel that the right-hand path was the correct route to take. The entire way back I had this inkling that the tunnel doors leading back to the two gargoyles at the fork in the road would be now closed. But this fear was short-lived, and when we passed through those glorious doors, seeing their mischievous smirks again was an ironic welcome sight! They might as well have been door-greeters at a grocery store!

The battle culture took a twist as we went into the right-hand tunnel. It was like a junkyard, gutted nanobots scattered everywhere (with parts floating around in the anti-gravity chamber). In fact, our five-bot ship seemed to be the only working nanobot in the tunnel. The haploids were making little movement ahead as they were busy wielding electrical tasers, rods, rubber hoses, and pipes during a moment of confused bedlam. Others took a more defensive approach, using nanobot shell casings as rudimentary body armor. This tunnel appeared to be more fight and less flight.

The haploids and their weapons posed very little resistance due to the low gravity and also the horsepower of our five-wing ship. After we knocked many soldiers back through space, many others decided to get out of our way altogether, as if making way for a presidential motorcade.

Sage smirked. "At least the ones getting out of our way understand the gravity of the situation. Everyone turn your nanobot clockwise. This will help dispel our adversaries to the sides rather than just knocking them in front of us just to have to bash through them again. It will also cause less wear and tear on our ship."

Our "starship" spun around like the Gravitron, making me quite dizzy. While my head was spinning, I was able to spot nearby gametes toppling to the sides like bowling pins (not to mention that sperm sort of resemble bowling pins anyway, well, without the cute little red necklace). But in this case, the nanobot was the bowling ball!

"Strike! Spare! Go back to the gutter!" shouted Levity with each and every hit.

"Strike!" shouted one cheeky haploid who whacked Brawn clean off his nanobot.

"See, Levity?" asked Sage. "Strikes may be a good thing in bowling, but not baseball. We have to save him!"

In the next three seconds, a hundred thoughts went swirling in my head. If something like that happened to me, what would I do? Would I shout "go on without me" like the suave and gallant heroes in old-time films? And for no more than 1/100th of a haploid second, my heart had the impulsive desire to leave him behind despite the fact that my mind desired to fetch him. Does anybody ever really want to be left behind? Is it just shame and honor that coerces some to utter those words? Are we all resigned to be such selfish and ignoble creatures? Is it just shame rather than bravery that makes the hero? Being left to die does tend to cramp one's style. If it boils down to winning vs. losing the war, is it ever okay to allow one to die so that a hundred may live? I know Sage doesn't think so. Me? I'm not so sure.

"Let's do a U-turn and fetch him," I proclaimed as if the decision was left for me alone. Despite the mass of haploids, Brawn's GPS tracker made it easy to find him (it was getting through the crowd to get to him that posed the challenge). It was a good thing that so many of the sperm were selfish enough to race on and leave us alone. I felt almost invisible as they came right on by.

We nestled the unconscious Brawn right in the middle of our five-nanobot "star" and resumed course towards the right uterotubal junction as before (but we ceased our clockwise spin as we didn't want Brawn to get dizzy). Seeing quite a few sperms ahead of me forced me to realize that coming back to fetch Brawn stole lots of valuable time.

Everyone remained quiet for the next portion of the journey as we jettisoned towards the right uterotubal junction. I couldn't tell if this was because of concern for Brawn or just being too tired to emote, think, or speak.

I spotted Brawn groaning and moving about. "Hey, Brawn is with us again!"

"You took quite the blow," shouted Sage as he stole a glance at Brawn before resuming his gaze on what was ahead.

"What did I miss?" asked Brawn. "I can't remember what even happened to me."

""You were out cold for thirty minutes," said Sage. "If

only white-out could erase a black-out."

"Good thing you had a GPS tracker," thundered Animus. "Cuz these machines don't come equipped with fish finders."

Brawn rubbed his eyes. "Did all those haploids ahead of us get that far on account of me holding you up? I am flattered you came back for me and all, but I'm not sure if it was very wise to the overall goal of our mission."

"Are you kidding?" I asked. "We had to save you. You are the brawn of the operation. Without you, it's just brain without brawn. We need them both, like Yin and Yang. Isn't that right, Animus?"

Animus paused. "Well, if saving Brawn's neck translates into saving ours, how can I disagree."

"I sense another half-compliment from our softy Animus," said Levity.

Brawn worked his way out of the crevice and mounted his nanobot. He rubbed his head with his hands.

"You sure you are okay?" asked Sage, stealing another glance at Brawn.

Brawn made a thumbs-up gesture. "Just a massive headache. You can go back to rotating our ship as before."

"This time, let's make it counter-clockwise," said Sage. "Just to put a different spin on things."

I could still spot a few thousand gametes ahead of us as we jettisoned towards the rocky entrance tunnel to the uterotubal junction.

"This last bunch of haploids ahead of us have all but ceased fighting and are racing to the finish line," said Brawn. "I say let's reprise our role as the bowling ball."

We proceeded to breeze through the medium-density mass, knocking many of them to the sides as before (in a sort of counter-clockwise pattern). The impact felt like a mere bump in the road due to the low gravity. But we were not in the clear.

"Hey, Sage," I said. "What's up with those five nanobots ahead? They are racing towards the right tubular junction, but they don't have any riders."

"Proceed with caution," said Sage. "Could be a bomb or trap of some kind."

I didn't even think that there could be a bomb involved. This put me in a bad situation. On the one hand, I knew how to defuse a bomb. On the other hand, that's the last thing I wanted to do. As they say, just because you are good at something doesn't mean you like it! I had better things to do than to blow myself to bits. And then that damn conscience had to rear its ugly head again.

"Come on, man, you gotta defuse that bomb!" shouted my conscience.

"Hey Sage, I know how to defuse nanobot bombs," I said in a meek voice.

"Say something, Levity?" asked Sage.

"I said I know how to defuse nanobot bombs!" I shouted again but in a much louder voice.

"You alright, Abacus?" asked Sage. "We should check it out. Your skills are valued."

"I suppose, if you insist," I said.

"It's up to you, Abacus," returned Sage. "We don't even know for sure if it's a bomb."

I nodded, and Sage steered our star-ship towards the five vacant nanobots.

"Shame makes the hero," I said as I took a gander at the nearest of the five. I squinted my eyes as if that would somehow keep the nanobots from blowing up. But closing my eyes only led to another problem.

"This is a stickup!" said the ringleader of the Harpoon Platoon as all five of them revealed themselves from behind their "vacant" nanobots. Each of the five aimed their harpoons at each one of us.

"Oh great, the Harpoon Platoon," said Levity. "That's the last thing we need."

"Brace yourselves," said Sage.

"That's hardly reassuring," said Brawn. "Sounds like another of Levity's fortune cookie rejects."

"Hide behind your nanobot and use it as a shield," added Sage. "Is that better?"

We did as we were told. But Sage miscalculated. They had no interest in aiming at us like before. This time, they modified their harpoons into make-shift tasers. The harpoons were connected to conductive wires. All the harpoons hit the nanobots and were knocked away.

A painful shock went through my body, but I did not lose my grip (if anything, the frazzle made my grip tighter). I could tell all my mates also felt the pulse, as I could see them shimmy and shake. But due to some miracle, none of our bodies were pierced by the probes.

"That current didn't even tickle!" shouted Animus.

Levity, Brawn, and Animus heckled and made faces at the gunners as we whizzed by them.

"They sure had poor aim," said Sage. "Even at point blank. We didn't defuse any bombs. But we did defuse the situation."

I felt ill at ease. Something didn't seem right. There's no way all five of them could have missed. Most scientists want to prove their theories right. In this case, I wanted to prove mine wrong. I tested the magnetic brakes on my nanobot (as the normal friction brakes would not work under low gravity conditions). Sure enough, the magnets were clapped out!

"They didn't miss," I shouted.

"You on something?" asked Animus as he and Brawn were doing some sort of drunken and uncoordinated happy dance.

Sage held up his hand to silence the others. "Quiet gentlemen. What do you mean, Abacus?"

I continued. "They used their electrified harpoons to demagnetize our nanobots."

"He's right!" said Brawn. "Our magnet brakes are kaput!"

The others tested theirs as well, to no avail.

But things were just getting started. Not long after our

tussle with the Harpoon Platoon an alarm sounded and repeated a message on all five nanobots. "Warning, impact imminent. Not enough clearance."

Sage shouted. "The uterotubal junction entrance is too narrow for our tethered nanobots to make it through. We are gonna hit the tunnel like a drain stopper."

Brawn screamed with a high-pitched voice. "What do we do? Thanks to the Harpoon Platoon, we have more inertia than a train and bowling ball combined."

Brawn, Levity, and Animus started arguing about who was to blame for this mess.

I raised my hand.

"Really, Abacus?" asked Animus. "You need to raise your hand as we jettison to our doom?"

"Go ahead," said Sage. "You have the floor."

I continued. "We have to slither in front of our nanobots so that when they strike the tunnel entrance, we will keep moving onward into the tunnel. If we stay where we are, behind the nanobots, we will be crushed like a bug on a windshield."

"That's my kind of obituary," said Animus. "Short, sweet, to the point, and action packed to the gills."

"Sometimes I wonder if our Animus has a death wish," said Brawn. "Let's listen to Abacus!"

We all shimmied to the front of the nanobots.

"Get ready," said Sage. "And don't get your tails caught between the nanobot and the tunnel wall."

"I shouldn't have hot-rodded the nanobots so much," I posited. "Putting too much emphasis on speed can compromise accuracy."

"Well said," said Sage.

Animus grumbled. "Brown noser."

The nanobot star clogged the entrance like a cork, causing the lot of us to jettison onwards. I could hear those behind us slam into the blockage. It was a sloppy organic sound like apple sauce smacking a brick wall. I wondered if the Harpoon Platoon was among them.

"Our make-shift drain-stop should keep the riff-raff at bay for a good while," said Brawn.

"Not for long," said Sage. "They will uncork the bottle as more and more of them slam into the barrier."

"Brace yourselves once again," said Sage. "We will be leaving low gravity soon."

As we went flying ahead, I saw the far wall get closer and closer. I closed my eyes, expecting to know what it feels like to be a bug against a windshield. Instead, the loving arms of gravity seized us and dropped us all smack dab in the middle of what appeared to be a battle arena! Are there angels among us?

"Talk about a dramatic entrance," said Brawn. "Or exit. I can't really tell."

"Well folks," said Sage, "we appear to have our gravity back. If you weren't grateful for it before, you are now."

The place smelled of death and looked the part. Even as I write this right now, there are hundreds of corpses on the walls rotting and wilting as if Halloween pumpkins the staff were too lazy to throw away by mid-November.

"There is nothing wrong with sugar-coating death," said Sage. "But this is glamorizing it to a whole new level. Is this supposed to be inspiring? Like we are special for making it this far?"

But the floor décor was odd, if not as gruesome. The floor mat depicted an insignia of what appeared to be two sperm wrestling over the coveted egg. Are we getting closer to the battle phase of this adventure?
Sincerely,
Abacus

P.S. I tried your morale booster of naming something positive about someone that rubs you the wrong way. As insufferable as Animus can be, I made a mental note to admire his strength and fearlessness. I do wonder what role "fear of death" plays into his level of fortitude. At any rate, I mentally burned the gratitude statement as soon as I mentally wrote it down. I hope it still counts!

CHAPTER 7

The G Letters
Subject: Battle at the uterotubul junction
Survival type: Cellular competition (fight class)
Author: Ron Une (Morale)
Date: February 14, 2182 (Thursday)
Location: Neuron
Recipient: Adventurer 1 (Abacus)

Greetings, Abacus (Adventurer 1), my interpretation of the insignia matches yours. But I also discovered that it's a modified yin/yang symbol as it has one dot in the middle instead of two dots. This symbol is very common in the world of humans, and it represents "balance," such as hot/cold, light/dark, sunrise/sunset, or good/evil. Feel free to have the honors of telling Adventurer 3 (Animus) that the fight phase will soon begin. And it goes without saying to relay any crucial intel to the others as well.

Brass tacks. There should be five thousand gametes there waiting for the next phase. And lucky for you, all the haploids that took the left path at the fork in the road are now dead, as they resigned their fate to a simple coin toss (which I must admit almost got you killed as well). I suppose I can forgive any insubordination associated with your concerted effort to take the left path (as long as you can all forgive me for almost getting half of your platoon killed). Although, to be fair, Sage almost got the entire platoon killed by having everyone take the left route. So maybe we can all forgive each other and call it a draw.

This will be a fight to the death. (Did you expect any other?)According to what I learned from Euclid's mind, only one thousand out of five thousand sperms will survive. This will be a "battle of five thousand armies," as we are each an "army of one" out for ourselves. For now, at least, we will have an "army of five." But I can't emphasize enough that alliances are temporary, and the best-case scenario is that four of you must die. But that's a story for another time (and the sooner you accept it, the less hurt you will be).

Do not expect a classy fight with all manner of formality, elegance, and comportment. This will be an all-out brawl without the luxury of "war crimes." It's every man for himself. Pull no punches. Pull no tail whips. When one thousand sperm are left standing, you will enter the Fallopian tubes. I had to abort my study of where these lead. So, let's stay positive and say that perhaps it's a subway tube that will take you straight to the egg.

One in five chance of survival is not too shabby considering some of our other tasks we have been through. These odds will be augmented and buffed further thanks to our genetic modification and strength/stamina upgrades. Work smarter AND harder.

It appears Euclid received his nanobot implants just under two years ago (human years). He had nanobots implanted into his muscular system (in the country of Musc) to enhance his muscle cells to keep his strength up as he struggles with Korsakoff's Syndrome (which affects not only him but all of us in Neuron as well). But that is not all, as the nanobot implants added a fringe benefit. His overall physique is more toned, strong, and muscular than most humans. It's amazing what nanobots, genetic modification, and somatic genetic editing can do. It is harder for us as we have to conduct science while also soldiering through battle. We are like those journalists who get caught up in the very war they are covering. They are not just passive observers beyond the 4th wall. There should be a proper title for soldiering scientists. Soltist? Scienter? I digress.

Drop me a note when you are nested in the safe haven of the Fallopian tubes. The nanobots will relay data about the upcoming battle, and I trust you will keep me abreast. I am working myself to the bone trying to ascertain why the sperm are so dead set on reaching this magical egg that may not even exist. We know WHAT we are doing, but not WHY we are doing it. Euclid has the answers we seek, but dragging them out of their hole is the challenge.

P.S. Don't die. That's an order!

The G Letters
Subject: Re: Battle at uterotubal junction
Survival type: Cellular competition (fight class)
Author: Adventurer 5 (Sage)
Date: February 14, 2182 (Thursday)
Recipient: Ron Une (Morale)

Dear Ron Une (Morale),
This is a rundown of what transpired during the "Battle of the Sentries" (as this is what we were all called by the battle staff (the workers, not to be confused with tall oaken clubs). As we soaked in our surroundings, our apprehension was palpable, as evidenced by our trembling limbs, sweat, and wavering words. This didn't seem taboo or unexpected. After all, we were all cogs in the same machine with a sort of collective consciousness.

Like the races before, the goal of the battle was survival and competition. Unlike the races, this was more fight than flight. The onset of the tournament began with the appearance of a retinue of ringmasters (the aforementioned staff, which were called "Prospectors"). They set up the game, removed the bodies after the battles, and operated the gates leading to the Fallopian tubes. These regal sorts were adorned with gold crowns, gold scepters, and what appeared to be diamond finials at the tips (you don't need a wine expert to tell you that gold and diamonds pair well together). They wielded these staffs as if air marshals with batons guiding airplanes. There were five of them, and they were herding the fighters into place around the circle. Why they needed gold scepters for such a simple purpose is beyond my pay grade and scope of practice.

The diameter of the arena was just large enough to couch all five thousand around the insignia, shoulder to shoulder. The five of us stood in the same line, next to each other. Three of the five Prospectors wandered together around clockwise in the middle of the ring, holding large oaken chests. Each gamete was given a choice of a bow/arrow (for distance) or a machete (for melee), depending on each individual's preference.

I whispered to Animus. "We mustn't get too comfortable. It's imperative we chomp at the bit and anticipate the starter pistol. When push comes to shove, it's better to "break a leg" than to "break your neck." We need a stronghold strategy. Let's have Levity and Abacus build a waist-high nanobot barrier using nanobot scrap while you, Brawn, and myself cover them. If anyone gets in their way, they can splay their melee weapons. Pass it on."

I felt like a teenager passing a secret (and it was indeed a secret). Animus whispered into Brawn's ear, and the message was sent between all five of us. I crossed my fingers that the message wouldn't become too distorted by the time it got to the end, like what often happens in the telephone game. For all I knew, Levity received instructions on how best to decorate a Christmas tree.

The message must have remained intact, as Animus, Brawn, and myself each opted for a bow and quiver for long-range attack. Abacus and Levity each took a machete for melee. I figured a machete would be more user-friendly for Levity and Abacus, given the fact that their only experience with a blade consisted of spreading jam on crescent rolls.

I scanned the arena to discern how many haploids were part of an alliance. Some of the alliances were easy to spot as the members wore the same uniform or gi as if they were in a biker gang. One ten-member alliance wore all green (with an emblem of crossed swords on the back). Another alliance consisted of each member wearing a gi with a chicken egg on the back (is that what human eggs look like?). A third alliance wore black belts (although it remained questionable how legitimate they were, anyone can put on a black belt without knowing a lick of martial arts). There were dozens more, with various types of identification, emblems, and symbols representing their unions.

Other alliances were more discreet and abstained from wearing any regalia (other than the emotions on their sleeve). I tried to discern the covert alliances by the manner of their body language, posture, and eye contact. I surmised that upwards of twenty-five percent of the gametes appeared to be in some sort of alliance (with anywhere between three and twenty haploids each).

In theory, an alliance is a lucrative strategy (as long as each of the members were loyal, of course). An alliance could surround an enemy and do a pincer attack. And if surrounded themselves, they could form an ironclad mass by standing with their backs against each other with eyes in all directions and their backs protected.

Two hours dragged by as the three Prospectors in the middle distributed the weapons. It was amazing how quiet the room was despite housing five thousand sperm (if I had my eyes closed and tried to guess how many were in the battle chamber, I would have guessed a few hundred at most).

When the last machete was handed out, all five Prospectors returned to their thrones behind what appeared to be weapon-proof glass. It piqued my curiosity as to the purpose of the window. My supposition was that it served a three-fold purpose. One, it protected them from being attacked by mutineers. Two, it allowed them the ability to "referee" the show. And three? That was the most disturbing proposition, and it became apparent when I spotted two of the Prospectors snag boxes of popcorn from behind their balcony. I guess they just wanted to enjoy our life and death as if it were just another day at the box office. I guess all really was fair in love and war.

The head Prospector stood up and proceeded to unroll a scroll.

"Somehow, I got the idea he isn't about to give a gentle reminder to floss daily," said Levity.

The Prospector cleared his throat. "You are all aces of the races, as evidenced by not only your survival instinct but also the gruesome and grisly deaths of millions of your fellow peers left behind in your wake. Your victorious stature is made manifest by the visible gore, audible shrieks, tangible wounds, smell of rot, and taste of blood. Even now, echoes of your victory can be heard from the wails of their family and friends. Do not shed tears for them! The slow do not deserve your haste. The weak do not deserve your strength. And the infirm do not deserve your anodyne or poultice.

You have proved yourselves to be "aces of the races" and have now been elevated to "Sentries." But do not mistake this for a coronation ceremony. The battle phase has yet to begin. There is only one rule in the Battle of the Sentries: Survive! This includes kill, be killed, run, or hide. You will not begin until I tell you to begin. If any of you should tempt fate by jumping the gun, you will be executed where you stand."

The Prospector's message may not have been as eloquent as FDR's Inaugural Address, but the message was poignant, loud, and very clear.

The Head Prospector continued. "The 'Battle of Five Thousand Armies' will commence when I count to three. One, two, and begin!"

Just as the head Prospector reached three, a blast of energy jettisoned from his gold scepter.

"What's wrong with a simple starter's pistol?" asked Levity.

Animus huffed. "So dramatic!"

"I thought I got shot before the fight started," said Brawn.

"I had to feel myself to make sure I wasn't bleeding!"

"Those scepters are not for show," I said. "Levity and Abacus, go and build our nanobot barrier near the wall so we have front and back cover. The rest of us will cover you. Remember to keep the wall waist-high so we can still aim our bows at their heads."

"Roger," said Abacus.

Levity nodded. "We got this."

There was a copious amount of nanobot scrap in the room for Abacus and Levity to build with as if the scrap was an erector set. There were also non-functional but intact nanobots strewn about as well, which were already close to waist-high.

"I will start building our nanobot wall," said Levity as he approached the nearest bot.

"Look out!" shouted Animus as one of the black-belt sperms popped out from behind the nanobot.

Levity spun around and was greeted by the sight of the black belt falling in defeat from one of Animus's arrows.

"Take his machete with you," Brawn shouted. "The less access to weapons they have, the better."

We were all staring at Levity and must have taken our own safety for granted.

"Hi," said one of the green-gi wearing gametes as he tapped Abacus on the shoulder. The latter spun around.

"Ah, hi?" responded Abacus.

Another green-gi haploid tapped Abacus from behind on the shoulder, and the latter spun around yet again.

"And bye," said the second green-gi.

"Look out!" I shouted.

My warning must have been unwarranted as both greens howled and fell to the ground before I finished the command, almost as if their voices and movements were choreographed. One of them fell from Abacus's machete, and the other from Animus's arrow.

"Well done," I said. "Thank you, Animus."

"I can't take full credit," said Animus. "Abacus took care of one of them."

"I don't even know what happened," said Abacus. "I just let my nervous jitters control my machete."

"It's called survival instinct," I said. "Even so-called cowards have it, and it's one of the very best assets any soldier can have. Just make sure you look before you leap, aim before you shoot, and listen before you stab. Survivor's instinct can be a blessing or a curse."

"Watch out for their 'Hi and Bye,'" said Levity. "It was very much purposeful and intentional how they try to stab you in the belly and back at the same time."

"Now we know what those crossed swords mean on their uniforms," said Brawn.

"Are you hurt?" I asked, noticing some blood seeping from Abacus's lab coat from his back.

"Their blades only entered half an inch," said Abacus. "Just a flesh wound."

"Spoken like a warrior," said Animus. "There is hope for you yet!"

Just after the two "green gi" fighters fell, Brawn and I spotted another "green gi" member begin to stab his fellow team members in the back! He took down three of them before the other five took him out.

"The crossed swords on the traitor's gi suits him," I said to Brawn. "The double-crosser that he is."

Brawn smiled. "If they kill each other, it's less work for us."

Animus guffawed. "Divide and conquer, oldest trick in the book."

Abacus and Levity retrieved the enemy weapons and then took to retrieving pieces of nanobots like beavers building a dam. It only required a total of fifteen haploid minutes to finish our barricade. Only three more gametes dared mess with them (from the chicken/egg gang), and Brawn, Animus, and myself each took one for ourselves.

"I will fetch our arrows," said Animus as he went head-first into battle wielding one of the spare retrieved machetes. He swiped the heads off two unaffiliated haploids en route and returned.

"All that work for three arrows?" asked Brawn.

"Worth every calorie," said Animus.

When the waist-high and crescent-shaped wall was finished, we had the nanobot wall for front cover and back cover from the wall behind us.

"Kneel behind the barricade to avoid arrows," I shouted.

We all hunkered down behind the coveted cover, me next to Abacus. I noticed that his white lab coat was not designed to keep a secret, and blood from the "mere flesh wound" on his back was seeping through plain as day.

"You really are hurt," I said, kneeling down next to him. "Why didn't you say anything? Such macho posturing is beneath you, isn't it?"

Abacus sighed. "Well, I wouldn't call it machismo. I didn't want to call attention to myself and burden you guys."

"Stubborn pride nonetheless," I said. "Whether from a worrier or a warrior. Levity, you render him aid. Fashion a bandage for his back."

"I have an idea," said Abacus as he began fiddling with components on the nanobot.

"Stop moving around so much," shouted Brawn.

Abacus continued working as if he didn't hear.

"Let him work," I said. Brawn, Animus, and I will cover for Levity and Abacus. I have an inkling Abacus is up to something. And from my experience, whatever he gets up to is most welcome."

"You remember when the Harpoon Platoon fashioned their harpoons into tasers?" Abacus asked.

Levity rubbed his own shoulder. "How can I forget."

"They must have used nanobot electricity to charge their

probes," continued Abacus. "If I can harness nanobot electricity, I can charge this entire barrier into an electric fence. But it's imperative that we don't touch it ourselves!"

It took about ten minutes for Levity to fashion Abacus's bandage (fashioned, yes, fashionable, no).

"Thanks, Animus," said Abacus. "And perfect timing, I just finished myself."

I motioned everyone to stand back away from the barricade. "Alright, gents, stand back. It's time to add some jolts to the bolts."

Abacus set the five-second timer on the nanobot and joined us as if we were taking a group photograph.

"Five, four, three, two, one," went the clock in a robotic female voice.

"It's working," said Abacus. "Despite the lack of noise. Now hide behind the barricade but at a safe distance of at least six inches."

We knelt down behind the wall. It only took five minutes until a group of at least fifty sperm ran towards us.

"Zap!" went the wall as the front lines died on impact. After about twenty of the fifty died, about ten tried jumping the wall while the other ten attempted to dismantle the charge. None of these strategies worked, as all fifty were smoldering by the end of the ordeal. We were thinning the herd. Still, I couldn't help but think that it was only a matter of time until other factions joined forces to smoke us out like gophers.

And do you remember, Ron Une, when you told me how one's cynical fears can make Murphy's Law come true? Well, I still don't believe it, but in this case, it may have happened.

"TA," shouted a loud voice from a loudspeaker.

"I know that voice anywhere," said Levity. "That's the creatures from the harpoon lagoon. No doubt about it. But what does 'TA' mean?

I sighed. "I can tell you that he is not soliciting for a teacher's aid. It means Temporary Alliance, and it's a call to arms to invoke an informal agreement that enemy factions will band together only long enough to take out a dangerous cell or faction. And before anyone asks, that faction is us."

You know, Ron, this "TA" thing made me wonder if all alliances were temporary, even in the civilian sector. Even those who lose a spouse will often take up another so-called "one and only" lover. This could be one of life's sad truths, after all. Some dreamers dream despite knowing full well they are in the throes of a nightmare.

"Okay, gents, hold your ground," I continued. "When the Harpoon Platoon gives the order, many factions will charge after us in concert. And with those numbers, they will breach our barrier. Not that it will make much difference, but at least my GPS tracker is letting me know that we are the only ones with genetic enhancements."

"Hold the phone," said Abacus. "How do you know that?"

"I connected the GPS tracker to the LAN earlier," I said. "The organ detection software is equipped to vet such things."

Abacus stood up.

"Easy, Abacus," I said.

Abacus scrunched up his face. "These bandages are helping. If I stay here, I will be trampled to death. Besides, the gashes aren't more than an inch deep."

"That's not even the thickness of a deep-dish pizza," said Animus. "That's the spirit!"

Abacus hobbled around the barricade and began pulling an intact (non-electrified) nanobot back.

"Let me help you," said Brawn. "Brains and brawn and all that."

When they appeared back on the scene, Abacus removed the tracker from his ear and connected it to the nanobot LAN as Brawn watched.

"Hey, this is no time to assess how much battle prowess we have," said Animus. "We are fish in a barrel against those kinds of numbers. Unless you are using your GPS tracker as a dog tag to identify your body later.

"If this is the end, let's hope our deaths are short, swift, and sweet," I said.

"So that's it?" Levity asked. "You all want to throw in the towel as if we are airing our dirty laundry?"

Animus huffed. "If I had more time, I would take you to task, Levity. Watch your mouth, kid."

Brawn, Animus, and I formed a line and clung to our machetes as if they would save us. We might as well have hidden under a desk during a nuclear war. Talk about having a Linus Blanket during a nuclear winter.

"Here they come," I said as I nodded towards the volley of haploids at the other side of the room.

"Like a swarm of killer bees," added Animus.

"Done!" shouted Abacus, clapping his hands.

We all looked over Abacus's shoulder to see what the fuss was all about. The screen displayed a red warning light with audio. "Ten minutes until activation."

Abacus was grinning ear to ear. "When Sage checked his GPS tracker, it gave me an idea. I just connected my GPS tracker to this nanobot, so the organ detection software will alert the nanobots which haploids are genetically modified (i.e., us). In less than a minute, every intact nanobot in the room will attack everyone in the room except the five of us. Just don't touch them. They are still electrified."

Brawn gave Animus a fist bump. "If Sage never mentioned GPS trackers having the ability to spot genetic anomalies, Abacus would have never got the idea. I think Sage just saved our necks."

"How about that," I said. "But we can't forget Abacus, who has saved our necks a few times. And to think we were going down with our tails between our legs, well, if we had legs."

"You still got that towel, Levity?" asked Animus. "I think you may want to hang on to it."

Everyone laughed. I guess there's just something about "not getting killed" that tends to put some pep in one's step. But we weren't out of the woods yet.

"Hunker down, gents," I commanded. We all knelt down behind the barrier and remained alert for archers. "This barrier should give us protection until the mob gets here."

I transfixed my gaze as the mass of "white paint" slithered towards us like a gigantic slime monster with a collective consciousness. The mob knew by now not to fuss with our electric fence, so they stopped short of our bunker and waited.

The Harpoon Platoon emerged from the white mass, harpoons in tow.

"We meet again," said Levity.

"Ever so dramatic," said the leader. "Don't worry, the pleasure is all yours. We began with harpoons. And then we leveled up to electrified harpoons. I don't know if you did your homework, but we learned our lesson. And that bunker will not save you. Our harpoons are now fitted with explosives so powerful each harpoon is like a hand grenade."

"If you toss it with your tail, does it become a tail grenade?" said Levity. "Prepare yourself. Things are about to get tubular in the uterotubal junction."

In a normal situation, I would have chastised Levity for egging him on and pushing his buttons like that. But in this case, his quip bought us some precious few seconds of time. And I think it gave us a boost of confidence, whether for good or ill.

Each of the five members of the Harpoon Lagoon looked at each other and nodded.

"Sex," said one.
"Drugs," said another.
"Rock," said the third.
"Roll," said the fourth.
"And murder!" said the fifth.

Their flippant remarks bought us even more moments of

precious time. But it was unclear if it was enough. All five of them aimed their harpoons at an eighty-degree angle, fixin' to get their harpoons to land behind our bunker as if they were lawn darts. Now I know why those things were made illegal in the world of humans.

"Nanobots are now activated," said the voice emanating from Abacus's nanobot.

And then it happened. What you ask? "It," I say! The nanobots went rogue. Every one of them. Even the intact ones that were part of our barricade. Five of the latter rolled after the harpoon platoon like police dogs to their subject. They brought their harpoons down and aimed them at the nanobots. Not only did the nanos sizzle them like bacon, but their harpoons discharged in their hands as well, leaving nary but smoke in their location.

Animus inspected the area, kicking up dust along the ground. "There's no way these guys are gonna get an open-casket funeral. In fact, by the looks of it, they don't even need a closed-casket one. There's nothing left of em.'"

But that was only the start of our grand entrance (or was it grand exit?). Hundreds of nanobots in the room gave chase to the throngs of haploids still running amok. And they were a fearsome bunch. There were moments when I wondered if they were motivated by anger and hatred. Some of them electrocuted the enemy, while others used their gene splicers to carve them up. We didn't just have a "war on." Now the war "was on!" As in, "it's payback time!"

Their primitive bows, arrows, and machetes were no match to the high-tech weapons of the bots. The nanobots went through the crowd like sheepdogs herding cattle. Hundreds of their sperm were shocked, sliced, or otherwise eradicated. And while their massive alliance was truncated, it was not disbanded. The haploids just changed their focus from us to the nanobots as being public enemy number one. They shifted the focus of their "temporary alliance" and left us alone to work together to dismantle the nanobot horde (it required at least five haploids to take down a bot). The haploid herd, as well as the nanobot herd, were being thinned.

"We can't just hide behind this bunker like cowards," said Animus. "We should attack while they are distracted, don't you think?"

I tapped my chin. "Hmm, you are right. But we don't need to go in guns blazing. Just keep our distance and pick them off from a distance. After all, Brawn can fire an arrow at twice the distance as your typical haploid."

"Brawn sounds like a regular little miss Annie Oakley," said Animus.

"Enough," I said. "Don't worry, Animus, you won't be upstaged. Your aim is twice that of your typical haploid."

"Animus is like a jealous little puppy when he's not being credited," said Brawn.

We slithered along, Brawn, Animus, and myself picking off the occasional haploid in the distance. There were dead bodies all around us, and it did precious little for my own morale.

"Hey Levity, look out, that one's playing dead!" Animus warned as he pointed ahead.

"Hi!" shouted a sperm "coming to life" in front of Levity, wearing a green gi from the "crossed Swords" battalion.

"Hiya!" shouted Levity as he brought his machete down into the haploid's chest. "What, no goodbye? How rude."

As we kept slithering, I cautioned my mates. "Keep on the lookout for haploids self-effacing, hiding, or playing dead. One cue is to see their bellies rising and falling."

If there is one thing I learned, Ron, it's that playing dead is a refined skill. And seeing others play dead is yet another. And some are more equipped than others. After all, it requires the ability to remain still in a tense situation, hold your breath, and quell your trembling nerves.

It wasn't long until the remaining gametes hovered around one thousand.

"Cease the battle or die," thundered the lead Prospector's voice through the loudspeakers. You haven't lived, Ron, until you have heard a stern message in 5.0 Dolby Surround Sound that you are allowed to live. Four of the five Prospectors left their post from behind the protective glass and used their gold scepters to usher the survivors into the "safety" of the fallopian tubes.

Once inside, we were "greeted" by a battle arena with the same modified Yin/Yang motif as before. But this time, it was much smaller, sized for the one thousand survivors. The walls of the Fallopian tubes were "decorated" with skulls and bones like the Paris Catacombs. There were three large statues equidistant from each other along the edge of the circular battle arena. One statue was a haploid holding a weathered scroll as if it had been unrolled many times and read aloud. Another statue was hoisting a boulder above his head. The third statue was of a haploid wielding a massive (and open) pair of shears above his head. I don't know what that meant, but I had the inkling these three men were not about to engage in an art project.

There were fewer nanobots this time around. And the ones present mingled around the Prospectors at their beck and call, as if serving their masters.

This next bit is rather difficult to say, even from the safety of my distance, pen, and parchment. But Remember a moment ago when I mentioned that one of the "Crossed Swords" gametes popped out and said "hi" to Levity? And how Levity said, "What, no goodbye?" Well, the green-gi wearing gamete did have a partner. He was playing dead near Animus.

"And bye!" shouted his partner in crime as he pulled back his bow and aimed towards Levity.

"Look out, Levity!" shouted Brawn and myself in unison as they poised themselves as human shields between Levity and the haploid's arrows. But the gamete was not fixing to kill Levity. And he was also not fixing to even use a bow. He tight-fisted two arrows in each hand, four arrows in total, and thrust them right through Animus's chest.

"Take a bow," said the haploid as he tossed his unused bow towards Animus. But Animus was not finished yet. With blood spilling out of four wounds, he managed to catch the bow in one hand and used it to prepare a bow for the haploid.

"Take a curtsy," shouted Animus as he shot an arrow from the enemy's bow from punching distance of the enemy's face. "It might be unexpected to use an arrow like a knife, but it's also unexpected to shoot an arrow at point-blank range at someone's head."

So enough on that. Animus died. That's all that we need to know about it. Does it really matter how he died? Does it give any sort of closure? By any rate, I will spare you any and all gruesome details.

One thing I learned is that bravery does not guarantee survival. There are times when it can provoke the opposite. And other times, it's just a smokescreen for stupidity. One weakness of his was that he spent far too much time taunting his opponents. What other point is there to "trash talk" than to enhance the aggression of the aggressor? Maybe it was his way of boosting confidence. Or cloaking his fear, like acting big and mighty in front of a bear. Or perhaps he became complacent and over-confident from being a super soldier. However you spin it, his version of courage was also the cause of his downfall. If Animus proved anything to me, it's that good people can be annoying. And he was one of the best at both.

Gory details aside, his last words were worth noting. The four of us surrounded him, Abacus fidgeting with his spinner and Levity in tears. Brawn's countenance was flat and apathetic, like a corpse. As for me? I don't know if anyone could tell, but I retreated into my brooding, safe place where nothing could harm me except for myself.

"I guess I have always been a sore loser," said Animus.

I put my hand on Animus's shoulder. "Literally and figuratively. Try not to speak."

Levity tears fell on Animus's cheeks like the first heavy

drops of rain before a storm.

"You should stand back," said Animus. "Some might mistake your tears for mine. And that's not the impression I want to convey when I croak."

"Did you get the obituary you wanted?" Levity asked, clutching his hand in his.

Abacus forced a smile as blood trickled from his mouth. "Short, sweet, to the point, and action-packed to the gills. It won't be a closed casket funeral, but it will have to do."

"You sure you are not playing dead?" asked Brawn, his eyes moist with tears. "You wanna jump up and bring life back to normal, please?"

"I'm about as good at playing dead as I am at playing the victim or playing dumb," said Animus. "I just don't have the impulse control to put on such an act."

We stood by him for five additional minutes, standing in solemn silence, until he breathed his last. It wasn't long after that when the Prospector seized the battle. When we got to the Fallopian tube, we zombie-slithered to one of the lone tables at the far end of the chamber. After racing through the five stages of grief, I invited everyone to say something positive about Animus.

Levity went first. "I admire Animus's uncanny ability to express his love by teasing you and how that signified that he liked you."

"His pit-bull aggression and stubbornness," said Brawn.

Abacus paused and thought for a moment. "It might appear that I took the brunt of Animus's beating. But behind that veneer of ironclad bravado, I could sense a genteel and sensitive fellow underneath."

I jumped in. "It's true, Abacus. In private, he told me that without you, we would not have made it this far. He was drunk, mind you, but that is when his words were the most sincere."

"What about you, Sage?" asked Levity.

I was so crestfallen I went with the obvious, if only to convey proper comportment as a leader. But the words were still true. "He died with courage, dignity, and selflessness trying to defend the rest of us." By any stretch, we ended with a moment of silence. At least verbally. My brain was far from silent. Was any of this worth it? What am I doing here? Why did I allow myself to get so close to Animus and the others? Now I know why so many humans refuse to ever get a dog again when they lose one.

If I may, I would like to delight in a "re-do" of my campfire memorial, but only to you. Death has a way of turning even the least of us into angels. Everyone has a story. Extreme "madness" cannot exist without an extreme "method." It's not as if living and breathing individuals are exempt from the laws of causality. All things happen for a reason, as our dear Abacus would be quick to point out. Despite having the bedside manner of the Grim Reaper, Animus had one laudable quality in particular that I would like to call to attention. Our irascible hero never beat around the bush. If anything, he would beat the very bush itself! He was more of a "front stabber" than a "back stabber." He would say it like it was, without reservation, right to your face. He was the kinda guy that would make your enemies "walk the plank" but reassure you that it was "above board." But his mercurial temperament was not just his curse but also his blessing. Contrary to public opinion, he was not heartless. The truth, however stark, was that he wore his heart on both sleeves.

It's amazing what can go through one's head during a "moment of silence." I also caught myself thinking about all the contention between the eleven countries on planet Euclid. Many in Neuron think they are superior to those in Cardio because they are intelligent brain cells. And just as many from Cardio claim that they have so much more emotional intelligence than those in Neuron. Or how those from Repro hurl toilet humor towards Uri and those from Uri hurl sexual innuendos towards those from Repro. "Tit for shat," as they say in Skel, as if the lot of us in Uri and Repro.were swine before pearls. I try to say that all eleven systems are crucial to keeping Euclid Hux alive. Creating a caste system based on which organ systems are more or less important is nothing short of futile and foolhardy. And with me being from the "vile and base" country of Repro, sometimes I wonder why I bother trying to defend and validate those who would not do the same in return. There are just as many battle flags as there are sperm, millions of one-man armies, each defending their own governing body. Each is a prisoner of war, confined to the cell of the cellular body. And what's the impetus? Same as always, fear and survival in the face of peril. To not be one of the helpless haploids pinned to the wall of the uterotubal junction. If only I could borrow some of Brawn's hubris. I fear that if I made such a requisition, he would most certainly command me to "leggo my ego."

P.S. It goes without saying or hesitation. Please do not tell the others about the plight of my dark thoughts I have been having as of late. Such weakness is unbecoming of a leader. I wonder if it's even prudent that I tell you as much as I just did. But there are days, My Captain My Captain, where I feel that if I wasn't a third wheel, I wouldn't be a wheel at all. All the death I have seen, the fear on the haploids' faces tells me they are not as riveted with adventure as they were on the day they set out on the adventure back at the Crystal Gate. Even the ones left alive do not seem like happy campers. Their smiles are fewer, and their laughs are more subdued and understated. And despite my best efforts, I have seen this same trend with my very own platoon. And how can I enjoy summer camp when my fellow mates, dead or alive, appear so dejected and despondent? Is it their fault that their less-than-desirable fate should rain on my parade? Why must we all die, even those of us who are lucky enough to live? So what of my emotions in addition to such intrusive thoughts? They share the caprice of a storm cloud, with all manner of thunder, lightning, and heavy rain. I fear to be alone and left to my devices (vices instead of vice grips). The more focused lucubration I dedicate, regardless of topic, grants me more confusion than peace. Some silver linings are more difficult to find than a silver needle in a haystack. Some things do have a rhyme and reason but still make no sense at all. "Death" and "breath" may rhyme, but the dead do not breathe. I am finding myself envious of the prize itself, this "egg" we are seeking. Why is the egg allowed to sit in passive resignation, safe and sound in her humble abode, with no death, with no competition, while waiting for the sperm to clash, smash, and thrash in all manner of warfare just for first access? What about the sperm that have no affinity to engage in such blood lust? Predators do not sign up to be predators. They get what they are given and must make the best of it, to the chagrin of those who are more inclined to pray for the prey. What came first, the chicken or the egg? This question does not just apply to the chicken or platypus.

CHAPTER 8

The H Letters
Subject: Fallopia Dystopia
Survival type: Cellular competition (fight class)
Author: Ron Une (Morale)
Date: February 14, 2182 (Thursday)
Location: Neuron
Recipient: Adventurer 5 (Sage)

Dear Adventurer 5 (Sage),

Is there a hard and fast rule that the first paragraph in a friendly letter must be reserved for small talk? I will break said convention. Despite my best efforts, the loss of Adventurer 2 (Animus) weighs heavy on me as well. I tell you, Sage (Adventurer 5), I must be without shame! I cried in the public marketplace square, and all eyes were trained on me as if police spotlights, their cringed/grimaced faces telling me everything I needed to know about their second-hand embarrassment! Let them look! They know not the loss I have been through!

But what if these well-intentioned, nasty people had a point? So, with a bit of elbow grease, I spent the better part of the last few hours telling myself that "losses are inevitable," "soldiers are disposable," and that "sperm are a dime a dozen." Losing Animus was a loss, to be sure, but this little psychological exercise helped a bit more than I thought it would. I suggest you all give it a go.

I, too, hate to be the harbinger of bad tidings, but some

things need to be said, even if it leaves the listener worse for wear. Do not take my "nagging" as evidence that I consider you all to be irresponsible. Such repetition is not meant as an insult to your intelligence. But it is imperative that I drive the point home, like a stake in a vampire. Getting too close to your mates will end in heartache, as we have just seen! We started with millions and millions of gametes. The fact we have come this far is a sublime blessing without disguise. Such miracles are rare indeed, and here and now, it is displayed in the open for all to see, as if bejeweled mannequin busts in a storefront window! The papers in Repro and beyond are abuzz with chatter about you all as if you were astronauts on a space mission (but please keep mum about this from Brawn, for I fear his head will expand to the point of no return).

Nuts and bolts (if you have not passed through the five stages of grief, I suggest you do it now). I engaged in further research and was able to breach some of Euclid's most secure memory locks, including ones to his unconscious memory. These included, but were not limited to, not only the generational memories of Euclid's family tree but also the whispers, ghosts, and echoes of entire generations from traumas long past and still embedded in the deep unconscious memories of humanity itself! These echoes are akin to audio fossils!

Despite their ceremonial garb and stately poses, do not be deceived by the Roman inspired monoliths and statues! They are not for show. Their "paper," "rock," and "scissors" motifs represent a popular luck-based method of "drawing straws" in the human world to settle disputes. Take it to heart. It works like this: paper beats rock, rock beats scissors, and scissors beats paper. It's no mere nursery rhyme. Like Tic-Tac-Toe, there can be a tie. But unlike Tic-Tac-Toe, and more like Bingo, this is a truly random affair (lest the rectitude of one's karma should affect the roll of the dice). So even still, hold the hope and keep the faith.

This next tournament will be a one-on-one affair. Holding a tournament where one thousand gametes engage in one-to-one combat would be foolhardy and time-consuming, to say the least. This is where quantum mechanics comes into play. Time and space will be warped and compartmentalized so that each one-on-one battle that ensues will play out in its own alternate reality, all at the same time. Each arena will be built for two, but it will be spacious enough to allow for range combat. The finer details are not important and will present themselves to you in due course.

I was remiss in sharing a detail prior, to which I must apologize (although even with the benefit of the Hawthorne Effect it may have made little difference). When the next skirmish begins, those who finished in the 50th percentile of the previous battle will gain an experience level. This status upgrade is based on battle prowess, which includes such ilk as body count, bravery, stealth, and even grace and style. I should have, and would have if I could have, warned you about these performance buffs. It was not enough to be in the surviving retinue of 1000 gametes! Still, let's cling to the hope that some of you will gain enough experience to level up to a "Sentinel." For those of you less mathematically inclined than Abacus (Adventurer 1), five hundred will remain Sentries, and five hundred will be boosted to Sentinels. But do not mistake this for a 50/50 chance. You must also factor in how the element of skill plays its role as well (in addition to your body upgrades). Keep positive! And please chronicle everything you can about the disparities between these "Sentries" and "Sentinels."

Don't brush aside the power of "feinting." You can bait and dodge the opponent's magic at just the opportune time, forcing the caster to wait five minutes until he is recharged and able to cast magic again. Seize this opportunity to put your skills to the test! It will also behoove you to know when your opponent is feinting as well.

I still have to learn more about these "Prospectors" as well. Other than running these games, I know very little about them. That can be one of your "homework" assignments (well, you can do the work part, even if you are not at home). I will leave it to you to educate me on what lies beyond the Fallopian tubes from the Graduate School of Hard Knox.

Going by statistics alone, a scant 200 of the 1000 haploids will survive this battle (20% chance, skill factors aside). As always, don't allow statistics to create any self-fulfilling prophecies. I still believe that the pros outweigh the cons in telling you such grim and stark reminders. Put your eggs in the "skill" basket. Your genetic upgrades should be a boon for all of you in this battle and any to come. Do not allow reality to quell your confidence.

I will now leave you to your devices (be they vices or vice grips). And if any of you remain a Sentry, do not fret. Where there is a will, there is a way (especially when the "will" is of the ironclad variety). Stop, drop, and rock & roll!
Sincerely,
Ron Une

P.S. Work smarter AND harder!! That's an order (and I don't mean from a Sears Roebuck catalog)!

The H Letters
Subject: Re: Fallopia Dystopia
Survival type: Cellular competition (fight class)
Location: Fallopian Tubes
Author: Levity
Date: February 14, 2182 (Thursday)
Recipient: Ron Une (Morale)

Hi Ron Une, Levity here (no, duh, right? It says so just above). This is our update on what transpired (I had the gang proofread my letter and give suggestions). Take comfort in the fact that the very act of you reading this letter indicates some level of victory on our end, right? It only took an hour for the Prospectors to determine who would be elevated from a Sentry to a Sentinel based on the battle assessments conducted by the nanobots. Half of the thousand remained Sentries, and the other half were elevated to Sentinels, as we expected. To make a short story even shorter, I remained a Sentry (but only because I was holding back my true potential). But the fact I am alive right now should speak volumes, right? Brawn became a Sentinel, and so did Sage. Abacus? He was stuck with being a Sentry with me.

"The pen is mightier than the sword, my ass!" shouted Abacus. Definitely not one of his more scientific statements. I guess this was no place to showcase his calculus skills. But at least I wasn't the only Sentry, right? That's gotta count for something.

The Prospectors had everyone stand shoulder to shoulder around the perimeter of the Yin/Yang symbol as before, but this time, the arena was designed for only a thousand fighters. There were only three Prospectors this time around. Two of them claimed the inner sanctum of the circle as a matter of routine and walked together around the ring in a clockwise manner. One-handed out the electric daggers and bronze scepters to the newly Christened Sentinels. A second collected the bows, quivers, and machetes from the Sentries graduating to Sentinels. The third lead Prospector was behind a sheet of fire-proof glass as before (for extra security in the event of a mutiny).

"Isn't it backwards that the worse fighters are the ones that don't level up?" I asked the guy taking my melee weapons. "Shouldn't Sentries be the ones being elevated to Sentinels so as to create a more fair fight and level playing field?"

The Prospector handing out the bronze scepters and electric daggers took the liberty of answering my question. "You don't get it, do you? That is not how the food chain works according to the laws of nature. Leveling up is a privilege to be earned, not a right to be granted. The laws of nature trump the laws of society. Now, take your electric dagger or go with nothing."

I took my electric dagger. So much for "there are no bad questions!" Combatants were paired together using random assignment, regardless of whether they were a Sentinel or a Sentry.

"Remember, guys," said Abacus. "It's a random selection with replacement, so there is the chance of being selected to fight multiple times as names are placed back into the subject pool." I was starting to wonder if there was any difference between "random selection" and "natural selection!"

The head Prospector stepped up to the microphone with a smile as if an MC at a beauty pageant. "Listen up, everyone, I will only say all this once. Unlike the last free for all skirmish at the uterotubal junction, these will be one-on-one fights, each taking place in its own private venue and worldline. This is the main arena, and the three statues in the corners of the room hold the key to victory. Half of you remained Sentries, and the other half elevated to Sentinels. We already know what Sentries are. The School of Hard Knocks taught you that. Sentinels? So far, we know that they receive a regal scepter fashioned from engraved bronze, with a shiny emerald at the finial. But this is what you don't know. In every one-on-one battle, each Sentinel is privy to something called a "die-cast." I will toss a polyhedral three-sided die to determine the Sentinel's magic class (paper, rock, scissors). A large and visible insignia of a paper, rock, or scissors will be emblazoned above the emerald finial, as if by magic.

If two Sentries are chosen for battle, it's a one-on-one version of the battle at the uterotubal junction. Instead of bows, arrows, or machetes, all Sentries will be given a short-range electric dagger that they can wear sheathed on their hip. This knife will discharge a burse of electricity if the blade goes into the body an inch or deeper. Nobody has ever survived after being electrocuted by an electric dagger. When one electric dagger is discharged, this automatically de-activates the other electric dagger. This is a safety measure to prevent both haploids from shocking each other to death."

"What happens if a Sentry is pitted against a Sentinel?" shouted a rando Sentry in front of the crowd.

"I am glad you asked," said the Prospector. "This is a rather unfortunate position for the poor Sentry. Only the Sentinel is capable of wielding magic. Sentinels are privy to a "die-cast" using a polyhedral three-sided die."

"I guess I won't get a die-cast," I mumbled to myself.

Sage patted my shoulder. "You will have to resort to fortitude and settle for die-cast metal."

"If I wasn't a Sentry, I might use that for a fortune cookie," said Levity.

The Prospector continued. "This is where the rules of paper, rock, and scissors come into play. Depending on the die-cast, the Sentinel will be imbued with the ability to cast magic of that class (paper, rock, or scissors). One blessing for the Sentry is that the Sentinel's bronze emerald-tipped scepter must recharge for five minutes after each blast. This is a blessing if you are the prey but a curse if you are the predator. And you may find yourselves switching roles like a game of 'it' vs. 'not it.' But the Sentry has one last option that could save his life. If he can manage to steal the scepter from the Sentinel, he can cast magic. So if you are a Sentinel, keep your distance at all costs."

"And two Sentinels?" shouted a rowdy Sentinel not too far from the Sentry that asked the previous question.

"When two Sentinels are in battle, each will be granted a die-cast using the polyhedral three-sided die," answered the Prospector. "So what happens to the Sentinel that loses the die cast? He will still be a Sentinel, but his abilities will be stripped down to that of a Sentry, with one very important exception. In addition to the electric dagger, he can also wield his bronze scepter like a club. It will not cast magic, but at least it can be used as a blunt instrument."

"So I guess you better not lose the die-cast," I told Sage. "As if you have any choice in the matter."

"As with a Sentry, another option for the losing Sentinel of the die-cast is to steal the opponent's bronze scepter, which can cast magic. I understand that none of these alternatives are ideal, but it's just the luck of the draw. But at least you still have a fighting chance, as you can mitigate your lack of luck with the application of skill, strength, precision, mental stamina, and accuracy. It's imperative that you don't lose your confidence and dignity along with your magic. Do not add insult to injury or injury to insult, whichever should come first. Oh yes, and in the event of a tie, both Sentinels will have magic of the same magic class."

To cut a long story short, Morale, the Prospector, dispersed a flyer listing the names and brief descriptions of the three paper spells, rock spells, and scissors spells. He stressed that it's imperative we memorize the names of these nine spell types (although he said it was up to us to get acquainted with how the spell works and feels in battle as some might be more unwieldy than others). I will include the information from the flyer below that summarizes these spells for your research records (you can include them with the recorded footage of the battle from the nanobots in the arena).

The head Prospector introduced the various fights in the main arena. And before each one, he would wave his gold scepter in the shape of a star constellation, sending the two fighters to their own private worldline. Like a sports bar, there were twenty-five video monitors sprinkled around the main arena showing each private battle (for our own "enjoyment," I guess).

A bright spotlight shone on two Sentries from opposite sides of the room (in addition to their finials flashing on their scepters). When they meandered to the main stage, the head Prospector introduced them. "Next up on monitor 17, we have an old-fashioned knife fight with new-fangled sensibilities...electric daggers! If I were to go by appearances alone, I would wager that Gamete A has the advantage. Taller, heavier, and eyes full of shazam!"

Gamete B's face crumpled up, as if let down by the Prospector's less than cordial introduction.

"Those electric daggers are worse than pea-shooters," I said to Abacus.

Abacus smiled. "Still, pea shooters aren't quite so bad

when your opponent is stuck with one too."

The Head Prospector aimed his time staff at the contestants, waved it into a pattern of an unknown star constellation, and they were transported to their very own arena in their own worldline (shown on monitor 17).

Gamete A danced around Gamete B, striking fast and hard like a boxer. His strikes were dispensed with careful hesitation. He was making all front jabs rather than side swipes as if trying to get a one-inch deep stab to discharge the electricity. Gamete B played a more defensive game and swerved to and fro like someone playing "keep away." He also used his dagger as a shield and knocked away Gamete A's stabs and blows. During one moment, he took a ½ inch stab to the hand, but it wasn't deep enough to send the zap.

I argued with myself on whether I should fight like Gamete A or B. I mean, they both stayed alive for quite some time, and they both seemed just as winded after fifteen minutes. But then something unexpected happened. Gamete A tripped over his own tail. Either he was clumsy or old-fashioned terrified. Seizing this once in-a-(potentially short)-lifetime opportunity, Gamete B jabbed his dagger into the opponent's abdomen, twisting it and driving it deeper as if a corkscrew or ice auger. Gamete A shrieked in agony for all of ten seconds as he was lit up like a Christmas tree. I guess Gamete B just passed the practicum portion of his crash course in "Fundamentals of Electricity" 101.

I wanted to learn more about these nine magic types spanned across the three classes of paper, rock, and scissors. I really wanted to see two Sentinels do more than spar (less for entertainment and more for the interests of science). It wasn't long until we were able to find a fight to vet and critique.

The spotlight appeared on two Sentinels, both on the same side of the fighting chamber. The head Prospector raised his time scepter with hand and his voice thundered through the mic in his other hand. "What do we have here? Two Sentinels will go tale to tale on monitor 9!" They both ran to the stage as if psyching themselves up or giving themselves some much needed confidence and pep in their step. The Prospector did their die-casts.

Sentinel A scored "rock" on his die-cast. The Prospector spoke. "Rock is an excellent choice. Just remember that the Statue of Limitations rock spell is unique in that it can only be used once per battle due to the fact that the sentient cement will remain active for the entire five-minute duration of the spell. All you have to do is speak the name of the creature you wish the sentient cement to turn into."

The main Prospector next conducted the die-cast for Sentinel B, and the Sentinel was blessed with "paper." The Prospector waved his gold scepter in the same star constellation pattern as before and the two Sentinels were sent to their own private arena. It was at this time that the head Prospector helped another pair of fighters with their die-casts in the main arena. Sage, Brawn, and myself opted to watch the two Sentinels duke it out on monitor 9. I was new to the whole paper, rock, and scissors thing, so I had to remind myself that paper was "better" than rock (despite rocks being adequate paperweights).

"Swan song!" shouted Gamete B the very micro-second the battle commenced. He reminded me of one of those "city-slicker" hunters making a "sound shot" towards any hint of noise resembling rustling bushes. But I paid attention because I aspired to acquire familiarity with all nine spell types across the three spell classes.

Swan Song revealed itself as a swarm of origami swans gliding in a haphazard line towards Sentinel A. He didn't even need to hop, skip, or jump as the spell missed him by a city mile! Since it required five minutes for Sentinel B's scepter to recharge, we were treated to a prey/predator swap as Sentinel A chased B around the arena with his meager electric dagger. When the timer worked its way to ten seconds, Sentinel A hurled his dagger towards Sentinel B from a distance, a massive risk if you are not adept at knife-throwing. Sentinel B wielded his still-charging bronze scepter like a baseball bat and swiped the dagger away like a samurai splitting a bullet. The strident "clink" noise just added drama to the whole scene.

Time ticks down, as it always does. Soon, the ten seconds became zero, and Sentinel's B's scepter was recharged like a cell phone. Sentinel A no longer even had his dagger. Sentinel B poised his scepter towards Sentinel A like a deer hunter taking aim. He was so still he could have been mistaken for one of the statues in the room.

"Air Brush," shouted Sentinel B. A plethora of wet clumps of paper jutted themselves into Sentinel A's throat like wasps returning to their hive. I will never forget the wretched gurgling sounds emanating from his mouth as he died by asphyxiation.

We watched one more example fight on monitor 12, although I must admit my morale was going down instead of up (it didn't help that I couldn't get that gurgling sound out of my head). This time, it was between a Sentry and Sentinel. The Sentinel's die-cast revealed "rock," imbuing him with three different types of rock spells.

"Statue of Limitations," proclaimed the Sentinel. All this seemed to do was generate a massive puddle of wet cement. I made a mental note not to cast that one (well, if I ever became a Sentinel, of course).

"Concrete troll," added the Sentinel.

Sure enough, the wet cement coalesced into a concrete troll twice as tall and thrice as fast as the Sentry (so I take back what I said about the puddle of cement). The troll appeared like a living gargoyle, and it even spawned wings. I guess the Sentinel could say whatever treacherous creature he desired, and the wet cement would grant him that wish.

Sage whispered into my ear. "Wow, talk about applying Stanislavski's 'Magic If.' With that spell, it helps to be a concrete thinker!"

"Just be careful what you wish for," I returned.

The gargoyle hissed and flapped its wings as it became

oriented to its surroundings. The Sentry took advantage of these ten or so seconds and retrieved his electric dagger. The gargoyle spotted the Sentry's movement like a hawk spotting a mouse in a field. The gargantuan gargoyle swooped towards the Sentry like a dragon, screeching all the while. The Sentry stood alert with his dagger like a baseball player who already used up two strikes. Just as the gargoyle's claws gripped the Sentry's shoulders to carry him skywards, the latter thrust his electric dagger into its wing, releasing the electrical discharge throughout the gargoyle's entire body. The bird brain hemmed and hawed, spiraling out of control as if a top out of balance. And then it morphed back into wet cement once again. Did this nullify the rock spell for the rest of the entire battle?

The Sentry crept over to the gurgling puddle. When the puddle was no longer gurgling, the Sentry leaped into the air and splashed down into the wet concrete like a child jumping into a rain puddle.

"Talk about pounding the pavement," said Sage. "I'm not so sure how wise that is, though."

The Sentry grinned. "Is that the only trick in your top hat, Mr. Sentinel? Your troll is a one-trick pony. I would have had a higher challenge from an internet troll!"

The Sentinel sauntered closer to the crime scene. I can promise you that you underestimate this formidable opponent."

The Sentry scrunched up his face. "What is that supposed to mean? You talk a big game, but you have yet to deliver on your promises."

Before the Sentry could finish his sentence, the wet cement coalesced around his tail and hardened, ensnaring the mouse in a mouse trap (gotta love mouse metaphors). The Sentinel maintained his confident gait at one stride per second with the accuracy of a metronome. When in sufficient proximity, the Sentinel kneed the Sentry in the gut, inducing the Sentry to keel over in agony from having the wind knocked out of him.

By now, three minutes had passed on the timer. During

the fourth minute of the cement monster's tenure, the Sentinel used his scepter like a mace and pummeled his face with a strike velocity of two whacks per second. Again and again. The whacks and wails were audible as the blood flowed like wine from a spigot. Like a cat playing with its mouse before the kill, the Sentinel released the Sentry from his concrete prison.

"Alligator," shouted the Sentinel, and the wet cement formed itself into a thirty-foot alligator. If it was me, I would have conjured something a little more creative, maybe something like a concrete star-nose mole, Japanese spider crab, or colugo. That Sentinel is about as creative as the kid that says "astronaut" when asked what he wants to be when he grows up (I suppose it's the thought that counts). I don't know what I was thinking when I wanted to be a "notary public." Then again, writing pearls of wisdom for fortune cookies is even more niche!

But regardless of the Sentinel's level of creativity, when it comes to classic predators, you can do worse than alligators. I could hear every massive step the monster took become louder and louder through the monitor. The alligator reared up like a rattlesnake, unhinged his jaws, and got into position. The Sentry seized his precious microseconds to feint towards the right, hoping to provoke the alligator to strike at the predicted destination point just as the Sentry would dart back to the left. The plan wasn't a total bust, but he miscalculated the jaw velocity of this beast. The jagged teeth came crashing down like a guillotine and severed the tip of the Sentry's tail. And just moments later, the alligator vanished, closing the gap on the five-minute spell limit.

"And here I thought they would have to use the concrete to make his gravestone," whispered Sage.

"I wonder if the Sentry's tail will regenerate back like those cool lizards," I returned.

"That's a theory I'm not willing to test," said Abacus.

Brawn laughed. "Come now, it's in the interests of science!"

The Sentinel hobbled over to the "corpse" to ascertain why the Sentry was not yet dead and the fight called by the

Prospectors. He poked at the body with his scepter as if poking a bear. He even hand-delivered one final blow to the Sentry's abdomen. But the Sentry did not respond. The Sentinel tossed his scepter aside and clenched the Sentry's neck with both hands as blood began to pool out of the latter's mouth. With the same speed as the alligator's bite, the Sentry jabbed his dagger into the Sentinel's foot, sizzling him to the point that I could see smoke emanating from his body. The Sentinel began writhing and waiting for his ten-second torture to end, the longest ten seconds of his pitiful life.

"And that cements the Sentry's victory," said Sage. "There's your proof that a Sentry can beat a Sentinel. That Sentry took more blows than a helium balloon and endured a more raucous beating than a pinata. But like that pinata, the Sentry still had a prize inside. And there's our silver lining,"

Okay, Ron, I sort of lied, just a little. I mentioned that the fight I just described was the last example fight. I did watch another fight. It just wasn't an "example" one. Due to the will of fate or bad luck, Abacus and Brawn were selected to fight each other after the smash, clash, and bash with the rock goblin. Or maybe it was the universe's way of preparing me for the worst. After all, you warned us that even if all five of us stayed alive until the bitter end, only one of us would survive in the best case scenario.

A bright spotlight lit up over Abacus and Brawn (who were sitting on each side of me).

"Next up, we have the two gents near Monitor 12," said the head Prospector.

"The powers that be sure have a sick sense of humor," said Brawn to Abacus as the Prospector was prepping for the die-cast. "Is this some archetypal battle between Brawn vs. Brain?"

Abacus did not respond. He just pulled out his fidget spinner and gave it a few whacks to build up momentum. Is there a world record on fidget-spinner spin-velocity?

"Please don't fret," said Brawn, reaching over me to pat

his shoulder. "This hurts me more than it hurts you. I have no intention of killing friends and family."

Abacus stopped his fidget spinner from spinning. "Even if we weren't fighting each other, we would still be forced to fight some random no-name sperm. What does it matter if we know each other? Every rando out there has a story and a network of friends and family. Whether by vice or virtue, the sharpest scissors in the world could not cut the bonds we have forged. But it's no better than anyone else's story."

Brawn raised his voice. "But the fact remains, which of us is bound to die?"

"You are a Sentinel," said Abacus. "You have a higher chance of making it to the end than I do. All you have to do is do the math. You need to live."

Brawn sighed. "We both know that neither of us is fixin' to see the other die. After the die-cast, we will do our own die-cast, known in our circles as a coin flip. If it's heads, you kill me. And if it's tails, I kill you. Simple as that. No survivor's guilt."

"We let fate decide," said Abacus. "I suppose we would be arguing all day about it otherwise."

Brawn yanked a coin out of his tracksuit pocket to make sure he had one and put it back in his pocket. "You know what Animus asked me not long after we met?"

"No," Abacus retorted. "But I have a feeling you, or rather he, is going to tell me."

"What do platoons and spittoons have in common?" Brawn asked, mimicking Animus's boisterous voice.

"Sounds like boilerplate Animus," Abacus mumbled. "He and his military metaphors."

"They both get spit on," said Brawn, using his normal voice. "Do you know what latrines and marines have in common?"

Abacus rolled his eyes. "Please enlighten me."

"They both get pissed and shit on," answered Brawn.

Abacus sighed. "Somehow, I can't picture those pearls of wisdom to grace the insides of Levity's fortune cookies."

I pulled out a pen to remember what Brawn said. "Hey, wait, slow down, I gotta write these down. But how does that apply to us exactly?"

Brawn continued. "It was Animus's roundabout way of telling us that we have to stick together, acquire a thick skin, and do what's best for our team, regardless of what anyone says. And sometimes the worst insults are hurled from the sidelines by the very folks we thought were on our side to begin with."

Abbacus and Brawn faced each other and nodded, Brawn's bronze scepter and Abacus's dagger held high, as if agreeing to the terms of the battle. They held flat expressions as if their mouths could not decide whether to smile or frown. I couldn't tell if they were feeling sanguine or rather the sweet surrender that "letting go" and resignation can bring. Then again, I shared their sentiment, as I was still coming to grips with the fact that either Brawn or Abacus would die.

The Prospector performed the die-cast, and Brawn scored "scissors."

By the time Sage and I worked our way to monitor 21 to watch the battle, the very first thing we saw was Brawn pointing his scepter at his own head!

"What are you doing?" shouted Abacus. "What about our coin toss?"

"In this world of kill or be killed, I just can't kill you," said Brawn. "Please forgive me."

"Wait!" shouted Abacus. "I don't want any survivor's guilt either. How is that fair to me? It's clear we would both rather die than see the other bite the bullet. So let's just refuse to fight if we are not going to do the coin flip."

Brawn sighed. "You think the Prospectors are just going to shuffle us back in the deck as if we were never selected?"

"It's worth a shot, isn't it?" asked Abacus. "Admit it, neither of us is going to budge in our steadfast resolve. We might both survive this! It's worth a shot!"

"If push comes to shove, you think we can take out the

Prospectors?" asked Brawn.

Abacus nodded. "I would rather kill them than you. And I would rather die by them than you. It's the lesser of two evils. The old Scylla and Charybdis."

"We refuse to kill each other," shouted Brawn towards the camera as he cast his bronze scepter aside.

Abacus tossed his electric dagger aside. "He's right."

And then something unexpected and strange happened. Brawn and Abacus respawned in the center of the main arena. A giant spotlight glided over them as if they were playing a famous scene in a play. This moment was also being displayed on all twenty-five monitors in the main hall for all to see.

Sage looked around. "What is going on?"

"How would I know?" I asked, shrugging my shoulders.

The head Prospector was not visible, but his ominous voice could be heard loud and clear as it thundered through the loudspeakers and all the monitors of the main arena. "There can only be one winner in these fights. As such, it's not against the rules for one haploid to self-delete. But it is against the rules for them both to self-delete. All the weapons are programmed to cease working after one contestant perishes, via self-deletion or otherwise. The scepters and electric daggers will lose their charge as soon as they kill the opponent."

"We don't intend to self-delete," articulated Brawn with a loud and booming voice.

Abacus stood by Brawn. "Neither of us do."

"Is that your final answer?" asked the Prospector.

"Yes," said Brawn and Abacus in perfect unison. "Such hubris is meant for the ring."

The head Prospector entered through a door behind the bullet-proof glass barrier and met his other two compatriots. The spotlight above the arena fragmented itself into the shape of a lit clock that projected itself onto the circumference of the battle arena.

"You have one minute to change your minds," said the

head Prospector. "Now is the time to flip a coin if you have one."

The crowd went wild, screaming, shouting, and pushing. It was as if they were paralyzed by the impending drama of this ludicrous reality TV show. But that's the key word, "reality." And calling it ludicrous was a moot point. In this reality, it was just stating the obvious.

"And what happens when the minute is up?" asked Brawn.

The Prospector continued. "That's a risk you will have to make."

"Hold your ground, Abacus," shouted Brawn. "We can take em.'"

Abacus made a double take towards Brawn. "All three of them? And how do we know they are even going to fight us? What if they have something else planned?"

"What else could it be?" asked Brawn with his tail planted on the ground like a potted plant refusing to move. "Those gold scepters are useless without a die-cast. They are just head-thumpers."

"Don't do it!" I shouted, my meager voice shielded by the white noise of the auditorium. "One of you must take the bullet, or you both will die!"

There was so much ruckus, shouting, trash talking, and commotion only Sage and the haploid next to me heard the words I uttered.

"Speak for yourself," said the rowdy as he knocked me to the floor.

When I worked my way to a standing position, Brawn and Abacus were gone. What just happened?!!

"Let that be a lesson to you all," shouted the voice on the loudspeakers. "Mercy will only get you both killed. These gentlemen have now been dead for over 500 years. Gold scepters require no die-cast to send combatants back in time. There is only one form of mercy allowed here, and that's putting someone else out of their misery. Do not make the same mistake these fools did. Rules are only suggestions if they have no consequence."

Sage and I are alive (if not well). Three down, two to go. If there is any good news, Sage had no trouble with the rest of his battles in the Fallopian tubes, as he won all his paper, rock, and scissors die-casts. This was only augmented by his eloquent battle prowess, including foresight, stamina, and speed. Sage scored the "scissors" every time, so he was able to master "Shear Pain," "Cutting Room Floor," and "Melee filet."

I suppose I should count my own lucky stars as well. "You made it to the finish line instead of the 'finished line,'" reminded Sage. And I was just a mere Sentry! To be fair, it didn't hurt that I was pitted against Sentries each and every time. Let's just say I can now do more with a knife than wood carving.

Sage and I have not been shirking our responsibilities, and we have not been remiss in our task of chronicling information on all nine spells. But you are missing out if you haven't seen the fireworks up close and personal. I suppose it's kinda like embarking on a proper vacation yourself as opposed to enduring someone else's insufferable vacation pictures. I told Sage about this as well, as I needed someone to talk to. But Sage had his own take on things. "Comparing being brutalized by a rock troll to a vacation is like comparing a root canal to a root beer float." Still, there is no arguing that sentient cement should earn its place as the eighth wonder of the modern world.

By any event, the two hundred survivors were led through the plain and rusty iron door. They (we) were haggard and battle worn, as evidenced by their scratched and chipped armaments and their stumbling. And what prize did we get? We were greeted by another sectioned-off chamber of the Fallopian tube! It was as if the iron door just separated the wheat from the chaff, the first class from the commoners. The décor around the walls of the Fallopian tube included bejeweled indentations, flying buttresses, and giant ivory elephants. There were antique/ engraved grandfather clocks, mythical marble statues, and lighted jewels adorning the myriad of candelabras. These jewels consisted of diamonds, rubies, and emeralds. I couldn't help but wonder if the Prospectors were attempting to make us feel somehow "special" for climbing the ranks this far. I hope they understand that there is always that pesky chance of "dying" that can dampen one's spirits, no matter how pretty the walls are surrounding one's deathbed. No doubt about it, this had more in common with a fraternity initiation than any celebratory luncheon!

In the center of the enclosure was another arena, smaller than the last (I was starting to think these arenas were inspired by Russian dolls). As before, there were three massive marble statues positioned at equidistant points along the circumference of the arena. One was standing on a mountain of some sort, striking a confident and upright pose as if he had just climbed Mount Everest. Another statue was a snowman, of all things, with a mischievous frown and squinting angry eyes. The third statue was holding a set of wind chimes. You don't have to tell us that these themes represented portents of what's to come. But if the number of remaining haploids holds any clues, the two hundred survivors must be nearing the end of this mission. Like before, it's clear that these symbols represented a paper, rock, and scissors sort of ranking system. All three of them also held a silver scepter with a ruby finial.

Sage and I hobbled and limped to the hardwood seats surrounding the arena. I wasn't in the mood to entertain what was on the other side of the next iron door in the corner. I wouldn't be surprised if it was just another sectioned off part of the Fallopian tube as before! But where do you go from first class? To the pilot's cabin? Out the door to fall to your death without a parachute?

With only two of us in our platoon left, I feel closer than ever to Sage. Will the same fate befall us as between Brawn and Abacus? Sage is a wonderful captain, but he was wrong about this. We should have learned to hate each other from the start. Blood may be thicker than water, but thicker isn't always better, is it? After all, the expression "slower than molasses in January" is seldom used in a flattering manner. Nope, that expression is not fit for a fortune cookie.

Sage asked me to read the letter he received from you on January 4 to get up to speed on things. You made an odd comment that Sage may not have wanted me to see: "Sometimes the 'bravest' among us simply have nothing left to lose." Am I missing something? You have one of the most prestigious posts in the human body. And your country Neuron is envied by most of the other countries. I would say you have plenty to lose, right? Is there a deeper reason you are risking hide and hair for this boyhood fantasy of yours?
Sincerely,
Levity

P.S. Below is what Sage and I compiled so far. This information, coupled with the data recorded by the nanobots, should grant you all the answers you need in regards to your scientific inquiries.

The Rules of Engagement (Tier 1 Survival of Sperm and Eggs)

Sentry vs. Sentry
Location of battle: Uterotubal junction
No Scepters
Choice of weapon: bow and arrow (distance) or machete (melee)
Sentries at 50th percentile battle prowess elevated to Sentinels after battle
Nanobots measure battle prowess based on stealth, strength, grace, cowardice, speed, etc.

Sentry vs. Sentinel
Location of battle: Fallopian tubes
1. Sentry is given electric dagger (basic weapon)
2. Sentinel emerald-tipped bronze scepter can cast one of three classes of magic (paper, rock, scissors)

3. Three-sided polyhedral die-cast at onset of battle delineates what class of magic Sentinel can cast

4. The die-cast determines the class of magic splayed for entire battle (paper, rock, scissors)

5. Being hit by magic is not a sure death, and there are partial hits

6. Due to random assignment (with replacement), a combatant may endure multiple fights

7. Sentinel bronze scepter requires 5 minute recharge (causing a predator/prey reversal)

8. Sentries can defeat Sentinels, but their chances are lower

A Sentry can steal the bronze scepter from a Sentinel and cast magic

Each of Sentinel's magic classes has three spell types (3 paper spells, 3 rock spells, 3 scissors spells)

The type of magic cast is decided at the will and behest of spell-caster by speaking its name

Sentinel vs. Sentinel

1. Each Sentinel receives die-cast to determine their magic type (paper, rock, scissors)

2. Paper beats rock (1/3 chance)

3. Scissors beats paper (1/3 chance)

4. Rock beats scissors (1/3 chance)

5. If die-cast results in a tie, both combatants wield same magic class (paper, rock, scissors)

Sentinels also retain their electric daggers from when Sentry

Magic is not always deadly if a partial hit

Sentinels in the 50$^{th'}$ percentile level up to Brigadiers (based on battle prowess)

Each class of magic has three spell types (3 paper spells, 3 rock spells, 3 scissors spells)

The type of magic cast is decided at the will and behest of spell-caster

Paper magic (activated by speaking spell name)

Swan Song: Papercuts from 2000 origami swans (Medium range, Medium melee)

Blind Luck: Opponent is completely blind for the five-minute duration of recharge (NA Range/Melee)

Air Brush: Asphyxiation from crumpled paper entering the throat (Low range, High melee)

Rock magic (activated by speaking spell name)

Boulder-Dash: Large boulder jettisons towards fighter (Medium range, Medium melee)

Condoning Stoning: Pelted with a volley of smaller rocks and stones (Low range, High melee)

Statue of Limitations: Rock monster is forged and active during five-minute recharge period. This spell can only be cast once, and no other rock magic can be summoned (NA Range/Melee)

Scissors magic (activated by speaking spell name)

Shear Pain: One hundred pairs of scissors strike your body like daggers (Medium range, Medium melee)

Cutting Room Floor: One giant pair of scissors snips your body in half (High range, Low melee)

Filet Melee: Sharp shears filet the body like a fish (Low range, High melee)

CHAPTER 9

The I Letters
Subject: Fallopia Dystopia Phase 2
Survival type: Cellular competition (fight class)
Author: Morale (Ron Une)
Date: February 14, 2182 (Thursday)
Location: Neuron
Recipient: Sage

Dear Adventurers 4 and 5 (Levity and Sage),

I admire your fortitude and steadfast resolve to locate the tiniest bit of humor with the same tenacity as a fisherman catching a sturgeon. And to witness but one of you survive is a boon and blessing, to be sure. But good news and bad news go together, like Yin and Yang. Hand and glove. Jack and Jill. And when separated by mere seconds, it matters little what temporal order the sound waves of bad news vs. good news should penetrate your ears first. I will be here until the bitter end, rallying the troops until not one of you is left standing. And despite my lovely epithet, the two of you have elevated my own morale in ways you may not even realize. But the fact remains, even optimists need a bit of perking up now and then.

I still can't figure out how or why Adventurers 1 and 3 (Abacus and Brawn) were placed together in the ring. Is fate really so cruel? Did the Prospectors do this with intent and purpose? And while my head tells me it's a waste of time to ruminate about this, whatever semblance of a heart I have in this brain cell of mine continues to insist and persist, as if the act of worry in and of itself was sufficient to raise the very dead.

If I know land is just beyond the horizon, is it too late to declare land ho? We are almost there! A tiny piece of light is visible at the end of the tunnel. Be vigilant, even if luck is on your side! A competent Captain knows that a soldier's level of confidence should match their level of competence. Balancing the two is a skill. Too much confidence, you acquire hubris and resort to heroics. Too little confidence, and you are left with missed opportunity.

Brass tacks. I learned some from my latest visit to Euclid's mind. This next battle will introduce another class of warrior, called a Brigadier. A Brigadier outclasses both Sentinels and Sentries. As per the three statues, the Brigadiers wield silver scepters with rubies on their finials, and there are three new classes of magic: wind, snow, and mountain. Through deduction, we can make an educated assumption that following holds true.

Brigadier vs. Sentinel
1. Wind (beats paper and scissors)
Snow (beats paper and rock)
Mountain (beats rock and scissors)

Take note how the Brigadier's spells have a 2/3 chance of beating a Sentinel's die-cast. But also notice that there is still a 1/3 fighting chance that a Sentinel can still beat the Brigadier's die-cast. Remember to embrace the skill factor if luck is not on your side. There is always hope, as Levity proved in the previous battle by surmounting the Sentinels as a mere Sentry.

If two Brigadiers are fighting, we can deduce additional rules similar to the paper, rock, and scissors rubrik from before if we just think about it a moment.

Brigadier vs. Brigadier
1. Wind beats snow

2. Snow beats mountain
3. Mountain beats Wind

This is just another version of paper, rock, and scissors. Remember it. The Brigadier that loses the die-cast will be resigned to rely on his silver scepter (without magic). Sentinels and Brigadiers may also retain their electric daggers as fall-back options. Each spell class will likely include various types of magic. And this is where I will count on you to educate me on what these spells are and how they work.

Take comfort in the fact that nobody from here forward will likely remain a Sentry, based on what we have seen so far. The nanobots will likely assess who displayed the most "battle prowess" as before. My hunch is that one hundred will graduate to Brigadiers, and the other hundred will remain/become Sentinels. My hope is that since Levity was able to surmount Sentinels as a Sentry in the last battle, there's a chance he will be elevated two levels, going from Sentry to a Brigadier. And since Adventurer 5 (Sage) graduated from a Sentry to a Sentinel in the previous battle, my hope is that he could become a Brigadier as well.

I know you are both suffering. If you haven't told me directly, I have seen it alluded to me in passing. There is no shame in grief. How I pity the soldier without trepidation or the ability to cry at a funeral! It pains me that there are such tortured spirits among us! But such melancholy, if left unchecked, can wreak havoc on one's performance. Grieve in your own way, in your own time. But do not allow it to interfere with our mission. Put your heart on hold. Honor our fallen heroes in a manner that would suit their desires and wishes in the land of the living.

Animus would mutter: "Quit your whining and win some wars!"

Brawn would utter: "Save your energy for something constructive!"

Abacus would stutter: "It doesn't help the living or the

dead. Do the math!"

What comes next could be the final fight. Only one winner will surmount this obstacle. And if you and Levity are the final two in the ring, do NOT make the same mistake that Brawn and Abacus did. There are times when there is more madness to the method than the madness itself. Not only were their deaths most tragic, but they were unnecessary. All it did was take two lives instead of one. Flipping a rusty coin would have been a more auspicious affair! If the Prospectors pit the two of you together, be it by luck or trick, do not bicker about who should perish. We cannot lose the both of you! If this happens, I will kill you both myself!

You asked about what I said in my January 4 correspondence to Adventurer 5: "Sometimes the "bravest" among us simply have nothing left to lose." If you have read the January 17 correspondence, you noticed what Brawn stated to me: "You may want to put a cap on the nightcaps. I hear it can kill brain cells." Well, as Adventurer 1 (Abacus) would say, you can "do the math" from there and put two and two together. If you haven't figured it out yet, I am a dying brain cell. It turns out our human host, Euclid Hux, drinks in excess (morning and night). If you must insist and persist, this is a major player in why I am risking hide and hair for this little excursion of ours. I do hesitate to disclose this matter as I do not wish to diminish our morale. But since we lost three already, I figure you have both become desensitized to infirmity and death by now, or at least less enamored by it. Still, let's never speak of this again, as such trifles and tribulations will serve no benefit. The pain and suffering in the ring is plentiful. The last thing we need are self-inflicted wounds.

P.S. Share from this letter what you wish to your mates. I encourage you, Sage, to share with Levity what you shared in your postscript in your last bit of correspondence. This is not just for the sake of full transparency. If you both looked at each other face to face, you might as well be looking into a mirror. While the nature of your vulnerabilities are not the same, the fact that you both have them alone is the common ground you need to enhance your level of loyalty and trust in each other. This battle is taking its toll. There is no getting around it. Own it. Accept it. And use it to your advantage. Grief and loss are a common enemy. And we all know that common enemies make for strange bedfellows.

The I Letters
Subject:Re: Fallopia Dystopia Phase 2 (cellular survival games and fight class)
Survival type: Cellular competition (fight class)
Author: Sage
Date: February 14, 2182 (Thursday)
Location Fallopian tube (second chamber)
Recipients: Morale (Ron Une)

Dear Ron,

  I suppose it is my turn to wield the electric pen. I feel I must apologize on behalf of Levity. On occasion, it fails him to grasp the rules of proper comportment that you and I take for granted. But since things are now "out in the open," as it were, I must also offer my condolences. Being too uncomfortable to disclose your condition is unnecessary, prideful, and, on some level, telling of your lack of trust in our sympathies. If there is anything we can do to help reverse your deteriorating body, do not hesitate to request our audience. These are not disingenuous words meant only to "keep up appearances" or virtue signals for the sake of accruing my own karma. Levity and I are confident that the nanobots are capable of imbuing your cellular body with hormones, drugs, genetic material, and whatever other payload will aid in your recovery. Although this topic is beyond my scope, I do know that we must halt this insidious cell destruction before it's too late. If only Abacus were still with us, his knowledge of genetics and nanobots would be most welcome (I still can't believe he died over five hundred years ago now).

So we passed the plain and basic iron door into chamber 2 of the Fallopian tubes, as Levity had stated in his last bit of correspondence. It was sized to house 200 fighters and contained 15 screen monitors. They just spent the last two hours ascertaining who would be elevated from Sentinel to Brigadier (all Sentries are elevated to at least Sentinels). Levity became a Brigadier due to beating Sentinels as a Sentry. As for me? I did not make the cut, contrary to your lofty expectations (the nanobot analyses indicated I was too cautious and lacked reaction time). So I remained a Sentinel to wield the bronze scepter.

There was a massive crowd response when a big burly fellow by the name of "Sperm Whale" was Christened as a Brigadier. Who was this guy, some sort of celebrity? If I knew he was such a threat I would have watched him fight on the big screen back when he was a Sentinel.

"Can you believe that massive Sentinel dude?" said a rando Sentinel near us. "He lost every single paper, rock, and scissors die-cast but still managed to stick his dagger into his opponents as if they were melted butter. And now he's a Brigadier wielding a silver scepter with a ruby finial."

"We must keep all eyes and ears transfixed on this venerable fellow," I whispered into Levity's ear. "Whether that story is embellished or not."

"Yeah," said Levity, "Let's just hope all that fat is blubber instead of muscle."

And then we spent another two hours receiving our battlements. We anchored our tails on the line encircling the Yin/Yang symbol in the center of the compact coliseum. There were only two Prospectors here, the head Prospector behind the fire-proof window with his microphone. The other was pushing around a cart with one crate full of silver scepters and another to collect any leftover bronze scepters from Sentinels. They also handed out flyers, like before, listing and describing the nine spells that could be cast by a silver scepter (across snow, mountain, and wind magic classes). As before, Morale, we will include the information from this flyer below for your records.

You should have seen Levity's cheerful countenance and ear-to-ear grin as he collected his new silver scepter. One would think he just discovered some ancient MacGuffin (he did make it to Brigadier, after all). This was in stark contrast to the flat-faced Prospector (who looked as blank as someone handing out food rations). I could tell it was not his first rodeo. We mere Sentinels retained our bronze scepters (which felt like one of my appendages at this point). At least we had our trusty electric daggers (which I admit was better than being stuck BY them).

The head Prospector went over the rules from the main arena. "As before, the three statues of brigadiers are holding clues that will assist you in these one-on-one battles. One is a snowman. The second is holding up a mountain. The third is holding a set of wind chimes. This is a simple but more complex riddle than before, as we now have six classes of magic to worry about (paper, rock, scissors, snow, mountain, and wind). If you cannot figure out what symbols trump each other based on quick intellect alone, you still have a chance of learning through experience as to what symbols trump the others. In the event of a tie, both combatants will have the ability to cast magic of that specific class of magic. Only one fighter can self-delete. And you also can't refuse to fight, as we learned from those two unfortunate fellows in the last battle.

To the head Prospector, they may have just been "unfortunate fellows." But to us, they were inimitable. But there are millions of haploids. And the more of something you have, does this make each one less significant? Is one in a million sperm less significant than one in a thousand? Maybe that's why we are so disposable. Can we change this tragic state of affairs? Can we rebel against the food chain? Can we rebel against biology and nature itself? Why don't we get a choice as to who or what we can be?

Levity and I waited for a chance to watch The Sperm Whale, as we would have to face the big oaf at some point if we survived that long. Sperm Whale was famous for having bad luck with the die-cast and still managing to win the battles on battle prowess alone (not to mention he was even larger and stronger than our Brawn, even with the benefit of muscle enhancements). We decided we might as well learn from the best, not just in terms of what to do, but also in terms of what not to do.

"Up next, we have the one, only, and lonely Sperm Whale," shouted the head Prospector from the main arena. "Sperm Whale is now a silver scepter wielding Brigadier, and he is pitted against a mere Sentinel! Let's say a quick prayer for the Sentinel, as he has only a meager 1/3 chance of winning the die-cast. The poor fellow! There is a reason silver is better than bronze!"

"If Sperm Whale wins the die-cast, this is going to be a facile victory," I said. "Then again, you proved just how ironclad the 'will' can be."

Sperm Whale and the Sentinel met in the main arena, one on each side of the Prospector.

"What do you mean lonely?" asked Sperm Whale, clutching the Prospector by the throat..

After Sperm Whale released him, the Prospector cleared his throat. "You know, 'it's lonely at the top and all that.'"

Sperm Whale went through the motions of "dusting off" and "straightening up" the Prospector's attire as if an act of apology.

"Not to mention that Sperm Whale is enjoying 93% popularity, according to the nanobot battle assessments in addition to assessments of spectator body language."

After the initial pomp, the head Prospector in the main ring tossed the die, and the Sperm Whale was granted "wind," whose insignia appeared on his silver scepter's ruby finial. The hollers and shouts in the crowd were so raucous I couldn't make out anything anyone was saying.

"Why are they cheering already?" asked Levity. "We

have to wait until after the 2nd die-cast to determine the winner anyway, right?"

I paused. "It's a bias. They don't care what class of magic Sperm Whale gets, as long as it's Sperm Whale. It's like when someone hosts a gender reveal party, and everyone pretends that the revealed gender was the very one everyone was hoping for."

Levity tapped his chin. "But why would they cheer Sperm Whale on when they may have to fight the old brute themselves? He's the big cheese. The big Kahuna. Top dog. Top brass. Head Honcho...."

"I get it," I interrupted. "Another bias. They are cheering because they don't expect to make it that far. They are enjoying their final moments as if this was a simple baseball game. I think it has to do with accepting the fact you are going to die and rolling with the punches. It has something to do with Terror Management Theory and how individuals make sense of their numbered days."

After the crowd became as raucous as the Prospector could make them, the polyhedral die was cast for the Sentinel. If this was a movie, this part would be in slow motion (and I couldn't help but wonder if those gold time scepters had the capability). I thought about the die-cast and how the most minute muscle movement could affect the outcome of someone's life or death (despite the Prospector not knowing which way it would land). It really wasn't luck. The die lands the way it does for a reason. We just don't have the predictive ability to tell which way it would land. To spare you any further suspense, the die landed on "paper." If that poor Sentinel looked like he was heading for the electric chair before, his frown became even more pronounced (which was matched in full by the size of Sperm Whale's wider smile).

"Wow, look at that poor Sentinel's frown," I said.

"Yeah, and look at Sperm Whale's grin!" added Levity.

I nodded. "I can just hear Abacus reminding us that for every action, there is an equal but opposite reaction."

The head Prospector had another caveat. "Like the Statue of Limitations spell, the Windmill spell also has a one-time use limit. But it will last the entire duration of five minutes."

The Sperm Whale's luck had changed. He not only held the cards, but he had a good hand at that. Not that he needed any help. He did just fine before without any buffs, boons, or benefits. That poor Sentinel was not accident prone. He was death prone.

"Battle commence!" shouted the Head Prospector as he waved his time wand, sending the fighters to their own dimension (shown on screen 8). As soon as the fight began, the Sentinel slithered as far and fast as he could from Sperm Whale as if he was a repelling magnet (shouting all the while). It may have been a fear response, but all this just winded him.

"It looks like Sperm Whale is tracking a wounded deer," said Levity.

I kept my eyes transfixed on the screen as if missing a solitary second would prevent me from knowing all I needed to know to take down Sperm Whale in battle. I felt like the quintessential and archetypal underdog, but this did not guarantee victory like in the movies. In real life, underdogs tend to lose. It may not be romantic, but it is what it is.

Levity leaned towards me and whispered. "Running like that and shouting trash talk will keep you alive, but at some point, he has to fight, right?"

I kept my gaze on monitor 8. "Yes, Levity. But that is not trash talk. If you read his lips, he is muttering his last goodbyes to all his friends and family before he passes away into oblivion."

"Whoa, whoa, whoa, you are right," Levity continued. "And that isn't sweat on his face. It's tears."

Sperm Whale didn't give chase. He hoisted up his silver scepter like a patriot waving a flag pole, with the wind-chime insignia flashing on the ruby finial like a military crest. The scepter was charged and ready to "fire its fire." After memorizing the Sentinel's predictable "running pattern" as if a boss pattern in a video game, he was able to predict where the Sentinel would run. Sperm Whale took aim, like a hunter on a tree stand, and discharged his scepter with a deliberate and careful blast, keeping his aim even after he fired, as if that would help guide the shot.

"Windmill," shouted Sperm Whale. What appeared to be a massive metal windmill with a five-meter diameter materialized ten tails behind the Sentinel. It crept towards the Sentinel at a stealthy clip of 3 mph.

Levity pointed at the screen. "See that? The propeller keeps following him around like a horror movie stalker. If he's too slow, it will eat him alive."

"Yes," I returned. "But notice it's not a run-of-the-mill windmill. It sucks air inward like a jet engine."

Levity took a closer look. "You are right. You can see the Sentinel fighting to keep his distance."

"And from what I can tell," I said, "the closer he gets, the more suction he experiences."

"Talk about the Little Engine that Could," quipped Levity. "That calamity is persistent."

Since the windmill began at ten tails away, I took this to mean baseline distance. Allowing the blade to get much closer than that, and you would be yanked through and sliced, diced, minced, and/or cubed in that order.

The Sentinel was huffing and/or puffing, emboldened to trudge onwards (fighting the wind). He must have tapped into his spare gas tank that Animus told me about. The one where you tap into your "mental reserves" in addition to "physical reserves." How Animus put it, when you think you hit your limit, you can still muster through with enough willpower, as if you have a spare gas tank. It also helps when a little something called death is looming behind you. After all, that wasn't just a propeller. It was a very literal Grim Reaper enhanced with a blade upgrade.

Sperm Whale kept his distance as if giving his partner a chance to do some dirty work in this rag-tag tag-team. This charade kept up for five minutes, and the propeller maintained its course chasing the Sentinel (it was gaining on him, and the Sentinel struggled to surpass eight feet).

I whispered towards Levity as if I were a track coach. "So that will be the only spell he gets. For your sake, Levity, if you get blessed with 'wind' in your die casts, save the 'Windmill' spell for after you have used 'Extra-Terrestrial Wind' or 'Funnel Cloud' first. That way, you can maximize your spell casting."

"Why is Sperm Whale just watching from a distance?" asked Levity. "Is he allowing the Sentinel a final request to say his final goodbyes?"

"I wish that were so," I returned. "Unlike sharks, whales do have bones. But make no mistake. Sperm Whale has no empathetic bone in his body. He's just toying with his prey. I surmise that he is fixing to rob a certain guilty pleasure from savoring the sight of the Sentinel getting shredded, chewed up, diced, and pureed by that massive blade."

Levity nodded. "And Sperm Whale knows that if he gets too close to the Sentinel, he runs the risk of being sucked through the blade himself."

The Sentinel was now shouting his final farewells and goodbyes to every friend or family member he could recollect, even roaming into the territory of acquaintances (he even mentioned the name of his local mail-bot). Instead of attacking Sperm Whale, he resorted to running ahead, taking a brief breather, and rinsing/repeating. But we all know what happens when you wash your hands too often. They turn chapped, dry, or bleed. Chalk it up to another case of "it's better to be safe than sorry" until it's not (I should know).

The Sentinel carried on with his final goodbyes and well-wishes. "Hugo in Repro, Jason in Resp, Dennis in Cardio, and last but not least, Morale in Neuron. I love you all." If anyone needed a well-wish from a wishing-well, it was that poor Sentinel. And did I just hear him proclaim your name, Ron? What's that about?

Then, the unexpected happened. The Sentinel spun around on a dime when the propeller approached seven-tails behind him. Combining the suction of the blade with his own velocity, he slithered towards the propeller at maximum velocity. And with the tenacity of a long-jumper, he cast himself right through the propeller as if cheese through a cheese grater (and this cheese grater was sharper than any cheddar). At least he made jumping through a flaming hoop sound like the bunny hill. I have to admit. I was rooting for that Sentinel. I gotta give credit where credit is due. At least he was able to say his final goodbyes and feel a moment of peace of mind before pieces of his mind were strewn with an array of other body parts.

The Prospectors put the Master Class Sperm Whale up against a fellow Brigadier, shown on monitor 10 (Brawn told me to stop calling him Master Class). After the die-cast, Sperm Whale was assigned "mountain." Brigadier B's die-cast granted "snow," giving him the advantage (as snow covers the mountain). Sperm Whale's bad-luck streak returned. But this only elicited madcap excitement, shouts, and air-fisting from the crowd (after all, this was Sperm Whale's M.O. At this point). Sperm Whale's smirk and slight smile on his countenance remained unwavering and inscrutable as if he was flattered he was chosen by fate for such a monumental challenge. And I can only imagine that the crowd only amplified his confidence and blood lust (as he couldn't let them down).

"Ready to turn into whale blubber?" smirked Brigadier B. "My lamp needs a refill."

If Brigadier B was hoping for the crowd to cheer in his direction, he was mistaken. They just booed and shouted nay-says from the sidelines. Brigadier B just wasn't the household name that Sperm Whale was. I guess his name didn't have the same ring to it.

Sperm Whale grimaced. "And you think that just cuz' you prevailed in the die-cast that entitles you to such hubris? I have memorized your battle patterns. I know them better than you do. Your scepter might as well be made from fool's gold."

"Your good luck will run out," said Brigadier B, holding

up his silver scepter as if it was a Roman candle firecracker. "You only got this far because of it. You have no skill, and I will seize what's left of your poor excuse of a guardian angel!"

"Get your own guardian angel!" shouted Sperm Whale as he planted himself into position, matching Brigadier B's scepter pose.

Brigadier B must have known that his Brigadier privilege was all that he had, as he spent no time sparring. Instead, he slithered to a distant area of the arena and pointed his silver scepter in Sperm Whale's general direction. He squinted his eye as if looking through the scope of a rifle, but this was not necessary for obvious reasons!

"Shiver River!" shouted Brigadier B, opting to try a new snow spell he had not applied before. An icy stream of water jettisoned from his scepter as if from a fire hose. The hose was like an out of control snake, and Brigadier B was struggling to keep control of it. I noticed that the icy water transformed into glare ice as soon as it hit the floor. As Brigadier B was falling all over himself trying to manage the scepter, I noticed him step on the ice, and it seemed to have no effect on the caster, granting him an advantage with the terrain.

Sperm Whale continued to hold his position as if awkward silence was a weapon that could prompt the first move from Brigadier B. The latter put the reigns on the scepter and planted his tail onto the floor to give himself more resistance and stability.

Sperm whale feinted to the side to prime the Brigadier to overshoot the icy water as he backtracked to the safety of his original position. The water shot missed Sperm Whale, but it created an ice path between the two fighters. By now, the scepter ceased producing icy water, and Brigadier B was fussing around with the hose as if he could get it to shoot water again. I hope he didn't think it was a clog!

"This spell only lasts ten seconds," said Levity. "And I'm assuming you can recast snow magic after recharge, unlike rock or wind."

I think Sperm Whale knew this "haploid-factoid" already, as he seized Brigadier B's moment of confusion as an opportunity. As if a luge in the Olympics, he employed a slithering start and slid on the ice towards Brigadier B. If you prefer a different simile, Ron, it was like a slip n' slide.

"What the..." exclaimed Brigadier B as he caught a glimpse of the "train" rushing towards him on the icy "track."

"Tail-flail!" shouted Sperm Whale as he positioned his tail. When Sperm Whale collided, he used his own tail to snag Brigadier B's tail and tangled them up. Holding the Brigadier into place, Sperm Whale "pushed" the Brigadier backwards on the icy path towards the snow statue in the corner of the arena. And since the icy trail didn't lead all the way to the statue, Sperm Whale was able to halt when his tail caught the friction of the arena floor. But not before he flung the Brigadier the rest of the way towards the statue. The inertia and lack of friction from sliding on the ice only augmented the forceful impact. This was further evidenced by the snowman's head falling off on impact. Not that I needed any more evidence. I was properly convinced that Sperm Whale was a force to be reckoned with. With or without friction.

I turned to Levity. "Notice how he feinted Brigadier B's 'Shiver River?'"

"How could I not?" asked Levity.

"Well done," I said. "You are now my star pupil."

Levity laughed. "That's not hard, I am your only pupil."

"You are becoming more adept at physical battle," I said. "Abacus is a titan of intellect. But if he was in the ring with Sir Blubber-Head here, he may have 'fainted' himself, but in an entirely different manner."

Levity laughed, but his voice cracked a bit, and it made me wonder if he was about to cry. "I miss Abacus already."

I patted him on the shoulder. "You said it."

The Sentinel crawled with only his hands as if his tail was out of commission. As he reached for his silver scepter, Sir

Blubber-Head kicked it to the side. The Brigadier then went to plan B and tugged at the sheath to claim his electric dagger. But he was so shaky and slow that Sperm Whale was able to swoop in and claim that for himself as well so much for not "tail-whipping" a man when he's down.

"No, please," said Sentinel B. "Show some mercy, I beg of you!"

"Why, so we can both die?" asked Sperm Whale. "Like those idiots before?"

"Did he just say that?" asked Levity as he whispered into my ear.

I didn't say a word, and I kept my gaze fixed on the fight.

Brigadier B closed his eyes as he stuttered. "Then let's get this over with. Be quick about it."

"Don't tell me what to do," said Sperm Whale. "Just for that, I will not give you the pleasure. Both silver scepters need to be nice and charged."

Sperm Whale slithered to the downed silver scepter and obtained it. He held it in his left hand and the original in the right (and the opponent's electric dagger with his tail).

"Talk about a one-man band, a band of thieves," I said. "He still has his mouth to play the harmonica."

"They say the wait is the hardest part," asserted Sperm Whale. "I would say that applies to both of us. I have to be patient and wait until this scepter is charged before I can perform a dramatic snow spell end finisher."

"No, please," pleaded Brigadier B. "Get it over with."

"Hold your sea horses," said Sperm Whale. "If I have to learn to be patient, then you can too. It's a virtue, you know. But in the spirit of olive branches, I will allow you to choose what spell you want to die from," said Sperm Whale. "Do you want Shiver River, Ice-Sickle, or Colder Boulder?"

"Anything but Shiver River," continued Brigadier B. "Ice-Sickle, whatever. Something! Anything!"

Sperm Whale just stood there, savoring every moment of

Brigadier B's shaky body tremors and stuttering voice as he was knocking on death's door. Sperm Whale grinned as Brigadier B cried, moaned, and wailed.

Sperm Whale held both silver scepters above his head like a dignitary. "I am feeling rather merciful. Ice-Sickle it is."

Hundreds of sharp icicles shot from both scepters and pierced Brigadier B's body like a pin cushion. Seeing his body flip, flop, and flap gave the impression that he died a thousand times. I pray that the first icicle was the one that finished the job. While I am trying to make it to the egg, I don't get a thrill of seeing anybody suffer like that.

"I don't think I can handle much more of this," said Levity as he proceeded to get up. "I'm just gonna stick to using my feinting and hope for the best."

I put my hand on Levity's shoulder, and Levity sat back down.

"Hold up a moment," I muttered. "That poor Brigadier was playing Checkers, and Sperm Whale was playing Chess. Sperm Whale has mastered memorizing and predicting patterns, melee, range attacks, and now his tail-flail. You are both masters at feinting. One weakness is that he feints so much that it loses its value. He's like the Sperm that Cried Wolf. We need to anticipate the feint and not fire unless we are close enough that there is no chance of missing. And use wide-radius spells if you can."

"Yeah, assuming we win the die-cast, to begin with," returned Levity. "There's always that pesky element of luck. Let's hope the dice are not loaded."

"But are they ever anything but loaded?" I asked.

Levity knitted his eyebrows. "What do you mean?"

"If a die was truly fair, then why would it ever give anyone an advantage?"

"You will have to ask the head Prospector," said Levity. "That is beyond my scope of practice."

The finial on my scepter began flashing. "I guess I'm next. I knew this moment would come."

As I groaned my way up to a standing position, Levity followed suit and gave me a hug. "I will be watching you, Sage, on the big screen, sending you good vibes. Just think, you are a celebrity back home."

"I suppose war is the oldest reality show in the book," I said. "Talk about unnecessary drama."

I felt lucky, in a way, because, at the very least, I was able to witness all nine spells by now, be it from watching others or experiencing them myself (I preferred the former method). I had an idea of strategy and which spell to use for the right occasion. This knowledge gave me a defense advantage as well, as I also knew what to expect if my opponents won the die-casts, leaving me in the role of the running rabbit. Predator and Prey may begin with the same three letters, but that is where the resemblance ends. But if the absolute value of the prey's defense is higher than the predator's offense, the former will prevail. I do not buy into the idea that a good defense is a good offense. Something has to be said for wearing down the enemy's resources with a suffocation strategy (with less bloodshed).

At the start of the match, the Prospector performed the Brigadier's die-cast. It came out "Wind." I shuddered when I remembered that I had only a 1/3 chance to win the die-cast, as his "Wind" would beat both "Paper" and "Scissors." My only chance to win would be if I scored "rock." The Prospector didn't hesitate to roll the die. In that brief moment of time, I couldn't help but see the irony that my life was in that little die's hands (small wonder it's called a die). The Prospector's flat expression made him look almost bored, as if there was no point in rallying the crowd, as I would just be a facile victory or "easy out," as they say in baseball.

Whether by rhyme or reason, the die was tossed higher than usual, as if taunting me to revel in my trepidation for as many microseconds as possible. I let out an audible sigh of relief when I spotted that lovely rock settle into a stable position. At this point, I felt like I was the Brigadier and he was the Sentinel. He was the werewolf, and my bronze scepter was the silver bullet. I didn't let it get to my head, though (Murphy's Law and all that). He could still beat me to death with his silver scepter, make use of his electric dagger, or rob me of my bronze scepter. I "played the tape" and visualized every one of these scenarios play out as if they were alternate timelines in other dimensions. A "rock" may have graced the emerald finial of my bronze scepter, but Murphy's Law was my rock and coat of arms.

I never used "rock" spells before, but I admired how the "Boulder-Dash" spell was ranked "medium" for both distance and melee. This makes sense, as the boulder was quite large and could also go quite a distance as if fired by a small catapult. This spell suited my Goldilocks "sweet-spot" sensibilities.

Five minutes is an epoch in these battles, so I had to make sure my shots counted. Animus may have chastised me and my sweet spots, but I made sure Levity didn't take his word for it. As a mentor of Levity, I used "typing" as a metaphor. When typing, if you put too much emphasis on "quantity" (i.e., speed), you run the risk of being too hasty, and you are bound to make mistakes. But if you focus too much on "quality" (spelling), you will sacrifice speed. But there is that wonderful middle ground where you maximize efficiency. Efficiency! That might be my favorite word in the entire English language.

But I must have failed to find the sweet spot between confidence and competence. I was so shaky I thought every one of his jerky movements was an attempt to feint and bait my rock to miss him. As far as I knew, maybe that was his intention. To be as haphazard and random as possible. I steadied my scepter as I held it towards his general direction. Was this going to come down to luck? Just toss it and hope my horseshoe hugs the peg? Should I approach closer? What if he becomes winded or bored and charges at me?

I used the worst strategy in the book. I held the scepter at the "general epicenter" where my assailant, Brigadier, was "buzzing around." I closed my eyes and fired my boulder at a moment when his back was turned to the boulder (every second of missed anticipation on his part was a benefit for me). The rock lofted through the air like a cotton ball in the wind. The shadow it cast covered the Brigadier like a blanket, giving him all the information he needed to dodge the massive rock. Truth be told, it wasn't even a close call. I don't believe the boulder made any contact with him at all. But I learned one thing, this guy wasn't a feinter (nor was he faint of heart).

The bad news? I had to wait 5 minutes for my magic to recharge. The good news? He was the one running like a madcap fool, gasping for air and huffing all the while. At this point, it made sense to play defense and keep my distance until my scepter was recharged. He was already more out of shape than me (thanks to my upgrades, don't assume arrogance on my part). And this, coupled with his lack of energy, made it an easy feat to keep him at bay (it was like not stealing candy from a bubble gum dispenser).

With one full minute left for my scepter to recharge, he had a "charge" planned of his own. He slithered at me like a jouster at a healthy clip (healthy for him), and just as I raised my bronze scepter to defend myself, he brandished his silver scepter and clocked me in the jaw as if my head was an employer's old time punch clock. Suffice it to say he punched in on time for his shift. The whole ordeal made me wonder if he was "hustling" and malingering during his "tired" phase to carve out a false impression of his prowess and ability.

As I was reeling back, he unsheathed his electric dagger. I swung my bronze scepter and whacked it away. As dramatic as it appeared, I think my survival instinct exceeded my skill. It wasn't long after this, and my scepter was recharged and ready to rock and roll. If I learned anything from "Boulder Dash," it was that my confidence with range attacks exceeded my competence. So, this time, I decided to put more eggs in the "melee" basket. While this basket was not as pretty as a cornucopia, my hope was that it was still a horn of plenty.

It was time to get up close and personal. "Condoning Stoning" was a close-range spell that hit the spot, at least for me (whether it would hit the spot of its designated target was a different matter). This time, I did not have to worry about anticipating movements. I felt like a golfer taking his sweet time to putt the ball despite the fact that it was only a foot (i.e., tail) away from the hole. After all, I have seen golfers miss these "easy shots" before (which brings me back to Murphy's Law). I took the shot, and a menagerie of debris, rock, stone, and detritus showered over him like falling babies at a baby shower.

The velocity of the stones must have been at least a hundred miles per hour. The strident sound as the rocks pelted his head reminded me of hail stones hammering the wooden floor of a patio. Even after he was knocked out, the rocks kept coming, some blunt and others sharp, as if the rocks were perfectionists aiming to be "extra sure" that he was as dead as a coffin nail. Unlike Sperm Whale, I took no pleasure in savoring his death throes (I turned around, but I could still hear the noise). It's not easy to pat yourself on the back (literally or figuratively), but I managed it (despite giving my arm a charlie horse).

"Yeaouch," I said, a cross between "ouch" and "yeah!" If anything, my new word captured the spirit of the emotion well as I delighted in my victory. When I appeared back in the main arena, I hobbled back to where Levity was seated near monitor 8 and sat next to him.

"It's down to the trip wire," I said to Levity. "It's just Sperm Whale, you, and myself. One of us is going to have to fight Sperm Whale before the end."

"Welcome back to Repro," said Levity. "This is going to sound crazy, but I kind of hope Sperm Whale beats one of us. Isn't that bad? That way, we don't have to fuss about killing each other."

I paused. "The important thing for the mission is that Sperm Whale is defeated, regardless of our feelings towards each other. He cannot get to that egg."

Levity was an illustrious Brigadier, but many of his battles were against Sentinels. While this may have seemed like good luck, it also robbed him from gaining experience on how to take down Brigadiers. So is that really good luck? Perhaps this "blessing in disguise" would prove to be a "curse in disguise" after all. But I didn't want to mention that to Levity.

The head Prospector adjusted his glasses. "This fight will take place right here in the main arena. No alternate dimensions this time. After all, we have nary a spectator left, save for the Prospectors! Next up, we have a young Brigadier vs. the famous Sperm Whale!"

Sperm Whale charged towards the Prospector and grabbed his microphone. "You mean the infamous Sperm Whale!"

"My mistake," said the Prospector, taking back his mic. "I mean the infamous Sperm Whale!"

Levity shook his head. "I guess Sperm Whale is all gangster. Talk about bad publicity being good publicity."

Levity's scepter began flashing, his cue to take the stage.

"I guess it's me against Blubber-gut," said Levity.

I pivoted from war captain to boxing coach. "Don't forget to anticipate his feints. He's more predictable than he thinks he is. Not only are you master class at feinting your opponents, but you can also anticipate their feints when they return the favor."

Levity laughed. "A shame you don't have a bloody mouth guard to slap in my mouth. Don't worry, I know all the strategies. It's the statistics, optics, and logistics that worry me. You don't have to be Abacus to know that the odds are not on my side."

"Come now," I said. "You are as odd as the rest of them."

Levity smiled. "If you don't see me again, I want you to get to the egg without me. Do not allow my loss to hold you back. My ghost will be very disappointed in you!"

I patted Levity on the shoulder. "Such dramatic resignation is unlike you."

I pulled the towel out from the inside of my suit coat and handed it to Levity.

"What is this?" asked Levity. "It's got everyone's signatures on it. All five of us."

"Don't you remember?" I asked. "Back at the battle at the uterotubal junction? When I almost gave up? Remember what you told some of us?"

Levity paused. "Yeah, I was frustrated that some of us wanted to give up."

"That is right," I said. "You were dead set against us 'throwing in the towel' like dirty laundry, I think, is how you put it."

Levity held up the towel and rubbed his fingers on the names. "Are these embroidered? By each of us?"

I nodded as I spotted a tear run down Levity's face. "That's correct."

Levity smiled behind his tears. "How did you manage to get Animus to embroider?"

"Let's just say when someone cares about you, they will come to the fore in ways you don't expect. They will stand by you, even if it's not comfortable."

"Oh wait," said Levity as he reached into his pocket. "I might as well give you this."

It was Abacus's fidget spinner.

"How on Earth did you get this?" I asked, as I spun it around on my finger. "I thought it got sent back in time a few hundred years!"

"I picked it out of Abacus's fight before his match with Brawn," said Levity. "He wasn't fiddling with it as much as usual, so I thought if I took it, he wouldn't need it anymore. You know, like taking the training wheels off a bike. I'm not a tough love guy, but it pained me seeing Abacus so anxious. It's not going to be easy for you watching me up there. Take the spinner, and use it as much as you need. There is a really good chance I won't survive. That brute is a psychopath."

I continued to spin the spinner in my hands. "Reminds me of the Wind-Mill spell."

"Tell me about it!" said Levity.

I continued. "For this battle, I shall call you Bravery instead of Levity."

"If only a label could make someone so," said Levity with a laugh. "It's not like the spells where words are enough to elicit action. I'm afraid there's not much courageous about denial and distraction. And that's all humor serves, right? Flattery will not get you (or me) anywhere. Morale said so himself."

"Then use denial and distraction," I said. "If that is what wins the war. It's served you well up to now, right? Use your psychological walls and defenses to your advantage as if they were fortified bastions and ramparts. You will find that sweet spot between caution and confidence. I know you will."

"How do you know?" asked Bravery.

"I've seen it before," I returned. "From the very moment we snuffed out the Lagoon Spittoon Platoon. There's a reason we both made it this far."

"Where is this coward?" shouted Sperm Whale, sniffing the air as if Levity had a signature scent.

Levity tied the embroidered towel around his neck like a scarf as he run-walked to reach Sperm Whale and the head Prospector in the center of the arena.

At the very least, Levity and Sperm Whale were both silver scepter wielding Brigadiers. The first die-cast is never as nerve-wracking or dramatic as the second, as it's the second one that really solidifies who is in the driver's seat. The Prospector tossed the die for Sperm Whale first, and it landed on Snow.

"My favorite spell class!" shouted Sperm Whale, doing a little jig to taunt Levity.

"Oh great," I thought to myself. "Did he like snow because he mastered that magic class? Or did he just like frolicking in the snow?"

"You have no class," returned Levity.

Next came the daunting part. The Prospector tossed Levity's die, and it felt like time stood still. It almost seemed as if it took longer for the die to fall than it did to go up. Then again, I was holding my breath the entire time with my hand over my mouth. My instincts forced my eyes shut at the moment of the reveal (as if closing my eyes would hold off the inevitable). I let my ears decide who won the die-cast. The cheers were as loud as ever, and this was not a good sign. Only Sperm Whale could generate that kind of applause. I opened one eye and squinted at the fighters' body language. And Levity's crest-fallen gaze and Sperm Whale's unbridled jig only solidified the stark reality. I was hoping for a tie, at the very least. But in the end, the die landed on "Mountain." And Sperm Whale had the upper fin.

I went to the corner of the room as water flowed from my eyes as if they were founts. I felt as if I was already at Levity's funeral paying respects (something I never intended to put on my bucket list). When I heard gusts of icy wind, I plugged my ears so I couldn't hear Levity's death throes. But when ten minutes went by, and I unplugged my ears.Why were the spectators still cheering? Was Bravery still in the ring? Was it appropriate for a captain to give up on his crew, even with the best of intentions? I was not just a captain. I was also a motivator, cheerleader, coach, mentor, and even brother. Now was not the time to indulge in my own brooding and misgivings. I risked opening one eye. And there was Levity, with pep in his step, seizing control of gravity, friction, and the other laws of the natural world. And that is when I realized that Leaving your friends behind was not "taking one for the team." It was taking the easy way out.

After my pitiful display, I meandered back to my seat with the same quiet dignity as if I was just returning from the bathroom. I noticed Bravery make eye contact with me like that child at a recital hoping to see their parent in the audience. Did my absence lessen his morale? Or did it prompt him to try harder and work all the more to impress me? Either way, I knew where I needed to be. And that was with Bravery. In the crowd. And I didn't even use the fidget spinner.

They found themselves in a clinch and engaged in close

range melee. For a moment, it appeared they were taking turns smashing each other with their scepters. Bravery was nothing if not efficient, and he was inclined to take full advantage of the five minutes of downtime until Sperm Whale's scepter would be ready for another blast of winter fun.

At the last, a full minute before recharge, Sperm Whale raised his scepter as if making a toast at a posh banquet. He brought the ruby finial down on Bravery's head just as I crumpled up my face and shut my eyes (yeah, as if closing my eyes would stop the flow of time). Or so I thought. When I risked a peek, I caught the tail end of the best parry I have ever seen! Not only did Bravery block the blow, but he also managed to knock Sperm Whale's silver scepter out of his hand! And since Bravery already had his radar on for Sperm Whale's feints, his reaction time was impeccable in getting to the spinning scepter before The Sperm Whale stood a chance (not to mention Bravery was faster, but not by much, despite the body enhancements). The whole thing appeared like choreography to a figure skating performance. Just be sure not to tell Sperm Whale that.

There were only two minutes left on the clock until the snow magic would be recharged. Bravery used his "coward skills" (as Animus might say) and played keep-away with himself. As Sperm Whale got within spitting distance, Levity chucked the scepter to the other side of the arena before running past Sperm Whale to fetch it again like a dog chasing a bone. He kept up this strategy until his (stolen) scepter was ready for a snow blast. Bravery planted his tail and clutched the silver scepter as he allowed Sperm Whale to approach within "bad breath" range (Sperm Whale's breath, not Bravery's).

"Do you know why I shouted from the rooftops that I fancied snow spells?" asked Sperm Whale.

"Cuz you actually know how to spell snow?" I shouted from the sidelines.

"Audience shall now speak!" returned Sperm Whale. "It's because I know how to avoid snow spells!"

Bravery grinned. "I don't believe you that losing your scepter to me was intentional. You are just playing mind games with me."

"Have you ever seen a whale do a full body breach?" smirked Sperm Whale.

"No, but I will soon see a whale that has been beached," Levity quipped as if he had nary any fear left in him.

Sperm Whale grimaced. "The gig is on."

"And I say the jig is up," returned Bravery, giving me a wink as I sat in the audience and smiled like a proud father.

In any event, that was Bravery's storm watch and storm warning rolled into one. Sperm Whale approached but stopped at a moderate distance.

Bravery held up Sperm Whale's scepter. "Colder Boulder!" I knew that Colder Boulder was a high-range and low melee spell, so it was a tough call as to the chances Sperm Whale could take a beating.

A deluge of hail stones jettisoned towards Sperm Whale. The stones appeared like transparent crystals, some of them blunt and others sharp as daggers. Sperm Whale ducked, dodged, skipped, jumped, and parried as the hail stones soared past him. I guess he wasn't lying, he really could defend himself against snow magic. I made the mistake of getting my hopes up, which meant I broke Murphy's Law. And what's the punishment for breaking this law? Dashed hopes.

The weather let up. The storm had passed. And Sperm Whale was left standing as the recharge clock started over.

"You can call me Moby Dick," said Sperm Whale.

Bravery stood his ground. "How about I just call you Dick. You know, just to keep it shorter and more informal."

Sperm Whale remained cool and collected in spite of Levity's remarks. Instead, Sperm Whale began tossing the electric dagger up and down with one hand without even looking, catching it by the handle every time.

"You are not the only one who can do that," said Bravery

as he reached into his sheath.

Bravery looked around the floor around him. "Hey, where is my dagger?"

"Word of advice," said Sperm Whale. "Never play keep-away with a pick-pocket."

Sperm Whale was now juggling two electric daggers! And these were sharp. It didn't take much to penetrate them an inch deep. He may have had two daggers, but Bravery had two silver scepters. And the latter began to juggle them! I was starting to think our Levity borrowed some airs from Animus and Brawn.

Sperm Whale's poor ego must have become bruised as he resorted to tossing his daggers higher and higher as if this was some sort of brutish pissing contest.. And Bravery did the same. What was Sperm Whale up to? Better question, what was Levity up to?

After a series of high tosses, Bravery caught them both and tossed each one at Sperm Whale, one after the other. Sperm Whale kept juggling and dodged the first scepter. The second caught him off guard and whacked him in the jaw. Sperm Whale staggered as his own daggers rained down on him from the heavens. The first dagger hit his head via the hilt and fell away, causing no damage at all other than a bump on the head. But the second? That one hit blade-down, and it went deep enough to send an electrical current through his body! And then I realized why Levity was egging him on to toss his daggers higher and higher.

"Why you..." said Sperm Whale as he smoked, burned, charred, barbecued, crackled, snapped, and popped. And those were his dying words. Not very poetic, mind, but Sperm Whale never was one for William Cullen Bryant. And that was that the indomitable and abominable Sperm Whale was not only a sperm donor, but he also donated his body to science. Bravery seemed more shocked than Sperm Whale was, as evidenced by the diameter and circumference of his slack-jawed and wide-open mouth.

Levity staggered back to his seat next to mine.

"I don't look so good," said Levity.

I guided him down into his seat. "Are you kidding me? You never looked better. In comparison to how Sperm Whale looks, you could be a model."

Levity smiled. "Well, not for long. We will soon be in Brawn and Abacus's position. Brother against brother."

"We can make this easy," I said. "When we are called on stage, I will toss Abacus's fidget spinner. If it lands with the brand name face up, you can kill me. And vice versa. We will not make the same mistake as our fallen comrades."

"Talk about ending on a low note," said Levity. "But it's the best we can do."

Levity and I were lost in our thoughts for ten minutes as no words were spoken.

"What's taking them so long?" asked Levity.

I looked around, and the three Prospectors were scurrying around cleaning and tidying up chairs, monitors, and tables. "I guess we just wait."

"I appreciate the new name you gave me," said Bravery, "But I think I would rather go by Levity if it's all the same."

I was taken aback. "But it's true, is it not?"

Levity paused. "It's not just that. I mean, it sort of makes me seem cocky. But as far as nicknames are concerned, I feel like I should start calling you "compunction.""

"You are not blind or deaf," I said. "You are observant to a fault. Sometimes, it keeps me up at night. I mean that we have advantages that others do not have, like the genetic enhancements and top-secret intel from Morale. I know that all is fair in love and war. I get it. But it's almost as if the nature of this world is getting to me. Why must some suffer so that others should live? Sometimes life and death, pain and suffering, or even good and evil are zero-sum games."

Levity seized the role of Captain, if only for a moment. "All is fair in love and war. You know why they say that? It's because war is already a nasty business right out of the gate. War is never good, regardless of one's political affiliation. But it's not as if we are engaging in war crimes or such ilk. What we are obtaining from Ron is not the answers to test questions. It's "intel," a common war strategy."

I patted Levity's hand. "It's a myth that there is this mystical 'equal playing field.' If there was such a thing, all things being equal, we would need to control for everything: physical stamina, numbers, intelligence, personality, speed, strength, height, weight, luck, money, genetic makeup, situational variables, and whatever else. There is no such thing as fairness. If there was, a die would never land. It would roll around on the table forever. What separates every winner from every loser is some kind of advantage. If an event was truly fair, in every sense of the word, every contest, every race, every game, every tournament, every match, and every battle would end in a tie or stalemate. Even if you keep some variables constant, other advantages will reveal themselves in both sport and battle. Even in basketball, taller players will still have a physical advantage. Is that right? Is it truly fair? One could even argue that luck-based games like Bingo are tied to a 'luck advantage.' What is luck but a random advantage granted by the very gods themselves? It's tantamount to favoritism."

Levity sighed. "Somehow, I don't think the laws are fairness are worked into the fabric of the space/time continuum. Just don't forget, there were a few times when our performance enhancements were a disadvantage, if anything, like that damn slow-moving door."

Levity smiled. "How can I forget that? Wow, I am already enjoying war stories."

I couldn't help but smile. "Join the club. And I don't mean meeting the blunt end of a silver scepter."

"Or the kind with tree-houses and boyhood tomfoolery," added Levity.

I nodded. "Life, at its very core, is about survival. And

sometimes, we are in the unfortunate position to kill or be killed. And there are times when the decision is not mutually exclusive. By the end of the day, we all die. As for killing? That part is optional."

The head Prospector finally stepped up to the mic. "Okay, gentlemen, congratulations to you both. Rest well. Soon, you will make it to the final phase of the journey."

"And here I thought the Sperm Whale fight was the penultimate battle," I said.

Levity grinned. "You're telling me!"

"Just don't get too excited," I said. "We are just staving off the inevitable. If it's anything as before, you and I will meet for the final battle on a stage that is the smallest of the Russian Dolls."

Bravery, I mean Levity, is dead set on saving your life, whether you like it or not (and I can't say I blame him). He has taken to trying to guess Abacus's password to hack into his email (as he is quite keen on the idea that Abacus has all his knowledge of nanobots stored therein, including how to deliver a genetic or stem cell cure for what ails you). I remain convinced that he is not delusional, as I, too, seem to recall Abacus telling Brawn something about saving his research within the nanobot LAN. I suppose I was naive to think Abacus would never die. I should have "done the math" when it came to figuring out his odds and ends.

Contrary to your instruction and by misstep or fortune, we have evolved into a family of friends. You have been ingratiated into this coterie of brothers in arms. And be your sentiments requited or not, we are all brothers. Our feelings stand. We understand that not all can survive. But do not even cattle in the abattoir live in blissful ignorance until the day of the bolt-gun? I am inclined to think that Levity and I would not have gotten this far without our close bond. This is not just about being a decent person but also a competent soldier. Even businessmen understand that it's not good for business to eliminate the human element.

But oh Morale, I think of Levity as a son, and I cannot think of him any other way. You should have seen the sanguine Levity enjoying his knighthood as a Brigadier! He was strutting around like a puffed-up robin and boasting just like Brawn! I suppose it's true what they say. One's regalia can affect how you think, feel, and act. If you look confident, you become confident and all that. Despite his jovial countenance, I do worry about the state of his mental health. It's the fact that he doesn't seem to show it that bothers me most. Is he really doing this well? And while I do not think his personality is given to Weltschmerz like mine, I do know that his survivor's guilt in relation to our own little platoon and microcosm is telling, and it's weighing on him. Sometimes, I think I am more aware of it than he is himself. I will catch him staring into space as if he were a porcelain doll or storefront mannequin. I have seen (and heard) him awaken from nightmares with a strident cacophony of shrieks and shouts and comments such as: "I don't deserve to live or die!" As there is no third option to go along with life and death, I shall take this to mean that he feels death is too easy and life is too hard, and there is no reprieve from either one of them.

The letter he wrote you about the battle in the Fallopian tube? It was dictated by him. And be it a favor to a friend or a moment of weakness on my part, I "took the letter." Either way, it's a slippery slope, and I fear he may ask me to ghostwrite the next one with nary a contribution from him. So far, I have given an inch, but I refuse to give the mile. A leader must be stern in such matters, and I would be remiss if I didn't show some level of backbone and spine (despite sperm having anything but). Still, I would be a liar if I said I didn't feel Levity's sentiment, my stoic poker face notwithstanding.

As my Captain and confidant, I respect your opinion as if it was a fact. And I respect your advice as if it was a command (except for that little incident with the fork in the road, of course, which says more about my "soft spot" or Achilles heel than anything else). But I took your advice to heart and read in full my post-script to Levity regarding my dark thoughts and feelings. And that was the impetus he needed to open up further about his survivor's guilt. We now have a therapeutic alliance in addition to a battle one. We both indicated that we felt all the better for it, as if a huge weight were cast asunder or shackles were cut from their very stakes.

P.S. Consider this syllogism:

A game is an activity that involves competition.
Survival is a form competition (for scarce resources and safety).
Therefore, survival is a game.

Attachment: The rules of engagement.

Brigadier vs. Brigadier

Wind beats snow (1/3)
Snow beats mountain (1/3)
Mountain beats wind (1/3)
Die-cast tie results in both scepters casting same magic class
Brigadiers given electric dagger
Self-deletion of both fighters prohibited
Brigadiers are granted silver scepters with ruby finials

Brigadier vs. Sentinel

Wind beats paper and scissors, but not rock (2/3)
Snow beats paper and rock, but not scissors (2/3)
Mountain beats rock and scissors, but not paper (2/3)
Sentinels and Brigadiers retain electric daggers
Brigadiers are granted silver scepters with ruby finals
Brigadiers cast snow, mountain, or wind magic
Die-cast for Brigadeir and Sentinel

Self-deletion of both fighters prohibited

Wind Magic: (activated by speaking spell name)

Windmill: A large jet engine follows the prey from 10 (tails) behind at 3mph. If the victim gets too close, he is ripped to shreds. And while this spell can only be cast once, it will last a full five minutes. (NA Range/Melee)

Extra-Terrestrial Wind: The entire battlefield will be under heavy wind conditions for the full duration of the recharge period. The wind will not affect the spell caster at all. This spell can be recast after five minutes. (NA Range/Melee)

Funnel Cloud: This is a tornado that will jettison towards the victim. If they should make contact with the funnel, they will be sucked upwards and airborne. (Medium range, Medium melee)

Snow Magic:

Shiver River: A stream of icy-cold water is jettisoned from the finial, freezing upon contact of the adversary or terrain below. (Low range, High melee)

Ice-Sickle: Hundreds of sharp icicles are forged and shoot towards target as if daggers or sickles. (Medium range, Medium melee)

Colder Boulder: A massive boulder is carved from sheer ice and falls from the sky towards enemy. (High range, Low melee)

Mountain Magic:

Mountain Fountain: A blast of molten lava spills out of the silver scepter towards target at a high velocity. It turns to volcanic rock upon impact. (Low range, High melee)

Unfortunate Landslide: A menagerie of dust, debris, rock, gravel, and detritus is hurled towards target. (Medium range, Medium melee)

Mountain to Mohamed: A large hill is formed under spell-caster giving him a safe terrain and home-field advantage. It lasts the full duration of the recharge period and can be recast. (High range, Low melee)

CHAPTER 10

The J Letters
Subject: Luck of the Draw (cellular survival games and fight class)
Survival type: Cellular competition (fight class)
Author: Ron Une
Date: February 14, 2182 (Thursday)
Location: Neuron
Recipients: Levity and Sage (Adventurers 4 and 5)

Greetings, Adventurers 4 and 5 (Levity and Sage)! What a superlative blessing it is to hear (read?) that you are both alive and well! Words fail to describe how these visceral moments feel to savor with all of the five senses. It is days like this, I feel like indulging in all manner of accouterments, fine foodstuffs and wine, aroma therapy, and a tactile massage! Didn't I tell you that mind over matter can transcend statistics? And your genetic enhancements no doubt played a bountiful role. I do hope that my encouraging words played their part as well. After all, I would be remiss if I failed to justify and earn the epithet that you all handed me with such fervor and grace (despite my inability to get myself to say it aloud).

Brass tacks! I was able to break the locks of some of Euclid's deepest and darkest vaults of memory stores (I seized the moment when his inhibitions and defenses were down due to intoxication as if I was a robber stealing a key ring from a sleeping night guard under cover of darkness). And lest Euclid be a charlatan, or his memories be tainted by inebriation, this "magical egg" is very rare, but it very much exists. Not only is this revealed and verified by his more accessible academic knowledge stores, but his deepest private thoughts reveal that his partner in crime, Autumn Hux, is indeed "fertile" and manufactures these eggs herself. There is only a 1/20 chance of conception for any random act of copulation (why does everything have to be such low odds?) Whether by rhyme or reason, eggs are far less plentiful than sperm. But do not take this to mean any of you are disposable or insignificant! Remember, it takes two to tango. And both dance partners are very much equal. Don't lose hope!

When a sperm and egg meet, in the typical scenario, they will form a sum greater than the sum of their parts. They will merge to create a superbeing called a "zygote" (sounds like the name of an email virus). But make no mistake, this is a fully functioning organic robot with all the tools necessary to expand and grow. If you should be fortunate enough to find this egg, you will become "one" with it, and your personality and physical features will interact and combine with those of the egg. Your very sense of self may transform as you adopt additional personality traits or physical features. But do not fret, for you are not moribund! This is just part of the merging process. It is merely like adding (+) to (-).

Euclid and Autumn Hux are each the sum total of a sperm and an egg forming a zygote. There is a risk that whoever meets the egg will only maintain 50% of who he once was. This "egg" appears as a circle and has no tail like a sperm. There are also (rare) cases when two zygotes are forged instead of one (this is called having twins). And there are different kinds of twins.

Identical twins share 100% shared DNA and are caused by a fertilized egg (i.e., zygote) splitting into two.

Fraternal twins share 50% DNA and are caused when two sperm impregnate two eggs (forming two zygotes). If you are slow to the uptake, this means that there are cases where two sperm can survive! Such news is sure to pique your curiosity and give Adventurer 4 (Levity) cause for celebration. The fellow lacks a thick skin, and his soft down feathers are easily ruffled! If I could grant him a nice shiny coat of porcupine quills, I would!

The odds of having twins the natural, old-fashioned way is only 3/100 (about the same odds as being spit on by a camel at the zoo). Do not be deterred. We have been pushing our luck the moment we breached the cervical gate! And we have cleared more bottlenecks than what's in Euclid's liquor cabinet. In the interim, I will be soaking up all I can about how and why twins are born and to what extent we can set up the conditions to make this happen without depending on Lady Luck, a most untrustworthy and undependable woman.

I hate to say "told you so" (well, I wouldn't say I hate it per-se). But this entire "twins" business wouldn't be an issue if you two heeded my warning about not becoming friends or family, to begin with! Now you are stuck with each other like parasite to host. Part of me wonders if I should waste my time trying to save both of you knuckleheads! Some might say it's tantamount to enabling insubordination! You poor vacuous socialites! I should have never humored your use of colloquial vernacular! Even the Prime Minister doesn't have a name, nickname or otherwise, other than his title of "Prime Minister." And every cell here in Neuron is named "Ron Une." It's nothing special, I assure you.

But alas, I will keep poring over information in Euclid's gloomy low hanging head, for right or wrong. It is too late now. Our bonds are too strong, and turning coat on each other at this point would feel like a war crime. We are in too deep, literally and figuratively. And we know what happens when strong bonds are severed. They snap, and the backlash can be destructive and dangerous.

From here on, we need to be checking our electronic messages on an ongoing basis. You will need to have a nanobot nearby and on standby at all times. Just like with blood sugar, check the nanobot, and check it often. There is just no reason not to!

If the last battle taught us anything else, it's that these

Prospectors are not just staff at a sporting event there to stir up drama and excitement. They are top-tier fighters of the highest caliber, and they outrank both Sentinels and Brigadiers. The diamond finials on their gold scepters are not for show. They wield an elemental power that trumps every other kind, whether up against paper, rock, scissors, snow, mountain, or wind. The subatomic particles shot from their scepters can send the target back in time, anywhere between 500 and 1000 years, to die in accord with their own devices. Part of me takes comfort in knowing that Abacus and Animus have been resting in piece for centuries and may have died of old age in the presence of family and friends.

P.S. You asked about the gent who shouted my name from the rooftops, the poor fellow who received "death by engine." I'm only going to say this once (unless you re-read this email). I call him Adventurer 0. He was the very first to send a letter to the Prime Minister of Neuron regarding taking the "journey to the egg." Back then, I intended on having him go alone without a platoon (as I feared the risk of treason and backstabbing from his fellow mates). But as time went on, I could tell he had little interest in science. He cared more about destroying the egg and mounting it on the wall of his tiny house like a game hunter. He was the one who figured out how to make harpoons from scrapped nanobots. Not only that, but he also Christened the Harpoon Platoon (before, they didn't want anything to do with him either). Good riddance to bad rubbish. Then again, one man's garbage is another man's treasure.

The J Letters
Subject: Re: Luck of the Draw
Survival type: Cellular competition (fight class)
Author: Sage (Adventurer 5)
Date: February 14, 2182 (Thursday)
Location: Palace of Life (Repro 2)

Recipient: Ron Une
C.C.: Levity

Hello Ron, I wish you well. Levity asked me to be his ghostwriter, but I refused. This is a letter written by me (with just a scant few tidbits of news he requested me to articulate). Levity remains all smiles all the same, but when it comes to writing letters of a more serious tone, that is when his pen seems to run out of ink. Either such matters hit a nerve with him, or he can't be bothered by such serious affairs.

Two sperm can survive to create fraternal twins? We don't have to put all our eggs (and sperm) in one basket? When I read that in your missive, my ears perked up like a cat hearing a can opener. But they perked down just as quickly when I read the part about "only a 3% chance." Be careful with such "good news," Ron! I can't and shan't get my hopes up like that! It wouldn't, couldn't, and shouldn't be prudent for my long-term mental health! We will need to know more about the science behind all this. If you can improve the chances for creating twins, that is another story. For now, I will forget I heard anything about it and any presumptuous hope I glean from any of this in the interim, I will consider folly or moot.

The entire entourage of Prospectors led us through the iron door. And while we left the Fallopian tube in the dust, we did not find ourselves in the humble abode of the Captain's cabin. The exit was but an entrance to a sort of lobby. It appeared like a waiting room but without the magazines and inspirational posters. But there was something else that set it apart from the boilerplate waiting room. Everything was either gold-plated or solid gold (I wasn't about to scrape anything to find out). The floors, thrones, statues, candelabras, flying buttresses, fern pots, and chandeliers were all gold as well.

"They would make the plants gold if they could," said Levity. "I sense a theme here. I hope you don't mind being one of their golden boys."

"The pleasure is all theirs," I said.

The thrones were easy on the eyes but not so easy on the behind. The winding stairwell near our chairs blossomed into the heavens like a tulip (with a golden dragon winding its way up along the ivory banister). There was no doubt about it. We were at the final chambers of the magical egg.

One exception to this different take on their "Golden Rule" was that there were bronze torches with a green flame, silver torches with a red flame, and golden torches with a silver flame adorning the walls.

"They sure like their shiny things," said Levity.

"Chalk it up to the 'Karat and Scepter Principle,'" I returned. "I must admit that it's a more lucrative mantra for those of us who detest vegetables and crave the finer things in life."

Levity smiled. "Let's see how much they like our shiny scepters."

One of the gold walls was all bare save for the engraved words: Palace of Life. There were only two marked doors in the golden lobby. Each gold door had a marble plaque stating Door Number 1 and Door Number 2.

"Something tells me there's not a new car behind one of those doors," said Levity.

"That sentiment is very much requited," I returned. "And it's difficult to get excited about a movie sequel when you haven't even started Part 1 yet. Not that I want any spoilers. A bit of false hope or fool's hope is better than no hope at all."

The head Prospector returned and alerted us that we had four hours (haploid time) until we would fight each other. We had some time to kill before we killed each other. You wouldn't know from the sterile electronic font before you, but I am struggling to even write you this letter due to my shaky hands and tear-stained eyes. How can I compose a letter when I cannot compose myself? It's not wise to spill my guts like this when I need them for battle.

After I composed myself, Levity tried "educational guessing" at least fifty passwords to tap into Abacus's email, and then he gave up and tried to answer his security questions instead. One of them was: what is my favorite quote? First he tried "Correlation Doesn't Mean Causation." And then he tried "Do the Math," and even that failed! I suggested Levity to throw on an exclamation point at the end. He entered, "Do the math!"

"It worked!" shouted Levity.

I put my finger over my mouth like a librarian. "Keep it low, man! That Prospector could be anywhere! But hey, that's fantastic!"

So now we have access to Abacus's information on nanobots. Now, we can attempt to reverse your degenerative cell disorder if it's not too late.

P.S. When I hear individuals say that the only rule in these games is to "kill or be killed," it sounds like a rhetorical question. It seems almost obvious that anyone would rather kill than be killed. But the question isn't rhetorical. There is no obvious answer. To kill or be killed is a classic case of choosing the "lesser of two evils." They say it gets easier after killing your first. But who are "they" with these pearls of wisdom exactly? Serial killers? Decorated soldiers? Survivors of an apocalypse? Cannibals? In any case, I am not feeling better at all. What makes me more special than Animus, Brawn, or Abacus? In relation to war, even Levity seems more immured than immune. It's hard to explain, but he just seems distracted and distant, and I find myself repeating things at least three times before they register in his brain. He isn't snippy or snarky, just in his own world, wavelength, and dimension.

The J Letters
Subject: Re: Luck of the Draw
Survival type: Cellular competition (fight class)
Author: Ron Une
Date: February 14, 2182 (Thursday)
Location: Neuron
Recipient: Adventurer 5 (Sage)

I just spent the lion's share of three haploid hours perusing the stacks in Euclid's memory stores as if the place was a legal library filled to the gills with dusty (and musty) tomes. Good thing it isn't, as my nosy nose wouldn't be able to handle all the spores.

It pains me to say that, once again, I must reprise the role of being a harbinger of bad tidings! How I do hate to get your hopes up, only to have them dashed so! These words are not empty, disingenuous, or without compunction, I assure you! I am no savage, and I will do my very best to atone for such an egregious miscalculation!

It turns out the father has naught to do with whether a mother has twins or not (i.e., whether a fertilized egg splits into two zygotes to form identical twins or if two eggs are each fertilized by a sperm to form fraternal twins). So why can't we just tamper with the egg instead of the sperm? For one, the egg is heavily guarded (as there is only one egg and millions of sperm). Two, all human brains have executive functions (under the direction of that brain region's Prime Minister). It would be foolish to assume the Prime Minister in Autumn's brain region would acquiesce to handing out such information willy-nilly (she may not be a glutton for punishment like I am). And Autumn may be just as insecure about sexuality as Euclid Hux and have just as many defenses of her own to overcome.

In the spirit of being realistic, I'm afraid we must forego the dream that we can get you both out alive. I shouldn't have mentioned it until I learned more about the science behind it. It was like rubbing salt in the wound when I kept reading and discovered that there are ways to induce twin-prone eggs on the mother's side using genetic modification, genetic editing, nanobots, fertility drugs, In-vitro fertilization, and stem cell injections. Talk about leaping before the look-see.

I am being an optimist when I say use the rest of your four hours to accept the fact that the twins-idea is a bust. I suggest you find an excuse to despise each other. Cast insults if you must. It will hurt less in the end. Get used to that idea, and do it soon. Do away with the silly nicknames. Your partner is no different than the other millions of sperm that have died. We just don't know their life stories (outta sight, outta mind, and all that). One of you alive is better than both of you dead. Sometimes, there is just no sugar-coating reality, and sometimes sugar substitutes are even more unhealthy. Don't hold back. Keep telling yourself, "One is better than none." Flip that coin. Say your goodbyes now. Just don't make the same mistake Abacus and Brawn did. We are at the cusp of our victory. We cannot, and must not, hold back now.

Brass tacks. As minted Prospectors, you will each be given a gold scepter with a diamond finial. There will be no die-cast here. Both weapons will be hot and readied for battle. And since there are only two contestants in these battles, they are bound to get tired if the fight goes beyond an hour. Regardless, there will be a thirty-minute break if nobody dies within the hour (like a pit stop in a race or water stand at a marathon). That is what I know so far.

Remember, if one of you touches this time wave, you will be sent back in time between five hundred and one thousand human years ago (and Animus thought I was old). So take comfort that you aren't killing each other per se. These Prospectors will know if you are holding back. They are trained to watch for such subterfuge. So the only options are to fight for real and test your skills or decide a-priori who is going to die with that confounded coin toss.

P.S. You are not friends. You are not family. You are enemies trying to survive. It's a dog-eat-dog world out there. Go back and re-read our earliest correspondence. We were all strangers then, like any of the other millions of haploids in the race. Nothing changed since then. This is tough love. It hurts me more than it hurts you. Now go! Stop, drop, and rock & roll!

The J Letters
Subject: Re: Luck of the Draw
Survival type: Cellular competition (fight class)
Author: Sage
Date: February 14, 2182 (Thursday)
Location: Palace of Life, Door Number 1 (Repro 2)
Recipients: Ron Une

When in the Palace of Life, we didn't waste away our precious time with small talk (or sulking). We had an old "chin wag" about who was gonna bite the bullet or kick the bucket. Yes, deceased. The end of the line and all that. I asserted we should just flip a coin and let fate decide. But what does Levity suggest? He was blithe as always and spoke of the matter as if it was as insignificant as a beer drinking contest!

"I want to see who's the better fighter," said Levity. "Let's show off our fighting skills for reals. Ron says it's nothing personal, right? The reality is one of us has to die. We might as well make it count and go out with a bang. A blaze of glory. A dramatic exit. End on a high note...."

"I get it," I interrupted. "This is not easy for me, and I hope that underneath that ironclad veneer of bravado, you agree with me on some level."

I tell you, Ron, there are times I can't tell if Levity is oblivious to the world around him or if he is just off his rocker (are they mutually exclusive?). He is the only one I know who can make light of someone being burned at the stake. Maybe I should re-Christen him as "Naivety."

By any stretch, your suggestion of "hating each other" was off the table in favor of having a "bit of fun" with friendly competition with friendly fire. I suppose I can't say Levity is wrong. We might as well enjoy our last moments as if we were partaking in our final meals before the electric chair.

A different Prospector (wearing an amulet) returned and jerked his chin in a nonchalant manner towards the door marked

"Door Number 1." Why was this guy so nonchalant about it? Was he tired of his job? Were we just the "next in line" to him? Was he inviting us to "go for a spin" in his new convertible? By any event, I am the only one that takes death seriously around here. Levity and I followed him through Door Number 1. As I trotted along behind him, I continued to think about his amulet. It appeared to be made from massive amounts of diamond, fashioned into the shape of a snowflake (with emphasis on "fashion").

This new "Russian Doll" battle arena was reserved for two, but there was ample room for distance fighting. There were no other Prospectors in the battle area and no bullet or magic proof window. This battle didn't appear to be televised, as I did not spot any visible cameras or screens anywhere in the battle chamber. The room was a complete circle at around thirty haploid meters in diameter, surrounded by what appeared to be fusuma walls. There were large black candelabras around the enclosure, but instead of torches they held sticks of burning myrrh.

"At least they provide a pleasant smell in here," said Levity. "Fancy fighting, eh?"

"Careful what you wish for, Levity," I said. "Incense is often used to hide the smell of dead bodies."

"Is it too late to change my tune when it comes to incense?" asked Levity.

I sneered. "You picked a great time to be incensed by incense."

"You guys ready to die?" asked the head Prospector.

Levity smirked. "You must be fun at parties. Do you guys ever joke around?"

The head Prospector glared at Levity. "Around here, that comment passes as a joke.

I sighed. "It is true, an alternate definition of 'humor' involves bile, phlegm, and blood. I can only surmise that the latter definition will be much more relevant here."

I realize this remark was a bit more flippant than my baseline. I figured that since these were my last words, it didn't matter much at this point. But then this segued into another muse. How many words can someone have for their "last words" anyway? Is there a limit? All I know is I may need at least five hundred.

The Head Prospector ignored me in the end. "Sit tight, and I will fetch the treasure chest."

And with that, the Prospector walked towards the corner of the room, which housed a walk-in closet. He returned holding a wooden trunk with a rounded top that resembled a pirate's chest (not the hairy kind). He flipped open the lid without a key and revealed a small red flag emblazoned with the two-dot Yin/Yang crest we all knew (and didn't love).

The Prospector spoke. "Even though I run this phase of the contest without any colleagues, do not get any funny ideas. I am the Head Prospector of the head Prospectors. You see this amulet on my chest? It is not a necklace, and it's burned into my chest. It allows me to be immune to time magic."

"So how is the amulet passed from one Head of the Head Prospectors to another?" asked Levity.

"Are you serious right now, Levity!" I thought to myself. "What kind of question is that?"

The Head Prospector humored Levity's requisition. "When it's my time to die, the amulet is ripped from my body and melded onto the next. Simple as that. It's all in the rubric of the Prospector Policy and Procedures manual if you make it long enough to take a look-see."

I guess the Prospector spoiled the surprise. There were time scepters in that wooden box. Not all surprises are the stuff of cake, streamers, and party favors. We selected our instruments of mass destruction (after all, atoms have mass and are the building blocks of matter).

The head Prospector used his time scepter as a guide-stick and motioned us towards the arena.

"It's now or never," I said.

"What are we waiting for," said Levity. "We got a fight to

do."

The Prospector waved his red flag of battle. And with that, battle commenced.

"Today is the first day of the rest of your life," I said to Levity.

"Classic fortune cookie quote," said Levity.

I knitted my eyebrows. "But nowhere in that expression does it say you will live more than a haploid day."

"So let's make the best of it," said Levity. "The good, bad, and ugly."

As soon as Levity spotted the flag wave, he fired his time wave at me (meanwhile, I was still trying to get used to the idea that 'shit just got real'). I leaped out of the way and fell on my backside, missing the particle beam by nary an inch. By now, being battle worn as I was, I developed the reflexes of a cat (it's a shame I didn't have nine lives or the ability to land on my feet). But now Levity had to recharge his scepter for five minutes. I guess it was now my turn, one of those predator/prey reversals.

I didn't waste my first shot willy-nilly. One would think a "once in five minutes opportunity" wouldn't mean much when compared to a "once in a lifetime one," but in the heat of battle, these two opportunities are not all that different. In a place like this, seconds count. And you can lose your life in that five-minute period.

It's easy to get cocky during the opponent's recharge period. But it would be foolhardy to underestimate the brute and blunt force of the scepter itself. There have been times when a contestant was knocked out cold by being struck with the scepter, only to be killed five minutes later when the scepter was recharged. This was true whether the scepter was bronze, silver, or gold (none of them feel good, trust me). And whether the jewel happened to be emerald, ruby, or diamond. Precious gems and precious metals aren't always the stuff of opulence and luxury.

How far from him should I keep myself during his recharge period? I thought about the "sweet spot" when typing (and aimed for an efficiency equivalent of three hundred characters per minute when typing, with minimal mistakes).

I could do one of two things:

Keep myself at a far and safe distance (while compromising my accuracy)

Get up close and personal with a better chance of hitting him (but also setting myself up for a melee attack or strike with his blunt scepter as it was recharging)

Levity grimaced. "If you think you are gonna find that sweet spot of yours, you can think again. I know your strategy by now.

"Oh yeah?" I returned. "Soon, your face will 'join the club.' And I don't mean the Lions Club."

I tried to humor Levity's use of humor. But it was just too weird. Then again, that was his way of coping with crazy, not mine. Animus hid behind anger. Abacus hid behind intellect. Brawn hid behind bravado. And I hide behind my intellect and non-committal philosophy. But these are not just fronts, facades, smokescreens, or pretenses. They are survival modalities that have helped us survive and navigate life up until now. But defense mechanisms are bittersweet. There is a certain comfy-cozy in familiarity, and these time-worn old hats can hold us back when taken too far. As they say, if you stay in your cocoon too long, you will never become that butterfly (one of the scant few bugs not considered odious and reprehensible, along with the ladybug).

"Prepare for a blast from the past," said Levity, spinning his scepter like a baton in a marching band.

"Oh, is that how it is going to be?" I asked. "When you are hit by my time wave, you will learn the meaning of 'time is of the essence!'"

I positioned my scepter at Levity, with every intention in the world of splattering him. My instinct told me to close my eyes as if being the one tasked to put down the family dog for biting the mailman. In a way, we were doing each other a favor by taking this seriously. I decided not to waste my five minutes while Levity's scepter was recharged. I knew he was a master of feinting and detecting feinting. So I did not feint. But I did take a running charge towards him and body-checked him to the ground before he could fire. I didn't waste my moment willy nilly.

"Bam!" went the time wave from the finial of my scepter. I trusted on impulse, and my aim/accuracy had the tenuous dexterity, grace, and poise of a crime of passion. But Levity, being the "professional coward," slid out of the way like a mudslide. But the blast did nick his finger (sending it back in time over five hundred years ago).

"My finger is gone!" shouted Levity, holding up his non-bleeding hand. My face must have displayed my guilt like a computer screen. Just as I was opening my mouth to speak, Levity mouths words to me.

"Do not show mercy," Levity's lips displayed. "Or we will die."

Levity was right. And as a leader, I should have known this. But I just cost Levity his finger! Even still, I mumbled to myself. "Losing a finger is better than losing his life."

The oddest part was how Levity's wound did not bleed and was healed without any trace of blood or bruise (I guess all the blood went back in time as well). I cringed at what I had done, but I was glad he was still alive with wounds healed. And it didn't seem he had any pain, judging from his lack of body language.

"How dare you send my finger back in time to the Ming Dynasty!" shouted Levity. "Now you gotta recharge your battery."

Seriously Levity? How far will you take a joke? I thought I was pretty good at empathy, but Levity was hard to read during this battle. Did he have a death wish? This was feeling far too weird.

We ran at each other and clashed like jousting single-cell

titans, using our scepters as both shields and swords. We played cat and mouse until I had 2 minutes left on my recharge. He wasn't going easy on me, and he whacked and wailed the gold scepter against my head ten times in thirty seconds (approaching that ideal typing speed I mentioned). Not to mention, a diamond is one of the world's hardest substances. But I can't complain! It could be worse! I could have been burned at the stake.

Levity was quick to the punch, and every time I swung my scepter, he would duck, dodge, dip, and whatever other synonyms started with "D." "Whap!" went his tail as it struck my face. It all made me wonder if he used his time scepter as a time traveler to predict what I was going to do. I gave up on the melee and opted for old-fashioned running away. We were so far apart inside the arena that we were like repelling magnets. We kept this up until both our scepters were hot and ready, like a couple of branding irons. What can I say? Some like it hot.

I was on guard for his next time blast.

"Smash, crash, and thrash" were the sounds of his unleashed fury. He unleashed a volley of scepter, fist, and tail melee attacks on my sperm-person.

"Never assume that a hot and ready scepter is going to fire," said Levity. "I know you all too well by now. You will not anticipate my baits and feints. And the harder you try, those will be the times I use a bait and switch technique."

After the beating of a lifetime, I fell to the ground.

"You look like a wounded deer," said Levity. "You are not fit to be a leader."

Was this a continuation of his trash talk? Or was he right? Was I not fit to be a leader? After all, I was just laid to waste in this insidious war of attrition (I guess when he said he learned from the best, I should have been less flattered).

I didn't want to risk blasting my scepter during this close-quarters bar brawl, as I could easily shoot myself into the Copper Age. There was also the chance I might miss or even shoot myself in the tail. All in all, Levity was a much more formidable adversary than I thought. I had to turn down my ego a full three notches.

Levity feinted as if he was going to shoot his scepter but then backed off. Without taking my eyes off him, I walked backwards to give myself more distance. I was very apprehensive (i.e., scared), as I didn't know if he was going to feint, shoot, melee, spring, or predict my feint and adjust his aim accordingly.

We ended up pointing our scepters at each other, sizing each other up despite being very similar in stature. We stared each other in the eye.

"It appears we see eye to eye on this issue," I said.

"Consider it a stare down," Levity returned.

We hesitated a moment as the reality that this was a real game of cops and robbers came to our senses.

"So, who is the cop, and who is the robber?" I asked.

"Take your pick," said Levity.

I squinted my eyes. "Perhaps they need each other. Yin and Yang and all that."

"Your philosophizing won't save you now," said Levity.

"Keep fighting!" shouted the head Prospector, aiming his time staff at us from behind his tinted glass. I guess we were dawdling.

"Our poker faces hold all the clues," Levity returned.

I took a deep breath. "I guess this is it. This is the end of the line. We must finish this with a dual, wild west style.

"Who's gonna draw first?" asked Levity. "In the movies, it's the bad guy."

I smirked. "Ah, yes, so the good guy can be the one to react and call it self-defense. How quaint."

"We can recreate the Han Solo and Greedo debacle," said Levity,

I squinted my eyes. "Either way, you can't even draw a bath, much less a firearm."

"Wise guy, eh?" returned Levity.

I smiled. "They do call me Sage."

"I say the Prospectors are the bad guys," said Levity. "That means either one of us can draw first."

"Luck of the draw," I said.

"Luck of the draw," Levity returned. "Now, let's put our scepters down on the ground and stand straight up."

I pulled out Abacus's fidget spinner. "I will toss this spinner in the air, and when it lands, that's our cue to begin."

Levity nodded in agreement.

In truth, our reaction times were on par. And while I was not trying to lose per se, I did wish to give Levity a break after all he has done for me. I would surmise that I was putting 90% of my ability into it. But I knew that if I eased up too much, the Prospector would catch on.

We set our weapons on the floor and stood up with our backs straight and eyes fixed on each other. It was at that moment that I noticed that we were both shaking.

I looked at the fidget spinner and mused about the irony of how an object designed for stress relief could cause so much stress. It controlled the fate of the game.

"Toss it!" shouted Levity.

I sput it first and tossed it high into the air. The spin allowed it to achieve some bit of hover, and it stayed horizontal with the ground the entire time. The very second I heard the "thud," I hunkered down faster than falling and reached for my scepter. But the back of my hand knocked it away. Levity snatched up his scepter with his tail and shot from the hip. I had to check myself over to locate the wound. But it turned out that his aim was not as skillful as his reaction time, as the shot hit and knocked over one of the candelabras (I don't think he tried to miss, but I am not 100% certain). With this predator/prey reversal, I now had a full five minutes to plan my next shot before his scepter would be recharged.

"I guess you have me now," said Levity. "My lack of tail dexterity is my Achilles Tail."

Levity stopped in his tracks. He just closed his eyes as

if resigned and ready to take his medicine (the medicine bottle reading: "Put an end to my misery"). I knew if I waited too much longer, the Prospectors would kill us both, so I had no choice but to sight up. His closed eyes and shaky disposition told me that he was impatient to get this over and done with (anticipation anxiety being just as painful as the act itself). Even Levity had a limit to how much this was all "fun and games." But I couldn't get my finger to pull the trigger. It's a shame that my worthless finger could not have been sent back in time instead of Levity's.

"Finish him!" shouted the head Prospector. I held the scepter with nary a micro movement. I held this position for several moments. The Prospector held up his scepter as if prepping it to kill us both.

I had no choice. "Ready, aim..."

The J Letters
Subject: Re: Luck of the Draw
Survival type: Cellular competition (fight class)
Author: Ron Une (audio message via GPS tracker earplants)
Date: February 14, 2182 (Thursday)
Location: Neuron
Recipient: Sage

Hello Sage, please tell me you have not killed Levity yet! I am sending this message via audio as timing is critical. You might be fighting as I speak. I can save both of you! I repeat I can save both of you! Starting now, you must only pretend to fight with Levity (without killing him). I know it will make things all the more dangerous for you, but I command you to abstain from letting him in on this secret. He does not have the acting ability to pull off such a factitious battle. This will require legitimate acting skills (and real battle skills) on your part. It is a risk not letting Levity in on this, but it's a risk we must take. And I have faith in your battle skills to pull this off.

Keep up this ruse for the rest of the hour until the first

break. Do not allow the Prospector, nanobot, or Levity to detect that you are acting or listening to me. Keep it real. You may even have to tune him up a bit, with real injuries and the like, and shoot your scepter a time or two to give the impending drama more veracity (and your shots must be very close to hitting him). When you reach your break, check your email forthwith. You will find a detailed report to accompany this audio message. Save it for when you are safe and sound. The information is imperative, but not right now. There is a time and place for battle and a time and place for academia. If I don't hear back from you, I will know that one of you has perished.

The J Letters
Subject: Re: Luck of the Draw
Survival type: Cellular competition (fight class)
Author: Ron Une
Date: February 14, 2182 (Thursday)
Recipient: Adventurer 5 (Sage)
Location: Neuron
CC: Adventurer 4 (Levity)

With luck, you are both alive and well reading this missive together on your break in a safe, non-emergency situation. Do not bother yet if you are in danger. I trust you heard my audio recording with no interference. This is the more detailed email I was referring to. I obtained intel of a very valuable nature, so pay attention. I can only imagine that Levity is still coming to grips with the fact that you were only acting for much of the battle.

I have additional intel from Euclid. We already know Autumn's egg is not twin-prone. If it was, the Prospectors would not have arranged for you two to engage in battle in the first place (and you both would have been privy to the egg's access). In fact, your time scepters would not even be functional if that was the case.

You are no doubt wondering why I am even talking about

saving both of you when the egg isn't even twin-prone. Allow me to elucidate. I worked myself in a frenetic frenzy trying to figure out a way to keep you two alive. I went deeper and deeper into the catacombs of Euclid's higher-level academic stores from back when he was at graduate school. As we know, Euclid Hux is a master class when it comes to genetics and stem cells. He literally wrote the book on reproductive science ("Reproductive Science and Genetics: A Deep Dive" by Euclid Hux). The only reason we are on this journey to begin with is because our human host has this knowledge.

From my research into Euclid's mind, I learned there is a very rare third type of twin, called a "semi-identical" twin. They are neither identical (100% DNA similarity) nor fraternal (50% DNA similarity). They share around 75% DNA similarity. This is very important, as it occurs when a single egg is fertilized by two separate sperm! But make no mistake, these are extremely rare. There are less than five documented cases, at least when nature is left to its own devices, unchecked and unfettered.

But it gets better. As you may remember, it's generally the mother and her egg that dictates whether or not twins are born. It turns out that during his years at University, Euclid wanted to test whether "twin-prone" sperm from the father's side could act as the impetus or catalyst for the conception of semi-identical twins. This was revolutionary stuff and had many ramifications for parents who might wish to have twins. What does this mean for us? Well, this is the trump card to get you both out of here alive. The answer lies in semi-identical twins!

Euclid had many skirmishes with the IRB board due to his research being too bold and controversial. One time, he told the IRB Board: "This research will be just as monumental as creating options of male birth control." But lo and behold, the IRB denied the research as too risky for the unborn babies (including the increased chance of the neonate showing signs of brain damage or disability). So, the research was never carried out. But the knowledge is still there for the taking in Euclid's mind!

So what does this mean for us? I have access to Euclid's method and procedure for creating twin-prone sperm. Between Euclid's and Abacus's memories and research, we can give this a shot (quite literally, as there is a needle involved). Two years ago (human time), when Euclid received the nanobot implants, he made sure to make them capable of genetic editing (having the ability to re-write pre-existing DNA as if computer code). The topic is quite obtuse, but the nanobots are capable of both somatic editing (specific cells like muscle cells) and germline editing (reproductive cells). The editing is accomplished through a complex technology called "Crispr/Cas9" which uses proteins, enzymes, and naturally occurring bacteria in the body to create a sort of "cutting tool" (which can cut and replace parts of DNA strands). Or, as the story goes! Like I said, it's obtuse, and I am struggling to understand it myself, and I'm a brain cell.

Any nanobot can do genetic editing, as it does not always require a genetic payload or volley of chemicals to transfer between nanobots. And thanks to Levity, the instructions on how to program a nanobot to carry this out were safe and sound in Abacus's email account all along! I guess fate is never late. It strikes just when you need it to. We are on a hot streak, don't let it go to waste. After all, they say good luck and bad luck come in threes.

Using Abacus's email information on programming nanobots, coupled with Euclid's DNA blueprints for how to create twin-prone sperm, I was able to upload the blueprint into my nanobot. And thanks to our male-female LAN, I was able to program the nanobots in your immediate proximity to obtain this ability as well. But we still need to get you the injection!

All this must be done on the down-low so we can stay on the up-and-up. Prospectors cannot, and must not, "catch wind" of any of this. You can allow Levity in on our little clubhouse secret this time, as I dare not risk losing your life so late in the game. He is becoming a more skilled fighter all the time, and I fear he has a legitimate chance of taking you out (no offense to you).

After the injection, it will take a half an hour for your bodies to become twin-prone as the genetic editing process needs ample time to complete. So keep up this ruse as long as you can (and tell Levity to make sure his acting skills in battle appear as realistic as possible). There will be nanobots there to assess battle prowess as usual. Remember that nanobots also have the ability to spot twin-prone cells. Sometime early in your second round, the nanobot watching the battle should detect you both as twin-prone sperm, stop the fight, and allow you both to survive and make it to the next level.

We must give credit where credit is due. We are very fortunate to have Euclid Hux as our host. I would have never even thought about partaking in this adventure if he wasn't such a prolific (and illustrious) reproductive scientist. It was only when I was looking through top-secret files for a cure for my disease that I even discovered that Euclid Hux was an expert in reproductive science. This is not just a once in a lifetime opportunity. It's a once in a billion lifetime opportunity.

Let's hope Euclid and Autumn will make peace with the fact they are having twins. Knowing Euclid, he will be tickled pink that they were blessed with semi-identical twins (and might even find it a spiritual experience, given the extreme rarity of such an occasion). Of course, they may just mistake them for identical twins and be done with it!

The J Letters
Subject: Re: Luck of the Draw (cellular survival games and fight over flight)
Survival type: Cellular competition (fight class)
Author: Sage (with input from Levity)
Date: February 14, 2182 (Thursday)
Location: Palace of Life, Door Number 1 (Repro 2)
Recipient: Ron Une

Dear Ron Une,

Did you just use our nicknames in your last two bits of correspondence? Freudian slip, perhaps? I can't help but think you are warming up to us. I inquired with Levity to see if he and I wished to take turns writing you (not that we find writing letters to you to be a burdensome affair worthy of drawing straws). If anything, we clashed on who "gets" to write Ron, not who "has to" write Ron. I am improving at this "art of positivity" business. Still, Levity was still not feeling very congenial, so once again, I penned this letter (with a bit of help from him as he peered over my shoulder).

If you have not deduced from my lighthearted banter so far, we are both alive and well for the moment. We are sitting by ourselves in the Palace of Life during break, merry as elves, while the Prospectors are busying themselves with the minutiae of managing the battles. And the very first thing we did was consult the nearest nanobot for any of your communiques (and spotted your follow-up to the audio message). Call me quaint, but there's just something uplifting about not having to kill each other. The only loss we suffered was losing Levity's finger (which is a loss I do not minimize as it was the fault of mine). It may have wound up in a castle somewhere in the middle ages, for all we know. May it rest in peace. He's already laughing about it (while I still feel pangs of consternation). Trifles and tribulations aside, your twin-prone needle injection is the "needle in the haystack" we have been looking and waiting for this whole time. It's a veritable "Fountain of Youth."

Levity and I were approached by a nanobot not long after we received your audio communique (which was fortunate, as we could have mistaken the nanobot for trying to attack us with that massive needle! It took the lead as if a defibrillator and facilitated the entire process. It even spoke audible instructions, which put us in a vulnerable position as we waited for the Prospector to return. Now we know how you feel, always looking over your shoulder in your world of cloak and dagger espionage!

I allowed Levity to go first (Captain's honor and all that).

"Look at that needle!" exclaimed Levity. "You could knit a hat with that thing!"

I chuckled. "I can't help but Imagine Abacus's reaction."

During our time with the nanobot, the feeling of "time ticking" was palpable, as if every second was linked to a time bomb (especially with that confounded nanobot talking us through the entire ordeal).

"Five minutes of genetic transfer remaining," said the Nanobot as the IV feed was in my wrist.

"We are home free," said Levity. "Only five minutes to go. Reminds me of when I was laid up getting my IV back at the fork in the road before the uterotubal junction."

"Some memories we will never forget," I said. "That goes for good ones or bad ones."

The door creaked as the head Prospector stepped into the room. Levity and I shot stares at the Prospector (I tried my best to not look like the guy with his hand caught in the cookie jar).

"Four minutes and thirty seconds to go," said the nanobot.

The Prospector approached us. "What was that? What has four minutes and thirty seconds to go? What are you guys up to with that nanobot?"

Levity stuttered. "Ah, we were just, sort of, you know, oh yeah, checking our emails and stuff like that, you know, how it goes."

I was tempted to face-palm my forehead along with rolling my eyes. I could have concocted a more believable lie about using the nanobot to pleasure ourselves. Levity was good at many things. Lying (including acting) was not one of them.

The Prospector cocked his head towards Levity. "Checking emails? Why is there an IV in that other gentleman's wrist?"

Levity started to open his mouth, so I saved him from himself (and me, for that matter). "Sir, he's checking his emails while I take a dose of Alprozalam for the ol' nerves. You know how it goes."

I pulled the IV out of my hand early just so the nanobot would shut up. "There, all done. No hard done."

The Prospector squinted his eyes. "Why would that other guy be okay with you taking a drug for your anxiety? Are you guys in an alliance of some kind?"

"I took a dose as well, just before him," returned Levity. "It's only fair we both get to take it."

"Then why is he checking his emails?" asked the head Prospector, looking at me.

Levity raised his hand (as my inner self panicked for dear life). "I'm writing to my loved ones. It's my way of avenging that gent that said his final goodbyes just before he got sucked into that fan. I was rooting for him."

"But you already avenged his death when you defeated Sperm Whale, didn't you?" returned the Prospector, unable to let it go. "I have never heard of anyone avenging someone's death more than once."

I seized the floor. "There's no rule on how many times you can avenge someone's death. Besides, one was revenge, and the other 'avenge.' Surely, we can have one of each."

The Prospector slithered around the lobby for a moment to see if he could spot anything suspicious, even looking behind furniture. He sized up the nanobot as well, top to bottom. "Okay, follow me."

I think our plan worked (despite the chance of it becoming "planned obsolescence" at any given moment). My only concern was whether I would still be assessed as "twin prone" with five minutes left to go on my genetic editing. Can't anything just go right without a hitch for a change?

The Prospector led us back to the arena behind Door Number 1, where we would now "fake fight" like WWF Wrestlers, as per your instruction. And since the head Prospector was already suspicious of us, the last thing we needed was for him to further question our motives. So, Oscar-quality acting was imperative. I noticed that the same nanobot that did our genetic editing would also be the one assessing battle prowess during the fight.

"Let's hope that nanobot can keep a secret," said Levity.

I used this time to whisper into Levity's ear clear instructions: "When I raise my staff high in the air with both hands, prepare to dodge my time blast. When I raise my staff in the air with one hand, that is our cue to engage in melee battle. You can do the same. We will each have to shoot at least three times to make this fight look more believable. And don't miss by too much. Our shots have to be close to hitting each other to look as realistic as possible. The time blast covers a large area, so make sure you do not so much as touch the stream (as your finger learned from experience). The subatomic particles are not easy to dodge, even when expecting the blast at a certain time. It's imperative we do not blow our cover, even for a second."

Battle commenced. The first thing I did was whack Levity upside the head with my scepter, and it drew blood.

"You don't beat around the bush, do you," said Levity.

"This hurts me more than it hurts you," I said.

"You sure about that?" asked Levity, rubbing his chin. "Ouch."

"Now we are even," I returned.

Levity smirked. "I didn't know we were keeping score. Whatever happened to 'let bygones be bygones?'"

"Consider it tough love," I shouted.

"Tough love, eh?" said Levity. "Your love is not as tough as mine!" Levity countered my strike with one of his own.

Levity raised his scepter with both hands, indicating he was about to shoot a time blast, but his aim was so atrocious that I wondered if the Prospector would surmise he missed on purpose.

"You missed me literally and figuratively," I said. "You missed because you miss me. If you are that nostalgic, allow me to clock you good and keep you stuck in the past."

"Thwack," was the sound of gold against my chin as

Levity clocked my jaw. And he did not hold back. A bloodstream shot from my mouth like projectile vomit.

You know, Morale, this was not the Ice Capades, but it was legitimate fun compared to round one (even if we did take some additional blows). The Prospector didn't even react to Levity's blatant miss, so that was an unanticipated (and auspicious) bit of luck. I did not make the same mistake, and after I raised my scepter with both hands to cue him, I took careful aim. His reaction time was on point, and as soon as the time wave shot, he rolled out of the way (the shot was far too close for comfort, no thanks to my poor aim). It's a curious irony when a bad shot can be a good shot (I felt like that guy that either gets gutter balls or strikes and nary anything in between).

After several "close encounters of the third kind" (3rd kind of gold scepter, that is), we learned how to read each others' minds with the tenacity of fortune tellers. We had time scepters, after all. After two time blasts apiece, we backed off and got more up close and personal like wrestlers (the incessant clinching and flailing was a great time-waster). I could tell we both felt apprehensive of using our magic anymore due to hitting one another by accident. When lit, those things were more difficult to wield than a fire hose. Best not to push our luck (or pull it, for that matter).

Using a wrestling strategy held potential as it provided the impression that we were waiting for just the right opportunity for the "perfect shot." That cautious golfer will be extra careful when the stakes are high, even when the ball is a mere foot away from the hole. And since we were messing with black holes instead of golf holes, these matters were all the more crucial!

Things appeared to be going great (which is always a red flag). Over a half hour came and went. The nanobots did not yet stop the fight. Did I pull out the IV too soon? Did I pull the plug on our plan altogether? Damn, my confounded poor instincts!

Our choreography turned into improv, and we sort of worked ourselves into more close-combat melee, hitting each other seventy-five percent as hard as we could (we both

understood the life or death ramifications of not drawing blood).
As much as this hurt like hell, it was the lesser of two evils when
compared to killing each other. And this fight was taking longer
than expected, so we had to go a bit easier on each other before
one of us got hurt for real.

Levity as he swung his scepter like an aluminum bat.

"Whack!" was the last thing I heard. Levity must have
miscalculated his strength. I collapsed to the ground and was out
cold and out like a light at the same time.

The head Prospector knew that I was not yet dead (as per
the nanobot observing) despite my lifeless body on the ground.

"You are recharged," said the Prospector (according to
Levity). "Finish him, or I will finish you. And then I will finish
him!"

"But he's already dead!" said Levity. "See for yourself!"

"Then send him back in time!" shouted the Prospector.
"Why show mercy to a body that's already deceased?"

Levity stumbled over his words. "Don't you believe in
proper burials? Why can't we show some respect for our enemies
like the good old days?"

"Twin-prone sperm detected," said the nanobot five times
in a monotone voice. As soon as the nanobot called the game, our
scepters went limp as if they were never imbued with magic at
all. They may as well have been candlesticks.

"Consider yourself lucky," said Levity as I was just coming
to.

I staggered to my tail and brushed myself off. "I think by
now we can both consider ourselves lucky."

The Prospector was less impressed. "I'm the only lucky
one here. And this is the first time I have ever witnessed a
game being called mid-battle due to being twin-prone. I smell
something fishy."

Levity jumped into the fray. "Make no mistake, sir. We
look like fish and swim like fish. The resemblance stops there."

"Ahhh!" shouted Levity as the Prospector whacked Levity

in the chin.

I jumped in like a contestant in a game show, trying to hit the buzzer first. "It could be because we are semi-identical twins. Maybe it required extra time before we could be identified as twin-prone."

The head Prospector pulled up the nanobot assessments for battle prowess and twin-proneness.

"How about that," said the Prospector. "This is most unusual."

The Prospector turned his gaze to me and eyed me over. "How is your anxiety doing? Is the alprazolam helping?"

I nodded. "Yes, jolly good, thanks for asking."

"And you?" asked the Prospector, looking at Levity. Levity nodded in agreement.

The Prospector turned his gaze back to the assessments on the nanobot, back to us, back to the nanobot, and then back to us. It felt as if a roulette wheel was spinning, and he was deciding whether to believe me or not. Let's hope his decision would land on "believe me!"

"Come this way, back to the Palace of Life," the Prospector said. "We still have door number two to contend with."

"Is there a fabulous prize behind that one?" asked Levity.

The Prospector continued slithering ahead without looking back. "That all depends on how you define fabulous."

This is it, Ron Une. The last "hurrah," the proverbial light at the end of the tunnel. What kind of light this will be? We know not. It could be a blaze of glory. Could be a shooting star. Could be a tragic explosion.

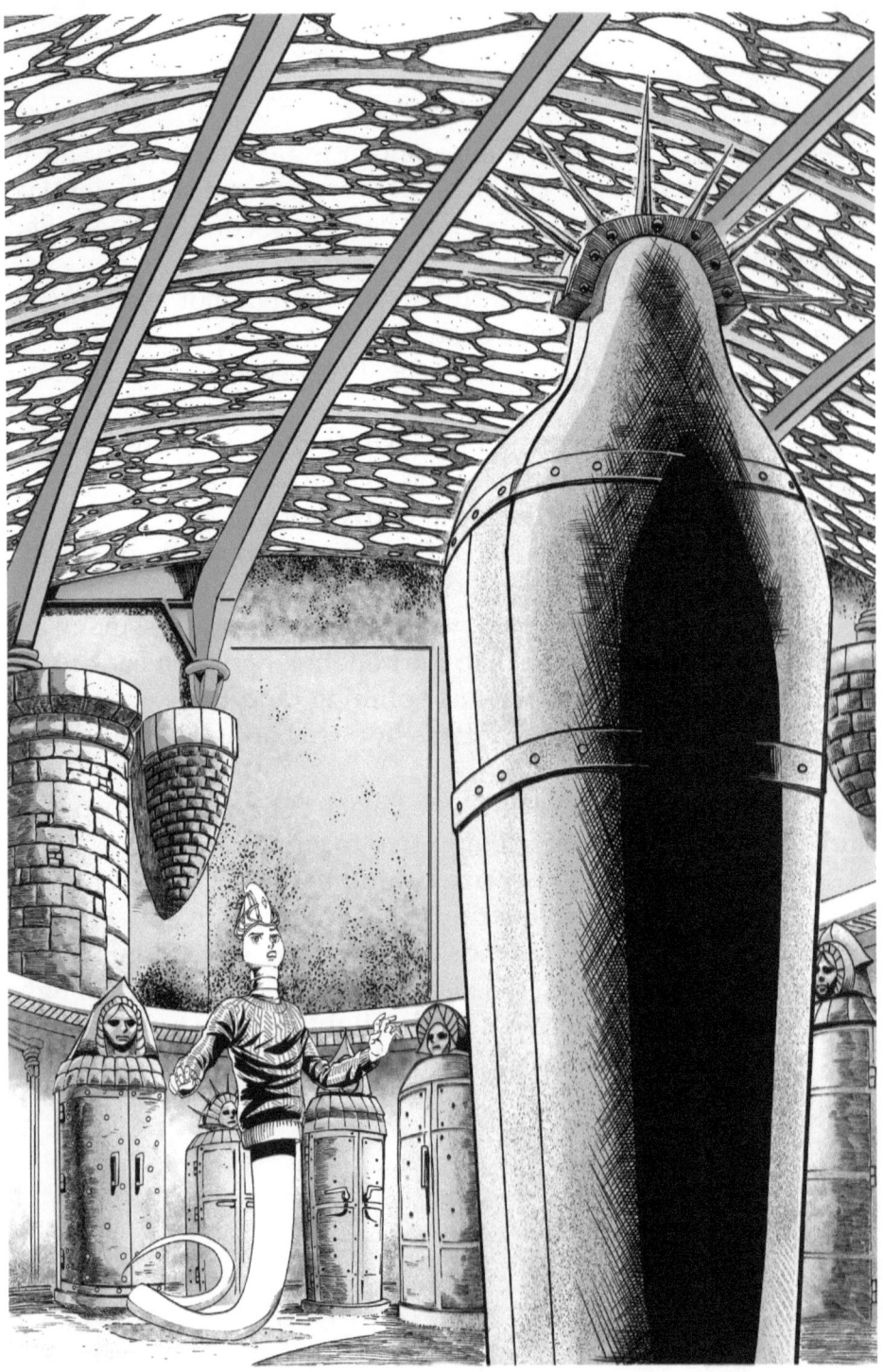

CHAPTER 11

The K Letters
Subject: Leap of Faith
Survival type: Cellular competition (fight class)
Survival type: Cellular competition (class = NA)
Author: Ron Une
Date: February 14, 2182 (Thursday)
Recipients: Adventurers 4 and 5
Location: Neuron

      Brass tacks. Right out of the gate. I have gathered some information to quell your curiosity, but it won't make things any easier. In fact, it may even make you more nervous, "outta sight, outta mind," and all that. This time, it won't be a battle or a race. It's a fight against a faceless enemy. The adversary will be the headless horse-woman, Lady Luck herself. You may have noticed I CC'd the rest of our platoon on this. Rest assured, I have not lost my senses (although they have been dulled). I suppose it sounds rather silly, but I had a moment of clarity and wished to include them. They can give their support posthumously from beyond the grave. They will/would appreciate being included. It's the least we can do.

      You will be (greeted?) by yet another small Yin/Yang arena, the diameter being just wide enough to house twenty iron maidens along the circle. This will be the final "Russian Doll." Only one of these doors may lead you to the fair maiden (i.e., egg). If you both enter through the same door, you will either live together or die together (after you make the decision, it's irrevocable, and you cannot change your mind). If you each select a different door, it increases the odds that one of you will make it out alive. The nineteen iron maidens that do not lead to the egg will chew you up without the luxury of spitting you out (to the chagrin of the poor Prospectors tasked with cleaning them).

The "lukewarm news" is that you will have twice the luck of others who have come before you (as you are twins). The bad news is the odds of survival are still very slim. But considering how far we have come, it appears fate has been on our side. Somehow, we have been ingratiated into the loving hands of the universe itself. But we mustn't push our luck (we must pull it if anything). Remember when Abacus would go on and on about the Gambler's Fallacy and regression to the mean? No? Me neither. But he would say there are no good or bad luck streaks. Odds will always remain the same. Flipping "heads" will always be one in two. The odds of one of you selecting a door that leads to the egg is one in ten. It's one in twenty if you both opt for the same door. I still like to think there is some room for luck being on our side.

Those with a positivist persuasion are inclined to say: "Don't sweat the small stuff." But even I am not so naive to think that any given cause for concern should be written off as mere "small stuff." This is the "stuff" of life or death. It may ruffle your feathers to know that I knew about the 1/20 factoid well before the "Battle of 200," but I thought relaying such troubling news at that dire hour would have been inopportune for your morale. But now, it's something we must acknowledge and accept. Sage and I can both agree that sometimes it's good to be realistic (cautiously optimistic or optimistically cautious).

Regarding your comments about the GPS systems, they are designed to help us navigate to body organs using map data and organ detection software (in conjunction with the male-female LAN), but they are not precise enough to locate the exact position of single cells like the egg. Remember the fork in the

road leading to the Uterotubal Junction? The best our GPS could do was locate the general direction of the ovaries.
Sincerely,
Ron Une

P.S. My cell structure is degenerating at a rapid pace. I do not know how many grains of sand are in my hourglass. Tell Adventurer 4 he needs not to feel that he failed me in any manner, way, shape, or form. He was never tasked with being my guardian angel, and it is not his responsibility to save my life. The world can be savage. It was what it was, it is what it is, and it will be what it will be.

The K Letters
Subject: Re: Leap of Faith
Survival type: Cellular competition (class = NA)
Author: Sage
Date: February 14, 2182 (Thursday)
Location: Pleasure Hollow
Recipient: Ron Une (Morale)

Greetings Morale,
        It was quite the hike, but we slithered behind the head Prospector up the twenty-story stairwell. About halfway up, I started feeling dizzy from all the circles. I have empathy for the fool who makes the trek only to realize he forgot his keys in the lobby! When we came upon the summit, we were greeted by a small lobby enrobed in gold and gems, just like the one below. But this time, there was a fluffy cashmere carpet that felt lovely on my tail. Across from the stairwell was a regal door with "Captain's Quarters" emblazoned on the wall above (I guess we did go above and beyond first class, after all). Another wall had six doors, and another wall had six more. One door said "Head Prospector," and the rest were dedicated for Prospectors two through twelve.

There was one wall left, and there was a marble base holding a gold bust of a mid-1800s gold prospector holding a gold scepter with a diamond finial. On the base were inscribed the words "Welcome to Pleasure Hollow. Enjoy the New Gold Rush."

"Quite the lavish lifestyle," Levity whispered as he rubbed his fingers over the bust. As for me, I seized one of the stacked wine glasses and poured myself and Levity a Pinot Grigio. I even prepared one for the Prospector.

"If you are Prospectors like us, why do you live here?" asked Levity.

I understand that there are "no bad questions" per se, but there are bad times to ask them!

The Prospector did not show any labile shifts in demeanor, indicating to me he was not offended (assuming he heard). And then the Prospector smiled and pointed his wine glass towards the golden thrones to cue us to sit down. He remained standing.

The Prospector cleared his throat like an orator. "As you may well know, Prospectors are 'prospective mates' for the egg, much like eligible bachelors in the world of humans. It is an honor to make it this far, as you well know. The odds are millions to one. The ten or so who reside here are much like yourselves and faced many trials and tribulations to make it here alive. I am the Lead Prospector because I held the highest battle rank among my cohort. When me and the others made it here, we were given a choice, by the then residing Head Prospector. We could opt out of the final phase of the journey, help with the tournaments, and live in luxury in Pleasure Hollow until the day we die in five days (human time) or seventy haploid years. Prospectors come and go like the dawn, and new arrivals replace the ones that have perished. Just like in the world of humans. Prospectors are a rare bunch, so we usually never have more than around ten residing here at any given time."

I took the next question. "Why would a Prospector get this far and not feel inclined to go the last mile?"

The Lead Prospector took a deep breath. "When newly Christened Prospectors are given this choice, many of them opt for the second place prize to live out the remainder of their retirement in a comfortable manner after their tour of duty. I experienced many grueling battles and races just to get this far. Call me a hedonist, but when the former Lead Prospector gave me the option to retire, I snapped it up like a dog to a steak. Despite the rumors of a paradise much greater than Pleasure Hollow, nobody knows what happens when the sperm reaches that coveted egg. Whether I am weak or selfish, it was a chance I was not willing to take. Besides, some Prospectors are needed in Pleasure Hollow to manage all the races and battles.

"So what's it going to be?" asked the Prospector after finishing the rest of his wine in one large gulp. "Now it's your turn to make this decision."

I jumped in before Levity started to get cold tail. "We will go the extra mile."

I did not even have to blurt this out, as Levity was nodding to the Prospector's question just as the words left my mouth.

"Well then," continued the Prospector, "just come back down to the Palace of Life lobby and knock on Door 2 in about an hour. I should have it all prepared for you."

So this is it, Morale. If you have any last words, tell us now. We are on death row, and none of our enhancements will help us. Iron maidens don't discriminate.

P.S. I may be leader, but you, Morale and Ron Une, you are our Captain. You have given our lives meaning. If we don't make it, get well soon and cure what ails you. Since I can't give you orders, the best I can offer is a very firm suggestion, and I suggest you take it, not just for your sake, but for ours.

The K Letters
Subject: Re: Leap of Faith (cellular survival games)
Survival type: Cellular competition (class = NA)

Location: Neuron
Author (audio message): Ron Une
Date: February 14, 2182 (Thursday)
Location: Neuron
Recipients: Sage and Levity

Attention, Sage and Levity! Please respond as soon as you can, for I fear I might be too late. Are you there? Answer post-haste so I can rest my troubled spirit! Do NOT march to your dooms just yet! There may be another way! The iron maidens in the enclave may not be all random!

I was able to surmount some of the additional top security locks in Euclid's mind. It appears that any "random" sexual encounter has around a 1/20 chance of impregnation. But there is something that can increase your chances. Remember back at the fork in the road when we learned how the ovary tends to shift positions every human month? There is something called an "Ovulation Period" that lasts around six days each month (and often around the same time of the month as well). If you are fortunate enough to confront the iron maidens during this ovulation phase, four out of the twenty doors will lead you to the egg, increasing each of your chances of survival to 1/5 instead of 1/20 (if you opt to take the same door). As usual, the chances of at least one of you making the cut will increase if you take separate doors (although this will guarantee that one of the twins will be miscarried).

I can't help but blame myself once again for placing you both in this less-than-savory position. Sperm can live about 75 days in the testes, so there would have been ample time for improved planning. But, due to the very sensitive nature of this knowledge, it may have proved impossible for me to break these knowledge blocks anyway.

But there is one final thing we can do. If it's not too late, ask that wily Lead Prospector if you can enjoy your luxury rooms in the Pleasure Hollow just for a few days (since sperm can live about five human days in the female reproductive system). I will do all I can on my end to ascertain when Autumn has her Ovulation Phase. If we are fortunate, it will occur on one of these next few days (if it hasn't begun already).

P.S. Please tell me I am not too late! And tell Levity to write the next letter! Tell him to cheer up, and that's an order!

The K Letters
Subject: Re: Leap of Faith
Survival type: Cellular competition (class = NA)
Author: Levity
Date: February 14, 2182 (Thursday)
Location: Behind door number 2 (Palace of Life)
Recipient: Ron Une (Morale)

Hey Morale! Wow, you were almost too late! Sage and I were just giving each other our hugs and goodbyes as we were prepping to step behind Door Number 2. Part of me felt as if we were marching to the gallows for an old-fashioned hanging. The door locks after you go through, so I appreciate your candor and timing! I am writing you this letter as per your request (this time with Sage peering over my shoulder).

The Prospector returned after an hour into the lobby of the Palace of Life to collect us for the final gamble behind Door Number 2. Sage and I stood up as if the Prospector was some regal dignitary.

"Say Prospector," Sage said, "can someone take a day or two to enjoy the accouterments before taking the plunge into the icy depths of oblivion?"

The Prospector smiled. "Of course! A Prospector can change their mind at any time, given they are still hale and hardy and not near death already. Any of the current Prospectors could change their mind right now if they wanted to and step into one of the iron maidens."

Sage paused. "Splendid. I want to take some time to smell the roses before we push up daisies."

I nodded. "And I want the same, thank you very much."

The Prospector put up his hands. "Don't you folks worry one iota. Enjoy yourselves. Take your time. And whenever you are ready to roll the dice of fate, just come back here to the Palace of Life and use that door knocker on Door Number 2. One of us will answer it forthwith."

So, at least we bought ourselves some time. Sage and I noticed that you have been using our nicknames! I know you have been in a hurry, and it's faster to use them, but I do hope there is more to it than all that sterile and practical nonsense! Many blessings,
Levity

The K Letters
Subject: Leap of Faith
Survival type: Cellular competition (class = NA)
Author: Ron Une (Morale)
Date: February 14, 2182
Recipients: Sage and Levity
Location: Neuron

Salutations, Sage and Levity!

Boy, am I relieved! Sounds like you guys almost met your deaths, like Caesar at the Ides of March. You both deserve a break, and now you can enjoy a few days in luxury. And tell Levity thanks for putting pen to parchment to send me a memo (if he is not reading this with you already).

By now, you may have spotted a more jovial tone emanating from these words you see before you. This is not wrong. Much of this is due to you being alive. But that's not the only reason. I probed Euclid's most private memories (which required breaking Euclid's last batch of iron-clad fortified locks). It turns out that Autumn's ovulation period will begin around

January 19 (in two days). This is fantastic news. But you should wait until the 20th to be extra safe. We just might do this!

As much as I enjoy the correspondence, I don't wish to hear from you until you reach the egg. If I do not get a letter, I will take that as evidence that neither of you exists any longer. Even if the ovulation phase does occur, we are still looking at a 1/5 shot that you two will locate the egg (if you choose the same door). I wish I could dissuade you both from choosing the same door so that at least one of you might succeed. Still, I have a feeling those words will fall on deaf ears. And you know what? For better or worse, you just may have won me over. Whether you broke me or woke me, I want to see you both to the end. All or nothing! Come one, come all. The luck of the draw!

P.S. I'm feeling lucky tonight, daddy needs a new tail-slipper.

Morale

The K Letters
Subject: Re: Leap of Faith
Survival type: Cellular competition (class = NA)
Location: Egg's final chambers (door 2)
Author: Sage
Date: February 17, 2182 (Sunday)
Location: Egg
Recipient: Morale

Salutations, Morale.

We are most honored to see you using not only our colloquial names but yours as well (they are much shorter, too, and they just roll off the hand when you type them). It has been three days since we last corresponded. The first day, we slept in our respective rooms most of that time. Neither of us even mentioned anything about the egg. It was a most lovely sojourn (in part due to the wine on tap). The second day, Levity and I shared stories about our journey with copious hyperbole and nostalgia (with many nods to our fallen comrades). One would be forgiven for thinking the Harpoon Platoon happened to be a rare race of sperm giants with drool emanating from their very fangs! The third day, we tried to re-enact the second day, this time in my room instead of Levity's. But Autumn's ovulation phase did not yet occur, and even on an unconscious level, this precluded us from tapping into our full enjoyment potential. After all, the war was not yet over, and no amount of wine could quell that factoid. There was one last battle, a battle against chance itself. And you can't tell a good war story if you are a casualty of that war. And lest there be a war with nary a casualty, I have yet to read a war story that ends with "they all lived happily ever after."

Instead, we resigned ourselves to our rooms to nap (as sleeping is like a fast-forward). My body was tired, but my brain was restless (for obvious reasons). I put some marching band music on a low volume on the wireless to help me while away the hours. The music was rather befitting. But I didn't know whether we were marching towards victory or failure. What kind of execution this would be remained uncertain. Would this be the execution of the rest of our plan? Or would this be the execution of our existence from this organic world?

I stared at my reflection in the gold ceiling. "My life really is golden. Only fun-house mirrors lie."

I don't recall feeling tired, but I did get some sleep, as evidenced by Levity's knocking on my door to rouse me up for our big day. In the end, I enjoyed the equivalent of a good seven human hours of sleep.

I opened the door and was greeted by Levity. And judging by his erratic movements and voluminous voice, he was ready and roaring to go (or maybe he took a morning swig of something).

I rubbed the sleep from my eyes. "It's still a good two haploid hours until the Prospector will collect us. You sure I can't borrow some of that energy?"

"Don't be fooled, Sage," said Levity. "I didn't sleep a

solitary tiddlywink. This is how I get when I am running on fumes. My body sputters and spits and goes into overdrive!"

"Makes about as much sense as anything else these days," I said as I motioned Levity in. He just sat his tail down on the cashmere carpet as I went to the bathroom to "freshen up" (one has to look his best in an iron maiden).

"Which iron maiden shall we open?" Levity asked as I was changing.

I called back. "I think we should go through door 3, you know, to honor the three fallen heroes, Abacus, Brawn, and Animus."

"Awesome idea," Levity returned. "It seems this is the only phase of the journey that is 100% luck. Our personalities, physical prowess, scepter magic, and other assets mean nothing. We could be the biggest thugging brutes of the bunch, and it doesn't matter, right? Or maybe the muscle enhancements made us too big to even fit inside. Fat chance."

"Luck is an asset," I said. "Sometimes I even think it's a skill."

Levity shouted from the other room. "Luck is a skill? Like Bingo?"

"Bingo!" I shouted. "You got it."

Levity sighed so loud I could hear it from the bathroom. "I think shell-shock must be setting in your head from all this war-mongering."

"Think about it," I continued. "What if good luck is a reward from above for our hard work, dedication, skill, or battle prowess? What if we are meant to make this scientific discovery, and fate is seeing us through to the end? If luck is a reward, then it may be based on some level of skill."

"This sounds a bit more optimistic than your usual banter," said Levity. "You hit your head or something?"

"Don't get me wrong," I said. "I am still expecting the worst but hoping for the best. I am just focusing on the latter right now. For my own sanity. After all, I am just about to knock on death's door, which today happens to be a door to an iron maiden."

"Mustn't be caught smiling or admit to feeling positive," continued Levity. "Heaven forbid your cynical reputation be called into question."

I laughed. "Well, at least Ron can't tell us we need any more iron in our diet. They say misery loves company. And here I am, chin-wagging with a literal comedian."

Levity and I meandered downstairs into the Palace of Life lobby. We stood in front of the door knocker on Door Number 2.

"Want the honors?" I asked.

Levity pulled the ring of the door knocker back and gave it three good raps. A few moments went by, and nobody answered. Levity and I looked at each other as we listened for tails-steps. Levity turned around and shrugged his shoulders. "Maybe this is a sign that we should call it a day and enjoy Pleasure Hollow for the rest of our days."

It was only just then that the door flung open, and we were greeted by the head Prospector, carrying a bloody rag.

"Hiya hiya friends," said the same Prospector wearing the amulet that we spoke with prior. "I was just wiping down the iron maidens. Sounds like you both want to step inside one of the iron maidens?"

Levity and I looked at each other and then looked back at the Prospector.

"I guess so," said Levity. "But when you put it like that....."

"We are ready," I said with a firm nod. "That is our resolve."

We followed the Prospector inside, looking around the room. I couldn't believe we were at the last Yin/Yang arena, the final Russian Doll. But the Yin/Yang motif was different this time, and it displayed two eggs instead of one, since we were vetting for twins. In other words, the emblem was identical to the Yin/Yang in the world of humans. The perimeter also had room for twenty iron maidens. But today was a good day, as there were only five iron maidens (as per your uplifting news).

Levity and I stood in the center of the arena. The Prospector turned around, fidgeting with his bloody rag as if it was Abacus's fidget spinner. "All ready to go, eh?"

"Not sure if 'ready' is the right word," I said. "But I suppose so, in a manner of speaking."

Levity chuckled. "I know that patience is a virtue, but in situations like this, it's wiser to get it done and over with, right?"

"I get it," said the Prospector. "Now you know why I opted out of this final phase to enjoy the rest of my days in luxury. Maybe that makes me a coward. But at least I'm a happy and comfortable coward. Besides, I get to wear this amulet as the Head Prospector in all of Palace of Life and Pleasure Hollow."

I paused. "No shame in that. You have come a long way. And this is the only part of this journey where you have to relinquish all control and put your life in the cruel, gnarled, and arthritic hands of Lady Luck. There is no sword or scepter large enough to give us an advantage here."

"Indeed," said the Prospector. "You lot are braver than I am. And speaking of scepters, the first thing I need to do is to collect your gold scepters. You will not need them here. They will go to other haploids that follow your tail-steps and become Prospectors."

I handed my scepter to the Prospector. "Fine by me. I never want to see that thing again."

Levity handed in his as well. "So now what?"

"There are five iron maidens encircling this arena, as you can see," said the head Prospector. You are luckier than most. I have seen as many as twenty doors in here. But there is still only a 1/5 chance each of you will survive if you take the same door. If you each choose a different door, the odds of at least one of you reaching the egg is 2/5. But the latter scenario will prevent you from becoming twins, as one of you will perish."

"Haven't you been curious to take a peek in the correct iron maiden to get a glimpse of the egg?" asked Levity.

The Prospector continued. "After you step inside, the doors slam shut as if by magic. There is no returning. And like I said, I am not willing to gamble with my life like you crazy lot."

"The human body sure is complex," said Levity.

Just then, there was a knock on the door. "Ah yes, it sounds like another Prospector may have had a change of heart and wants to play this lovely game. After all, once you knock on that door with that door knocker, there is no turning back."

More knocks followed, louder than before. The Prospector scurried over to the door and opened it. "Come on in. There's plenty of room."

And who was it? The lanky head Prospector that MC'd the second battle at the Fallopian tubes!

Levity elbowed me in the ribs. "Isn't that the chap that gave Sperm Whale such a grand entrance back at the Fallopian tubes?"

"The one and only," I replied.

"Let's do this now," said the Prospector. "I don't want to think about this more than I have to. Where's the iron maiden?! Where is it?! I demand to step into it Now!"

"Calm yourself, boy!" shouted the Head Prospector (wearing the amulet) as he dragged him by the arm towards us. "Right this way. I have some friends here who would appreciate such a visual demonstration. Why the sudden change of heart, if I may ask?"

The shaking haploid continued. "I'm going to die anyway. Please let me see the egg! It's killing me inside! What if I find the ambrosia of sweet immortality!"

The Head Prospector straightened out the trembling Prospector's suit and tie for him and guided him towards the iron maidens. "Worry not. You came to the right place."

The Head Prospector jerked his head for Levity and me to follow them. Levity looked at me. We followed them but kept some distance between them and ourselves.

"Step right up, step right up," said the Head Prospector,

pointing his time scepter towards the array of iron maidens. "Take your pick. They are all the same. All we know is that the egg is in one of them. Do you wish to hear the formal speech?"

"No way, Jose," said the frenzied haploid as he stepped into the closest one. The Head Prospector waved his time scepter in the shape of a star constellation, and the iron maiden slammed shut, blood, guts, and organic material seeping out of the sides of the coffin like an overfilled burrito.

Levity and I stared, slackjawed.

"Well, that's how it goes," said the Head Prospector, already in the process of opening up the iron maiden and cleaning away with his same bloodied rag. "Poor fellow. He did not choose the right one. At least his death was short and sweet. Hopefully, you gents weren't going to choose that one. But the odds will not change, as it's all 'with replacement.'"

"I was just going to ask about that," said Levity. "I say we get this over with."

"So here is how it's going to work," added the Prospector, fidgeting with his rag. "When you select an iron maiden, the door will open. Don't be alarmed when you see the spikes on the door. All the doors have them. But only one coffin has a false bottom you can drop into."

Levity cracked his knuckles. "Like the false floor on a magician's closet?"

The Prospector nodded. "Yes. As soon as you take one step into the Iron Maiden, that is when your fate is decided. If you find the iron maiden containing the egg, you will drop through the floor as if it were a portal, and the spikes will not crush you."

Levity stuttered. "And we all know what happens if you don't choose wisely."

"It's now or never," I said. "Read us your formal words for the interests of science."

The Prospector stood behind the podium in the center of the arena and revealed a scroll from behind it. "You are here today on your own accord. You have made a very important decision to take part in this final challenge. The reward is said to be a paradise that is leagues above the creature comforts of Pleasure Hollow. But as with any game of competition and survival, there is the possibility of death. But rest assured, the death will be swift. You will not suffer long, as the doors of the iron maidens will close with immediate haste, like a mouse trap."

Levity leaned towards my ear and whispered. "Did he just say 'rest assured? I hate to think what his version of an unrestful sleep looks like."

"At least he clarified it with a nice mouse simile," I whispered.

The Prospector rolled up the scroll and placed it back behind the podium. "Now it's time to choose your door. If you choose the same door, another iron maiden will rise from the floor right behind it but facing the opposite direction. The two iron maidens will be back to back. So, as you each step inside, you will either both be killed or whisked away to the egg at the same time. So now is the time to make your decision. Do you, Levity, wish to enter one of the iron maidens. And if so, which door do you choose?"

"You make it sound like we are getting married," said Levity.

"Indeed," I returned. "Despite our commitment to these other fine and fair maidens that grace us with their amorous presence."

The Prospector must have been unamused as he continued to stare at Levity, waiting for his answer.

"I do," said Levity. "And that door is number 3."

The Prospector turned towards me. "Do you, Sage, wish to enter of the iron maidens. And if so, which door do you choose?"

"I do," I said. "And that door is number 3."

"Third time's a charm, eh?" said the Prospector.

"We had this picked out ahead of time," asserted Levity. "We chose door number three to honor the deaths of our three brothers in arms in our alliance, Brawn, Abacus, and Animus."

"Sentimental softies, eh?" laughed the lead Prospector. "You have more faith in spermanity than I do. If you ask me, 'sperms are germs,' like the folks in Digi or Uri like to say. To be frank, I wish I lived in a more prestigious country like Endo or Lymph. I get tired of everyone looking at us in Repro like we are depraved reprobates."

"You should be proud of who you are," said Levity. "You can't help where you are from. It's not like any of us can choose our bodies like characters in a video game."

The Prospector paused. "I suppose it's all too easy to look down on yourself when others look down on you first."

The Prospector led us to Iron Maiden number 3. Both doors opened as if by magic (and could have hurt somebody if too close!). Blood and residue were dripping from the spikes like spittle from a rabid dog's fangs. The blood stains and bits of dried guts didn't help. These were definitely not the good kind of spikes that keep you alive, like the pitons used for mountain climbing.

Levity stood in front of Iron Maiden 3. I stood in front of the "other iron maiden 3," facing away but back to back to the other one.

Levity crept inside his as if entering a cold swimming pool. "At least we are going to be stabbed in the front and not the back."

I stepped inside mine. "At the very least, good friend, we will have each others' backs."

"The doors are going to close," said the Prospector. "If you are lucky, the floor will open as the door is closing, sparing you from the spikes."

Levity sighed. "So, how fast will the door close? Is this like a slow and painful death?"

"Not at all," said the Prospector. "It's fast but still gives you time to fall through the floor if you choose the correct door. Now enjoy."

So, if you have not deduced, Morale, we made it to the finish line. Levity and I both. We just arrived in the egg chamber, and Meg is very much real! She is right here with us as I am finishing up this very letter (she just said hi, by the way). Levity and I, and Meg, for that matter, can't believe this is really happening!

I will write more soon, but I did not want to keep you waiting to hear the big news that we are all very much alive and very much well. In fact, Meg is so smitten by what we have told her about you that she intends to write you a personal note of her own very soon!
Sincerely,
Sage

P.S. All three of us just burst into peals of rapturous laughter. It was great fun, and I tried to picture your reactions to our bouts of mindless banter. I can't deny that part of this gaiety is no doubt due to the champagne (but in our defense, we have to be sober for the next nine months, human time!). We don't want the twins to develop Fetal Alcohol Syndrome, after all.

The K Letters
Subject: Re: Leap of Faith
Survival type: Cellular competition (class = NA)
Author: Meg
Date: February 17, 2182 (Sunday)
Location: Final chamber of the egg
Recipient: Ron Une (Morale)

Hello Mr. Ron Une!
It's a pleasure to meet you! Sage and Levity have told me so much about you, and with so much excitement and zeal, that I am fully convinced they are over the moon for you, and their respect is off the charts.

It was pretty lonely here in the egg chamber, and according to some of the stories from these two lovely gentlemen, they went through some right scary and dangerous adventures to get to me. And while I am very flattered that they risked their lives to find me, I do feel bad for putting them through all that trouble on account of little old me. I hope it will be worth it for them. Despite being pigeonholed as the prize in this whole affair, I really don't see myself as any more special than them. Is such humility wrong of me?

When my egg splits into two, Levity's wifey will be named Megg, and Sage's wifey will be named Meggg. We are planning our "Big Fat Gamete Wedding" next week, and it's all thanks to you, Mr. Ron Une. We just had an argument on what kind of cake to have (marble, white, or chocolate). Sage, Levity, and I had a moment of philosophy intermixed with our fun banter about wedding cake.

"You think we will forget who we were?" asked Levity. "That's a scary thought, right?"

"I was wondering the very same thing," Sage said. "How much self-awareness will we retain?"

"I do know that zygotes share the genes of both parents," I stated. "Maybe the best parts of us will carry over."

"A pleasing thought," Sage said. "Perhaps our consciousness will be superimposed onto the neonates."

Levity frowned. "Almost feels like we are shedding our past selves like a snake. Maybe my personality will merge with Meg's for one twin, and Sage's personality will merge with Meg's for the other."

I smiled. "I can live with that. But don't forget about Euclid and Autumn. Both twins will be an extension of their personalities and physical characteristics as well. After all, Levity and Sage are extensions of Euclid, and I am an extension of Autumn. But what about my splitting into two? Will Megg and Meggg just receive an exact copy of my personality and physical traits? Or will my existing personality be 'shared' between them?"

"We are forming semi-identical twins," Sage assured. "Which means each zygote should share 75% genetic similarity."

"Personalities are like snowflakes and fingerprints," I

said. "No two alike. Even Megg and Meggg will display some individual differences, no matter how minute."

Sage interrupted. "I fear this topic has become subversive to the jovial spirit of things. We should get back to delighting in more pleasing matters, such as whether we should have red vs. blue balloons, streamers, or other party favors."

After a bit of heated argument about fruit punch, I blushed. "I better enjoy the now while it lasts. After all, I only have two husbands for a limited time only!" Thanks again, Ron Une, for helping to align the stars and hang the moon in such a way as to bring us all together.

Much love,

Meg

The K Letters
Subject: Re: Leap of Faith
Survival type: Cellular competition (class = NA)
Author: Levity
Date: February 17, 2182 (Sunday)
Location: Final chamber of the egg
Recipient: Morale

Hi Morale,

I'm a bit drunk, but I wanted to express my many thanks to you for being the best "Captain of the Captain" Sage could ask for. So far, we have cried, laughed, and pounded our fists. Our goal is to experience twenty different emotions before day's end.

It will be amusing to see how Megg and Meggg will compare and contrast with each other and also with the original zygote Meg. So what is Meg like? Sage took it upon himself to give her the same icebreaker he gave the five of us at the beginning of our journey (her results are below).

Meg
Age (haploid years): 29

Favorite outfit: Maxi skirt
Strength: Massive amounts of patience, can sit doing nothing for days (haploid time)
Example of strength: Sitting in one spot, waiting for sperm to show up
Weakness: Fear of the unknown, rebellious, reckless, impetuous, sensitive to criticism
Example of weakness: I don't know what will happen when I grow into a zygote, and that is unsettling for me.
Most embarrassing moment: I was trying on wedding dresses when Sage and Levity crashed into my dressing room.
Favorite expression: "It takes two to tango."
Hobbies: Photography

Meg shared that her human host (Autumn) was an "endangered species biologist" who works on saving certain animals on the verge of extinction (including animal habitats that are overpopulated). It sounds to me like Autumn and Euclid's careers may not be identical, but they are quite complementary. I do wonder if Autumn's penchant for immediate gratification may clash with Euclid's penchant for proactive deliberation.

Meg loved hearing about our journey as long as we glossed over some of the dangerous or sad parts, such as the passing of our friends. We didn't need to exaggerate anything, and it wouldn't have impressed her anyway.

I also realized the importance of Euclid and Autumn in all this. If Euclid and Autumn didn't have their messy romantic entanglements, Levity, Meg, and I wouldn't even be where we are at right now. And the twins would be an afterthought.

While Sage and Meg were putting the world to rights, Sage made a comment about sperm being "drafted" to undergo in vitro fertilization. And it was pure serendipity that he used that term.

"Draft?" I asked. "I never checked Abacus's draft folder! Didn't he say he was working on finding a cure for Ron?"

Sure enough, Abacus had copious notes in the draft folder, and I spent some time poring over them as if reading a riveting work of fiction. As we know, there are nanobots in the country of Musc that can use genetic modification on muscle cells and adult stem cells. But did you know the brain is considered a muscle, despite that neurons do not reside in the country of Musc? You are related to a muscle cell! Unless you have been rendered dense or daft, the THM (take home message) is that we can reverse your cellular degeneration! I am highlighting the key parts of Abacus's draft email to send to you. All you will need is the genetic materials for muscle enhancement from the nanobots in Musc. All you have to do is the same thing you did when you sent nanobots from Musc to us at the start of our adventure at the Crystal Gates. Make no mistake. This procedure is a risk. We don't know for sure how the muscle enhancers will affect a brain cell. When it comes to survival, everything comes down to risk vs. reward. I think we all learned that more than anyone. It's just the luck of the draw.

P.S. I am giving myself permission to speak freely. And in so doing, I apologize if I speak out of turn. I also can tell you without hesitation that I also speak for Sage. It is my belief, however absurd, that Sage and I would not be alive, and we would not have been able to reverse your cellular degeneration if we did not become a family of friends. This was no mere temporary "alliance" of fellow enemies or frenemies (keeping friends close and enemies closer and all that). It was an ethical dilemma and a risk we felt compelled to take. Not just for our own survival but for the survival of those we cared about. If only every sperm, all millions and millions of them, could get along this, it would be a beautiful thing. If I could change the very fabric of this world, I would, if only to unsee all the expressions of loss and heartache we have endured. In my perfect world, nobody is ignored. Nobody is killed. Nobody is stepped over. The slow, weak, and infirm are not left behind. And the very idea of competition is cast to the wolves. But alas, such maudlin sentiment is reserved only for the intoxicated or the delusional. But if alliances can form between warring factions against a common enemy, couldn't that common enemy also be a friend? We are all in this for Euclid Hux, who is not a common enemy. He is a common friend. Every cell in every organ system, from Neuron to Repro, are in this with the very best of intentions. Is it so far-fetched that alliances can be formed by love, kinship, and common bonds and not by common enemies?

We all knew the risk, and it was a risk that we felt compelled to take. We hope you can understand our moment of weakness (and insubordination). This very kinship gave us the compassion (and the motivation) to help each other when in need.

And then there is you, Morale. Your presence in our lives, even from afar, has left an indelible impression upon all of us. Not only did you grant us the opportunity for science and adventure, but we had the chance to get to know you (and maybe save your life).

P.S. Number 2 (by Sage): It's a crazy world down here. The science is both inexplicable and ineffable, a tried and true miracle to be sure. I will never understand why humans relegate such topics like sexuality as taboo and "sordid." Without it, the human race would be moribund. We would all perish. Sperm are not "vile and base." We, too, are life bringers and harbingers of miracles. Those who reside in the urinary system (country of Uri) and the reproductive system (Repro) carry the brunt of this shame. Humans are quick to acknowledge and respect the "ends" (neonate) with their "aw how cute" banter but are remiss in garnering the respect and appreciation of the "means" to reach that goal (i.e., the very process of sexuality and reproduction). But if I learned one thing, it's that "survival" is very much a morbid game. And if you look up the word "game" in any dictionary, the quest for survival meets every criteria.

The K Letters
Subject: Re: Leap of Faith (cellular survival games and fight and flight)
Survival type: Cellular competition (class = NA)
Author: Ron Une (Morale)
Date: February 18, 2182 (Monday)
Location: Neuron
Recipients: Sage, Levity, Meg

Dear Sage, Levity, and now Meg!

I have well wishes! Take ample time to celebrate and reminisce. Your effervescent and gregarious interactions warm my heart. Is this what they call love? Just don't forget that your adventures are just beginning. You will experience the world of humans first-hand as the zygotes grow into semi-identical twin sisters. You will enter the world outside of the human body. Let Meg know that Megg and Meggg will have different names given to them from Euclid and Autumn when the twins are born. But let Meg know that she can keep calling them Megg and Meggg as long as she needs to.

I am beside myself with your acts of generosity in helping me with my cellular degeneration (which you made poignantly clear would not have happened if we abstained from befriending each other). I will not hesitate to work on curing my neural degeneration, and I am confident I will pull through (tell Sage that's the mindset of an optimist). Euclid's overindulgence in hard liquor isn't helping his brain cells much. But I will get the nanobots to help me even if it kills me!

I have scoured every corner of Euclid's brain. It turns out there is a whole world out there beyond. All manner of flesh robots. Fish that can swim. Beavers that can build dams. Bees that can make honey. Eagles that can soar. It seems that plants, animals, fungi, and even cells have the same goal you mentioned: survival.

The topic of sexuality appears to be taboo for humans.

I had to break over ten of Euclid's shame and embarrassment locks just to learn more about the realities of "human attraction." There are many elephants in the room. From what I can gather regarding coupling or mate selection, be it from academia or the locker room, humans talk about this "love," but it seems to be very conditional and self-serving. More often than not, this "love" appears to be contingent on things like beauty, money, clout, or resources. I just hope Euclid doesn't find out that I am studying his love life. It's tantamount to having access to twenty volumes of diaries in there!

I am alive, and I will be alive, thanks to Levity and thanks to all of you. You are not acquaintances. You are not an alliance. You are not even friends. You are family! Keep in touch as long as you can, all of you. I am always here in Neuro. I love the lot of you, including Brawn, Animus, and Abacus. May they rest in peace.

Perhaps whenever Euclid uses his brain cells to interact with his twin daughters Megg and Meggg (or whatever their new names will be), this will be proof positive that the lot of us, Sage, Levity, Meg, and myself, will be together again and supporting each other, offering advice, setting the world to rights, or bantering about this, that, and the other thing.

The End

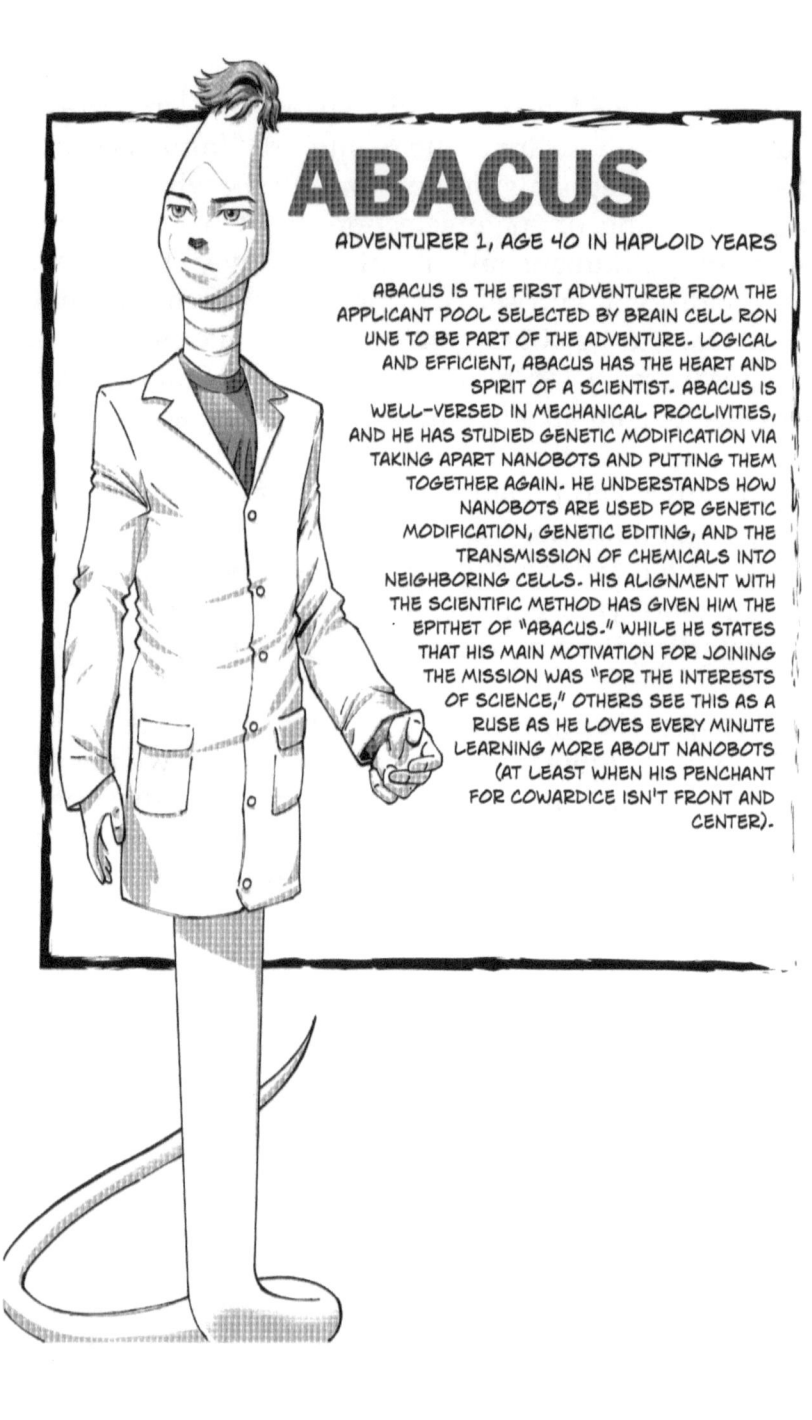

ABACUS

ADVENTURER 1, AGE 40 IN HAPLOID YEARS

ABACUS IS THE FIRST ADVENTURER FROM THE APPLICANT POOL SELECTED BY BRAIN CELL RON UNE TO BE PART OF THE ADVENTURE. LOGICAL AND EFFICIENT, ABACUS HAS THE HEART AND SPIRIT OF A SCIENTIST. ABACUS IS WELL-VERSED IN MECHANICAL PROCLIVITIES, AND HE HAS STUDIED GENETIC MODIFICATION VIA TAKING APART NANOBOTS AND PUTTING THEM TOGETHER AGAIN. HE UNDERSTANDS HOW NANOBOTS ARE USED FOR GENETIC MODIFICATION, GENETIC EDITING, AND THE TRANSMISSION OF CHEMICALS INTO NEIGHBORING CELLS. HIS ALIGNMENT WITH THE SCIENTIFIC METHOD HAS GIVEN HIM THE EPITHET OF "ABACUS." WHILE HE STATES THAT HIS MAIN MOTIVATION FOR JOINING THE MISSION WAS "FOR THE INTERESTS OF SCIENCE," OTHERS SEE THIS AS A RUSE AS HE LOVES EVERY MINUTE LEARNING MORE ABOUT NANOBOTS (AT LEAST WHEN HIS PENCHANT FOR COWARDICE ISN'T FRONT AND CENTER).

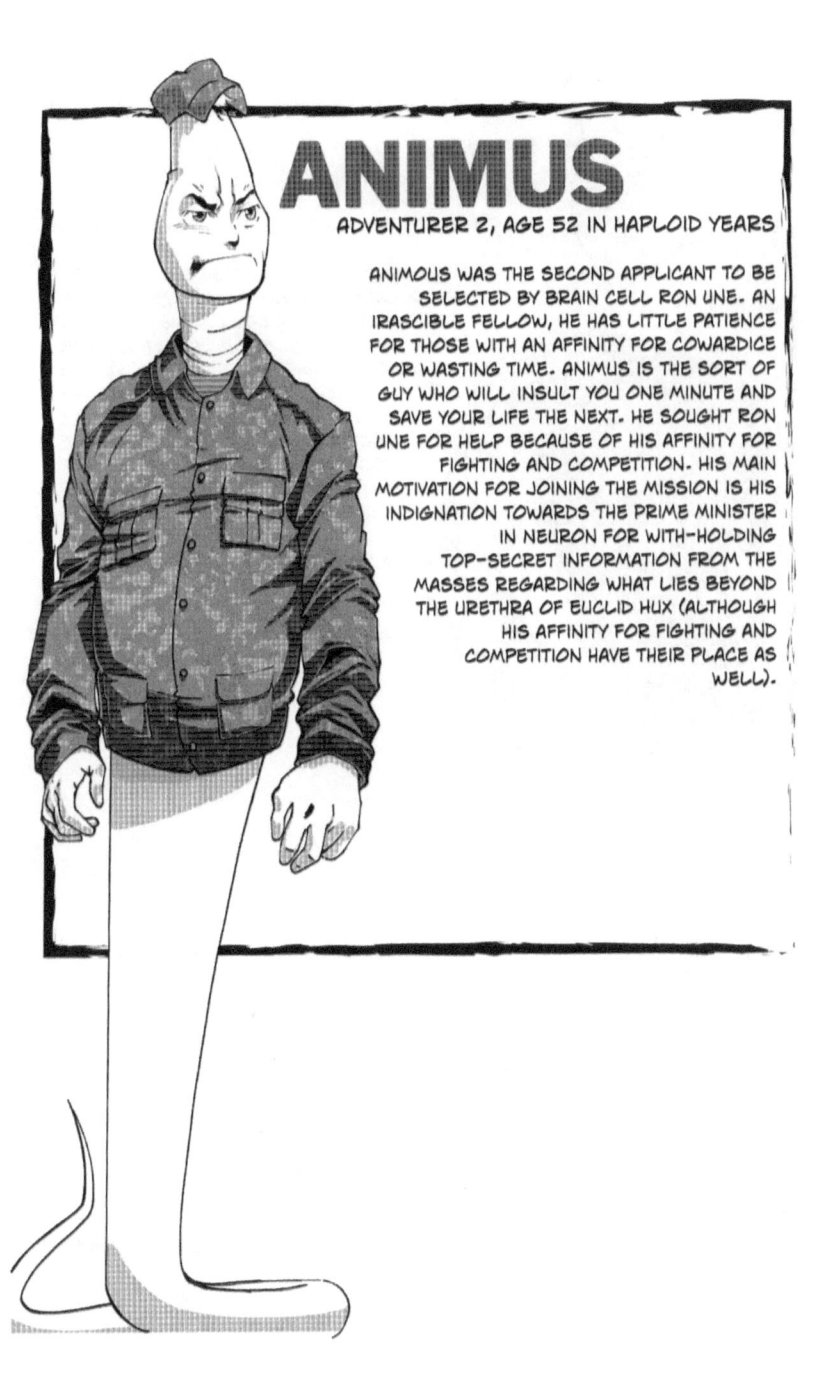

ANIMUS

ADVENTURER 2, AGE 52 IN HAPLOID YEARS

ANIMOUS WAS THE SECOND APPLICANT TO BE
SELECTED BY BRAIN CELL RON UNE. AN
IRASCIBLE FELLOW, HE HAS LITTLE PATIENCE
FOR THOSE WITH AN AFFINITY FOR COWARDICE
OR WASTING TIME. ANIMUS IS THE SORT OF
GUY WHO WILL INSULT YOU ONE MINUTE AND
SAVE YOUR LIFE THE NEXT. HE SOUGHT RON
UNE FOR HELP BECAUSE OF HIS AFFINITY FOR
FIGHTING AND COMPETITION. HIS MAIN
MOTIVATION FOR JOINING THE MISSION IS HIS
INDIGNATION TOWARDS THE PRIME MINISTER
IN NEURON FOR WITH-HOLDING
TOP-SECRET INFORMATION FROM THE
MASSES REGARDING WHAT LIES BEYOND
THE URETHRA OF EUCLID HUX (ALTHOUGH
HIS AFFINITY FOR FIGHTING AND
COMPETITION HAVE THEIR PLACE AS
WELL).

BRAWN

ADVENTURER 3, AGE 23 IN HAPLOID YEARS

BRAWN WAS THE THIRD MEMBER SELECTED FOR THE JOURNEY. HE IS THE MOST PHYSICALLY FIT AND FASTEST SPERM CELL IN THE PACK (AND WON'T HESITATE TO LET EVERYONE AND THEIR CAT KNOW THAT). HE TRAINED HIS WHOLE LIFE TO JOIN THE RACES TO EXIT THE URETHRA, WELL BEFORE RON UNE EVER GOT INVOLVED AND BROADENED THE SCOPE OF THE MISSION TO INCLUDE SEARCHING FOR THE MAGICAL EGG. BRAWN SOMETIMES CLASHES EGOS WITH A CERTAIN FELLOW TEAM MEMBER, AND IT'S NOT "BRAIN" (I.E. ABACUS). HIS MAIN MOTIVATION FOR JOINING THE RACES IS TO SIMPLY "BE THE BEST" AND "BECOME A CELEBRITY" IN ALL ELEVEN COUNTRIES WITHIN PLANET EUCLID.

LEVITY

ADVENTURER 4, AGE 29 IN HAPLOID YEARS

LEVITY IS THE FOURTH HAPLOID ELECTED BY
BRAIN CELL RON UNE TO PARTAKE IN THE
JOURNEY TO SEEK THE MAGICAL EGG. WHILE
HIS EPITHET WAS INDEED EARNED AND
GRANTED TO HIM BY HIS COMRADES, HE
ALSO SEES IT AS A TITLE TO ASPIRE TO IN
HIS MISSION TO LIGHTEN THE MOOD OF
HIS COMPATRIOTS IN DARK TIMES. HUMBLE
AND INNOCENT, HIS PENCHANT FOR HUMOR
CAN BE TAKEN TOO FAR, ENCROACHING INTO
THE REALMS OF NAIVETY OR AVOIDANCE. BUT
IF YOU ASK ANIMUS, HE MIGHT SAY LEVITY IS
JUST YOUR RUN OF THE MILL CLASS
CLOWN, COURT JESTER, OR COMIC RELIEF.
HIS MAIN MOTIVATION FOR JOINING THE
MISSION WAS "FOR SOMETHING TO DO."

MORALE

RON UNE, AGE 55 IN NEURON YEARS

MORALE IS THE ASSISTANT TO THE PRIME MINISTER IN THE COUNTRY OF NEURON AND HE RESIDES IN THE PROVINCE OF THE HIPPOCAMPUS IN THE TEMPORAL LOBE. WITH TOP-TIER (ALBEIT ILLEGAL) ACCESS TO EUCLID'S MEMORIES AND KNOWLEDGE STORES, HE IS IN A POSITION WHERE HE CAN GATHER INTEL REGARDING WHAT KIND OF WORLD EXISTS OUTSIDE THE HUMAN HOST OF EUCLID HUX (INCLUDING ALL MANNER OF KNOWLEDGE RELATED TO HUMAN REPRODUCTION AND BODILY SYSTEMS). RON IS RESPONSIBLE FOR ORGANIZING THE RABBLE OF REBELS AND THEIR JOURNEY TO THE EGG. FOR RON, LEGENDS AND TALES ARE JUST HYPOTHESIS WAITING TO BE TESTED. WHILE SUFFICIENT FOR MOST, EXITING THE URETHRA IS NOT ENOUGH. FOR YEARS HE HAS BEEN CAPTIVATED BY WANDERLUST FOR THE WHEREFORE AND WHY AND TEMPTED TO TAKE A PEEK AT WHAT'S HIDDEN IN EUCLID'S MIND. LIKE MANY OTHERS, HE HAS HEARD THE STORIES ABOUT A "MAGICAL EGG" WAITING AT THE END OF THE JOURNEY: "A VERITABLE FOUNTAIN OF YOUTH" OR "POT OF GOLD AT THE VESTIGE OF THE RAINBOW." WHILE HE IS EMBOLDENED TO BOOST MORALE, HE HAS BEEN KNOWN TO EMBELLISH AND PLAY DOWN THE DANGER IN SERIOUS SITUATIONS. DUE TO THE THREAT OF BEING ACCUSED OF TREASON, HIS ULTIMATE MOTIVATION FOR TAPPING INTO EUCLID'S MIND AND ORGANIZING THE ALLIANCE REMAINS A MYSTERY.

SAGE

ADVENTURER 5, AGE 35 IN HAPLOID YEARS

SAGE IS THE FIFTH AND FINAL SPERM CELL
ELECTED BY BRAIN CELL RON UNE (IN THE
COUNTRY OF NEURON). HE WAS ELECTED
LEADER OF THE RABBLE OF REBELS TO
CHRONICLE THE ENTIRE JOURNEY OF WHAT LIES
BEYOND THE URETHRA OF THEIR MALE HOST
(EUCLID HUX). SAGE IS BLESSED AND CURSED
WITH A PATHOLOGICAL CURIOSITY. WHILE HE
IS ENCHANTED BY THE AWE AND WONDER OF
UNCHARTED TERRITORIES, NEW FRONTIERS,
AND FRESH IDEAS, HE IS ALSO HAUNTED BY
THE UNCERTAINTIES OF THE UNKNOWN
AND THE MYSTERIES OF THE WORLD.
SAGE IS A PHILOSOPHER TO A FAULT,
AND HE HAS FIVE QUESTIONS FOR EVERY
ANSWER. FOR THIS TORTURED SPIRIT,
EVERY CAUSE IS JUST AN EFFECT (FROM
A PREVIOUS CAUSE) AND EVERY EFFECT IS
JUST A CAUSE (TO A FUTURE EFFECT). HIS
MAIN MOTIVATION FOR JOINING THE
ADVENTURE WAS "MORBID CURIOSITY."

Appendix:

The Specific Rules of Engagement (Tier 1 Survival of Sperm and Eggs)

Sentry vs. Sentry
Location of battle: Uterotubal junction

No Sceptres
Choice of weapon: bow and arrow (distance) or machete (melee)
Sentries at 50th percentile battle prowess elevated to Sentinels after battle
Nanobots measure battle prowess based on stealth, strength, grace, cowardice, speed, etc.

Sentry vs. Sentinel
Location of battle: Fallopian tubes

1. Sentry is given electric dagger (basic weapon)
2. Sentinel emerald-tipped bronze scepter can cast one of three classes of magic (paper, rock, scissors)
3. Three-sided polyhedral die-cast at onset of battle delineates what class of magic Sentinel can cast
4. The die-cast determines the class of magic splayed for entire battle (paper, rock, scissors)
5. Being hit by magic is not a sure death, and there are partial hits
6. Due to random assignment (with replacement), a combatant may endure multiple fights
7. Sentinel bronze scepter requires 5 minute recharge (causing a predator/prey reversal)

8. Sentries can defeat Sentinels, but their chances are lower
A Sentry can steal bronze scepter from Sentinel and cast magic
Sentinel's magic class has three spell types (3 paper spells, 3 rock spells, 3 scissors spells)
The type of magic cast is decided at the will and behest of spell-caster

Sentinel vs. Sentinel

1. Each Sentinel receives die-cast to determine their magic type (paper, rock, scissors)
2. Paper beats rock (1/3 chance)
3. Scissors beats paper (1/3 chance)
4. Rock beats scissors (1/3 chance)
5. If die-cast results in a tie, both combatants wield same magic class (paper, rock, scissors)
Scentinels also retain their electric daggers from when Sentry
Magic is not always deadly if a partial hit
Sentinels in the 50th' percentile level up to Brigadiers (based on battle prowess)
Each class of magic has three spell types (3 paper spells, 3 rock spells, 3 scissors spells)
The type of magic cast is decided at the will and behest of spell-caster

Paper magic (activated by speaking spell name)

Swan Song: Papercuts from 2000 origami swans (Medium range, Medium melee)
Blind Luck: Opponent is completely blind for the five minute duration of recharge (NA Range/Melee)
Air Brush: Asphyxiation from crumpled paper entering the throat (Low range, High melee)

Rock magic (activated by speaking spell name)

Boulder-Dash: Large boulder jettisons towards fighter (Medium range, Medium melee)

Condoning Stoning: Pelted with a volley of smaller rocks and stones (Low range, High melee)

Statue of Limitations: Rock monster is forged and active during five minute recharge period. This spell can only be cast once, and no other rock magic can be summoned (NA Range/Melee)

Scissors magic (activated by speaking spell name)

Shear Pain: One hundred pairs of scissors strike your body like daggers (Medium range, Medium melee)

Cutting Room Floor: One giant pair of scissors snips your body in half (High range, Low melee)

Filet Melee: Sharp shears filet the body like a fish (Low range, High melee)

Attachment: The rules of engagement.

Brigadier vs. Brigadier

Wind beats snow (1/3)
Snow beats mountain (1/3)
Mountain beats wind (1/3)
Die-cast tie results in both sceptres casting same magic class
Brigadiers given electric dagger
Self-deletion of both fighters prohibited
Brigadiers are granted silver scepters with ruby finials

Brigadier vs. Sentinel

Wind beats paper and scissors, but not rock (2/3)
Snow beats paper and rock, but not scissors (2/3)
Mountain beats rock and scissors, but not paper (2/3)

Sentinels and Brigadiers retain electric daggers
Brigadiers are granted silver scepters with ruby finals
Brigadiers cast snow, mountain, or wind magic
Die-cast for Brigadier and Sentinel
Self-deletion of both fighters prohibited

Brigadier vs. Brigadier

Wind beats snow (1/3)
Snow beats mountain (1/3)
Mountain beats wind (1/3)
Die-cast tie results in both sceptres casting same magic class
Brigadiers given electric dagger
Self-deletion of both fighters prohibited
Brigadiers are granted silver scepters with ruby finals

Wind Magic: (activated by speaking spell name)

Windmill: A large jet engine follows the prey from 10 (tails) behind at 3mph. If the victim gets too close, he is ripped to shreds. And while this spell can only be cast once, it will last a full five minutes. (NA Range/Melee)

Extra-Terrestrial Wind: The entire battlefield will be under heavy wind conditions for the full duration of the recharge period. The wind will not affect the spell caster at all. This spell can be recast after five minutes. (NA Range/Melee)

Funnel Cloud: This is a tornado that will jettison towards the victim. If the should make contact with the funnel, they will be sucked upwards and airborne. (Medium range, Medium melee)

Snow Magic:

Shiver River: A stream of icy-cold water is jettisoned from the finial, freezing upon contact of the adversary or terrain below. (Low range, High melee)

Ice-Sickle: Hundreds of sharp icicles are forged and shoot towards target as if daggers or sickles. (Medium range, Medium melee)

Colder Boulder: A massive boulder is carved from sheer ice and falls from the sky towards enemy. (High range, Low melee)

Mountain Magic:

Mountain Fountain: A blast of molten lava spills out of the gold scepter towards target at a high velocity. It turns to volcanic rock upon impact. (Low range, High melee)

Unfortunate Landslide: A menagerie of dust, debris, rock, gravel, and detritus is hurled towards target. (Medium range, Medium melee)

Mountain to Mohammed: A large hill is formed under spell-caster giving him a safe terrain and homefield advantage. It lasts the full duration of the recharge period and can be recast. (High range, Low melee)

Prospector vs. Prospector

Final two sperms in a cohort graduate to Prospectors and are given gold scepters with diamond finials. These scepters wield "time magic" that can transport an individual back in time between 500 and 1000 years (randomly).
Only the very last two surviving sperms of a cohort engage in the final fight of Prospector vs. Prospector.

There is no die-cast. Prospectors also retain their electric daggers from before as secondary weapons.

Winners of this final battle can choose to live out the rest of their days in luxury (while helping with the tournaments) or engage in the final test of choosing a random iron maiden in hopes of finding the coveted egg inside.

A riddle of sorts:

Hint: Is that a waltz I hear?

Tractors
Theatre
Elephant
Fate
Game
Call
Late
Tomorrow
Tofu
Alligator
Lure
Later
Unified
Umbrella
Lantern

Blake Alb (Snowcrow, The Fairgrounds) is a North Dakota native with a passion for stories that stray from the beaten path. He has an MS in psychology and has worked extensively in the field of mental health. He attributes his psychology background as playing a significant role in providing a wellspring of ideas for storytelling. Blake Alb has a penchant for all things geeky, including but not limited to: Japanese anime/manga, fantasy, science fiction, and video games. He also enjoys British comedy, word-play, and performing improv comedy. He has published a variety of short stories and novels.

Brazilian native Lieh Pena has been drawing as a hobby since childhood and professionally since 2009 when he illustrated his first book, "Zamba's Journey" ("A Jornada de Zamba" in Portuguese). He also illustrated "The Little Cowboy" parts 1 and 2 — a Northeast Brazilian parody of "The Little Prince". His illustrating works also include covers for other books, academic text papers, and a health booklet. In the field of comic books, his works include a few independent productions (yet to be published) and a political comic, plus his own comic project (yet to be finished). He also has a degree in English Language Teaching & Literature from the Universidade de Pernambuco (UPE). However, his love was always Sequential Arts in any form (cartoon, manga, graphic, etc.). For that reason, as a self-taught artist, he always tried to develop abilities related to such media, like penciling, inking, digital coloring, and lettering.